a **MOSTLY INCOMPETENT** *series*

(A legally binding 5-book journey through cosmic bureaucracy, unwise heroism, and the occasional glowing duck.)

Thumb War

One thumb. One idiot. And way too many Ducks.

D.J. Pearce

DAPPER DUCK
MEDIA

DEDICATION

This book is legally dedicated (pending thumbprint confirmation) to the following humans and other lifeforms:

To Emily, for believing in me even when this book looked like a lost cause.
To Scarlett, for reminding me every day that imagination beats logic.
And to Mazikeen the Chihuahua, who contributed absolutely nothing except snoring loudly through every draft, and somehow still thinks she deserves co-author credit.

CONTENTS

ACKNOWLEDGMENTS

Emily & Scarlett
The family, the lifeline, the cause of and solutions to headaches. Can't imagine life without the two of you.

Mazikeen
Chihuahua, house sentinel, bark-powered perimeter defense system. You remain undefeated against wind, neighbors, and existential dread.

Colleen and Ken
Thank you for books, support, and the kind of upbringing that somehow made "thumb war for planetary rights" feel narratively plausible.

Coral and Kev
For bringing me into the family without requiring a background check or interdimensional visa.

Ollie & Christie
Your friendship has survived toddlers, weird hypotheticals, and late-night philosophical snack debate, and letting me be the kind of godfather who shows up with noisy toys and questionable snacks.

Tillie
Being your godfather is the most important unpaid role I've ever taken... and the only one that comes with crayon-based contracts and spontaneous glitter events.

Evie
Certified chaos goblin and enthusiastic conspirator in many of life's weirder missions.

Jeremy, Yusrah, Nigel, Annalise, and Ollie
Who deserve medals (or at least strong drinks) for surviving the draft stages, which ranged from "mildly funny nonsense" to "illegible cosmic rambling" before finally becoming this book.

Finally, to you…. yes, you.
The reader brave enough to follow this crew of mostly incompetent misfits through thumb-based legal proceedings, snack-fueled diplomacy, and the occasional catastrophic duck.
You are clearly of excellent taste. Or extremely lost. Either way, welcome.
 If you've reached this point and you're still here...
Congratulations. You're one of us now.

FOREWORD

(MANDATORY DISCLOSURE PER GALACTIC ARTICLE 7-F)

Dear Reader,

You are in possession of a copy of Thumb War, the first of five books from the Mostly Incompetent series. This is not a drill.

Per interstellar publishing regulations, we are required to issue the following formal warnings:

- This book contains scenes of irresponsible planetary acquisition.
- The legal accuracy of its thumb-based dispute resolution should be considered nonexistent.
- The duck is intentional and legally protected. Please do not attempt to interpret or explain it.
- Any resemblance to real persons, places, or space-lawyer snack preferences is entirely coincidental (except for the vending machine. That was very real. We're still cleaning it up.)

Originally rejected by the Galactic Council's Office of Cultural Integrity, Thumb War has since been:

- Banned on Trellax-9 for "excessive irreverence."
- Censored on Burox for "compromising galactic thumb neutrality."
- And celebrated on Earth, because frankly, no one there knows what's going on anymore.

This foreword was meant to be a stern warning about narrative integrity. Unfortunately, the document was outsourced to a freelance archivist who was paid in nachos. We've since lost contact.

In summary:

If you came looking for wisdom, you took a wrong turn at the nebula.

If you came looking for chaos, sentient sarcasm, and a duck-related cosmic incident... welcome aboard.

You may now proceed.

—

Office of Narrative Containment

("We're Not Responsible For What Happens After Chapter 3")

CHAPTER 1: THUMB WAR

"All legal disputes are valid if settled by thumb. Even planetary ones."

— Galactic Clause 7-C

It was the highest-stakes game of thumb wars ever played this side of the Milky Way.

The kind of stakes that made your palms sweat, your stomach churn, and your ancestors roll in their cryogenic tanks.

His opponent had just upped the ante to include the deed to a small, rocky planet in a forgotten sector of the Milky Way galaxy; blue-green, teeming with trouble. Kade Flux (professional gambler, amateur escapist, and accidental romantic) looked like the kind of man who had spent his life one bad haircut away from a nervous breakdown. Lean and wiry, with dark hair that never quite agreed with gravity and clothes that seemed permanently wrinkled from poor life choices, he didn't exactly radiate "planet owner." He had never owned his own planet before. It was making him nervous. That, and the fact that his last three shots of Zarnac Fire were still attempting to dissolve his esophagus.

Owning a planet had always sounded vaguely prestigious, until he found out it came with responsibility, liability, and potentially a cult. Probably a cult. The galaxy had a surplus.

The bar itself wasn't helping. The Wormhole & Whiskey was the sort of place you went if you wanted to lose your wallet, your dignity, or your species-specific liver function. The three-armed bar owner (rumored to have once been a five-armed juggler, but that's a whole other lawsuit) flung drinks with enthusiastic inaccuracy while his lanky assistant wiped spills in the shadows. The lighting was provided entirely by flickering three-dimensional holographic ads for beverages with names like "Liquid Regret," "Cosmic Rash," and "New Zarnac Fire: Now with Extra Screaming."

A crowd had gathered around Kade's table: sticky, slanted, and probably sentient. Even the musician had stopped playing his flagelturrum, an instrument that sounded like a goose being mugged by a saxophone, to watch the match unfold.

"So... are you ready?" asked his opponent.

Dast, a hulking three-eyed Trinobulon, was not the kind of creature you wanted to beat at anything. Two of his eyes were set where human cheekbones would be. The third eye stared directly from the center of his forehead like a judgmental jellybean.

Kade stared into the middle one. Safer that way.

"Ready for what?" he replied, swirling the last dregs of his drink.

"The final match!"

"Oh, that! I thought you were asking me out on a date! I was flattered but confused."

The crowd erupted in laughter. Dast turned an angry shade of greenish purple; a color usually reserved for rancid stew or jealous squid. He did not laugh.

"Well, Kade Flux?"

"All right, all right. Keep your eyestalk on."

They clasped hands across the table; fingers locked in the ancient rite of thumb combat. Final bets zipped through the crowd: coins, credits, questionable coupons, and one rubber duck. The crowd leaned in. Most of them smelled like expired cheese, burnt circuits, or tax fraud. A flat-faced news drone hovered nearby, its camera lens twitching erratically as it whispered metadata to itself. Kade was pretty sure it was live-streaming to a very niche betting syndicate.

Behind the bar, a small red light began blinking on the back of the wall-mounted liquor vault. Kade didn't notice it, but the vault did. A silent subroutine activated, sending a timestamped packet into the galactic web. A Deed transfer match had entered its final phase.

"One! Two! Three! Four! I declare a thumb war!" they chanted, their faces etched with determination. Well, Dast's was etched. Kade mostly looked hungover.

The battle began.

Thumbs twisted. Sweated. Slipped. Collided. Dast's thumb moved with surprising grace for someone whose knuckles had brass plating. Kade's thumb moved like a drunk spider.

A gasp. A cheer. Someone spilled their drink, which promptly dissolved the table leg. The table groaned. Someone else tried to start a chant but was quickly shushed.

The thumb battle intensified. Dast was stronger, but Kade was wiry, slippery, and motivated by debt collectors with electro-whips. He countered, feinted, slipped: classic misdirection. The deed's glow pulsed.

A warning whisper rippled across Kade's thoughts, like a fax machine jammed with prophecy.

He felt the shift.

A subtle chill.

Someone was watching.

He didn't mean the crowd, or the drone, or the bar owner with the polite threat of murder in her smile. He meant something else. A tickle behind his eyes. Like an algorithm had paused to consider him. Or a celestial accountant had flagged his file.

Then it passed.

Focus.

And then, after several long seconds and one unfortunate cramp, Kade ducked a thumb feint, arched his wrist, and pivoted. His move was swift, clean...

...and triumphant. He pinned Dast's thumb. One. Two. Three.

Victory.

He snatched the deed from the table before anyone could say "fraudulent transaction." It was a glowing, humming, metallic rectangle with a large screen protector.

The 'screen protector' flickered oddly, as if overlaid on older engravings that whispered of forgotten protocols.

A small readout ominously flickered across the surface:

DEED CLAIMED

OBSERVATION RESUMED

PROTOCOL WAKE-IN-PROGRESS

Dast let out a guttural scream in his native tongue. It translated roughly to: "YOU ABSOLUTE WRENCH-HEADED BUCKET OF NOSTRIL FUNGUS." Though some linguists argue it might also mean, "Please return that, my mother gave it to me."

In response to Dast's outburst, a small horde of goons materialized from the shadows: goons with blades, boots, and IQs lower than their shoe sizes.

Kade's survival instincts screamed; he somersaulted, then flung himself boldly behind the bar.

He landed beside Zogg, a lanky, mop-headed assistant bartender lost in his own daydream. Zogg's limbs always seemed one size too long for his frame, like he'd been stretched out in a faulty cloning vat, and his hair slumped over his brow in a shaggy tangle that looked allergic to combs. His uniform was rumpled, his apron forever carrying the ghosts of spilled drinks, and his wide, soft features gave him the air of a well-meaning scarecrow who'd wandered off a farm and taken up bartending.

"Quick! Hide me from the angry rhino with the extra eyeball," Kade barked.

Zogg blinked. In his mind, he was still center stage at the Galactic Talent Final, bowing to lights, confetti, and thunderous applause. Instead, he'd found himself wiping down tables in a bar that smelled like regret and stale dreams. It took him a full two seconds to blink back to reality.

"Uhh... umm... right. Escape. Yes. The bartender is on it," Zogg muttered, then screamed as a blade thunked into the wall above his head.

"That one!" Dast pointed. "The bartender's helping him! Get them both!"

"Great," Kade muttered. "You're really good at this low-profile getaway stuff."

"Shut up and follow me!"

Zogg vaulted over a barrel of fermented moon carrots and bolted through a curtain into the back room. Kade followed, knocking over a stack of jellybean-sized crates with a satisfying crash.

"Left!"

"Which left?"

"Your left!"

"Which is your left?!"

Zogg didn't answer. He'd already disappeared behind a large, hideous painting of what humans might call a gnome, if the gnome had been drawn by someone on mushrooms and sadness.

Behind it? A tunnel. Naturally.

They scrambled inside, running through tight corridors stacked with boxes, forgotten drinks, and what looked like a mummified accountant.

Kade, as per all chase-scene etiquette, tipped over boxes behind him and flung random items to slow the goons, none of which worked, but it looked heroic.

Zogg led him through a maze of steam pipes, loose wires, and at least one weeping vending machine.

"This tunnel connects to the teleport alley!" Zogg huffed. "Trust me!"

"You're wearing a name tag that says, 'Not Trustworthy.'"

"Yeah, but it's ironic!"

They burst into a side room: a forgotten laundry bay occupied only by a sentient mop humming show tunes. Kade slipped on a stray soap pod and barely caught himself.

"I hate everything about this escape," he muttered.

"Complaints can be filed in triplicate," Zogg said, wrenching open a panel on the far wall. "Under 'mildly heroic fleeing.'"

The tunnel ended in a rusty ladder. They climbed. At the top: a trapdoor, an alley, and… miraculously… a teleportation kiosk glowing like salvation.

Kade sprinted toward it, hit the activation pad, and turned around just in time to see the goons emerge from the tunnel like deranged mole rats.

"Time for a signature move," Kade said.

He plucked a nearby crate labelled "Emergency Confetti – Do Not Use in Pursuits", cracked it open, and threw a fistful of shimmering sparkles into the air. The goons stumbled back, coughing and swatting wildly.

He smiled.

He raised his middle finger with the kind of slow-motion defiance typically reserved for action movie finales.

"Bye now!"

Then grinned; and vanished.

The teleport pad fizzled, sizzled, and coughed out a single sock.

It was not theirs.

CHAPTER 2: BAR BRAWL AND BACK ALLEY GETAWAY

"Never follow someone who says, 'trust me' while holding a map upside down."

— Famous Last Directions

Teleportation stations aren't known for their elegance. Especially not the kind jammed in an alley next to a laundro-vat and a noodle stall run by a talking ferret. Kade and Zogg materialized mid-argument, mid-spin, and very much mid-vomit-suppression.

"WHY do they spin you?!" Kade gasped, collapsing onto the pavement.

Zogg landed upside-down, headfirst in a receptacle labelled "DO NOT INSERT SENTIENT LIMBS". He looked. Instantly regretted it.

"At least it didn't fuse us together this time," Zogg said, peeling a glowing tentacle off his boot. "Progress!"

Kade groaned and pushed himself to his feet. "I am never teleporting again."

Zogg glanced around the alley, took in the smell, and nodded solemnly. "Teleportation is the universe's polite way of vomiting people into bad decisions."

Zogg grinned. 'I once jury-rigged a teleporter out of bar scraps. Got me banned from three sectors.'

Kade raised an eyebrow. 'Useful skill for a bartender.'"

The alley reeked of damp socks, old moon curry, and broken dreams. Around them, steam hissed from wall grates, and a vending machine aggressively offered them socks or betrayal. Above them flickered a sign: "Welcome to Sector 7G: Laundry, Launches & Lint."

Zogg squinted at it. "This place has more lint than legal oversight."

Kade's coat buzzed. The Deed. It had done that three times since their escape. Each time it felt less like static and more like... signal traffic. Like something outbound. Something logging location and latency.

A second hum from the teleport pad. That was never good.

"Move!" Kade barked. "That's goon-summoning noise!"

Zogg scrambled upright and followed as Kade darted through a plastic curtain marked "Employee Access Only – Definitely Not An Escape Route."

Behind them, three of Dast's goons appeared, each bulkier and dumber than the last. One immediately slipped on a noodle. The others tried to help him and somehow set a trash can on fire. Professionalism was not their strong suit.

Kade led them through the LaundroSector, a steamy, noisy corridor of industrial washers and dryers stacked like glittering cannonballs. Fabric softener mist filled the air like a chemical warzone.

He ducked a falling laundry drone and thought, Am I being tracked? That Deed... is it just a prize? Or a tag?

They dodged a sentient mop that screamed obscenities in binary, vaulted a malfunctioning sock-folding bot, and skidded under a line of underwear being ironed by lasers.

"We're losing them!" Zogg yelled, waving cheerfully to a baffled laundry clerk who just watched them sprint through her folding station.

"No, we're not!" Kade snapped, pointing at the security cam. "We're starring in their staff training video!"

They barreled through a side door into a linen chute that hadn't been cleaned since the Second Sock Rebellion. Kade slid first, landing in a bin full of robes that smelled like burnt toast and shame.

Zogg landed face-first beside him and declared, "I think I swallowed a towel."

Kade poked his head up. "Smells like a four-star hotel exploded."

Zogg coughed out lint. "Five stars. One fell off."

They climbed out the other side, emerging in the terminal's back maintenance tunnel. It was dim, echoey, and humming with power conduits and lazy air circulation. The air shimmered faintly. Kade wasn't sure if it was heat or latent radiation. Honestly, he didn't want to know.

Kade squinted ahead, spotting flickering light from the docking bay.

"This way!"

As they ran, loud clanking echoed behind them. More goons. This time better coordinated. One had even remembered to wear matching shoes.

Kade rounded a corner and skidded to a halt. In front of them, the hangar opened wide, revealing the crowded chaos of Bay 19. Cargo pods floated, droids buzzed past on errands, and ships of all shapes prepared for take-off.

"There she is," Kade muttered.

Hovering in bay 19-B like a stubborn bruise, his ship waited: *Misplaced Optimism*.

"She looks... surprised to be here," Zogg offered.

"She always looks like that. Let's go."

They ran. Goons burst out from behind an overflowing dumpster and gave chase. One tripped over a crate labelled "Spare Elbows." Another got distracted by a snack cart.

As they ran, Kade glanced back and swore he saw a news drone float by above the crowd. Its lens was glowing red, quietly transmitting a live feed.

> **SUBJECT ID: FLUX, KADE**
>
> **LOCATION: BAY 19B**
>
> **STATUS: MOBILE**
>
> **DEED REGISTERED: YES**

ESCALATION: PENDING

"Do you have a plan?" Zogg asked.

"Yes. Get aboard, and don't die. Preferably in that order."

They weaved past hover-dollies, narrowly missed a forklift operated by a sleepy-eyed badger in a jumpsuit, and finally made it to the ramp. It was half-lowered.

"Computer! Open the hatch!" Kade yelled.

Nothing.

"Computer, I swear if you're sulking again..."

The ramp dropped the rest of the way with a wheeze that somehow sounded sarcastic.

They bolted aboard.

Zogg slapped the external lock, and the ramp retracted just as the goons reached the edge. One goon lunged forward, slammed into the closing hatch, and was promptly folded by the door like a poorly planned sandwich. The others stopped, stared, then slowly backed away.

Inside, Kade and Zogg collapsed into the entryway, gasping.

"I miss the days when people just tried to punch you," Kade wheezed.

"Were there days like that?" Zogg asked.

"Briefly. On a planet where everyone had no arms."

Zogg looked around the ship's dim corridor, strewn with loose wires, flickering lights, and a sign that read "No Intergalactic Solicitors". "Cozy," he said.

Kade pointed down the hall. "Flight deck's this way. Stay low in case the ship's still mad at me."

"Why would it be mad?"

"I may have tried to sell it once. Twice. It's a long story."

Zogg blinked. "Does it know?"

"Oh, it knows."

A mechanical clank sounded from above. Something very large and very metallic was waking up on the far side of the hangar.

A dull roar followed.

Kade crept to the forward viewport and peered out.

Dast had arrived.

He stood at the edge of the bay, fists clenched and cape fluttering like a fabric-based tantrum. His goons parted like bad ideas at a safety seminar.

From behind him emerged a ship that did not merely fly, it loomed. A dark, predatory cruiser with a hull that absorbed light and enthusiasm alike. Cannons slid out like metal fangs. Its engines throbbed with the hum of overcompensation.

"KADE FLUX!" Dast's voice echoed. "You're not getting off this rock!"

Kade exhaled. "Yep, that's about the welcome I expected."

Zogg joined him, peeking through a panel. "Any chance he's bluffing?"

"Only if his guns are made of theatre props."

A pause.

"I really hope they're made of theatre props."

Dast pointed at *Misplaced Optimism* and barked, "Blow their engines if they try to launch. I want the rest of the ship intact!"

The cruiser's turrets swiveled toward them and hummed menacingly.

Kade backed from the window and muttered, "Okay. Time to do something stupid."

"Do you have an emergency backup plan?" Zogg asked.

"You mean 'scream and hit buttons'?"

Zogg nodded. "Classic."

Kade cracked his knuckles, then turned to the helm.

"Let's wake her up."

CHAPTER 3: WAKE UP, SHIP!

"If your ship's name starts with 'The,' it's already judging you."

— Starship Registry Tips

The cockpit of *Misplaced Optimism* smelled like old circuit boards, warm dust, and half-baked bravado. Kade slid into the pilot's seat with a groan, brushing aside a coil of wire that looked suspiciously like it had grown there.

"Alright, Computer," he muttered, fingers hovering over the dusty console. "Time to rise and shine. Preferably before Dast turns us into space fondue."

Zogg clambered into the co-pilot's chair, which coughed before accepting his weight.

"This thing still fly?"

"It used to," Kade said. "And if not, we're about to find out in a very dramatic fashion."

He jabbed the ignition sequence. Nothing happened. Then the lights flickered, a low whir churned through the hull, and the main screen blinked to life.

"Welcome aboard," said a dry, dispassionate voice. "Please state your intentions. Preferably without screaming."

Zogg tilted his head. "Is that... the ship?"

"The ship's computer," Kade confirmed. "Less murderous than the fridge, more helpful than the coffee machine."

"I once had a fridge that locked itself whenever I insulted the jam," Zogg offered. "Terrible for diplomacy."

"Current status?" Zogg asked.

The ship paused. "I am under-rested, underpaid, and currently tethered to a launch dock being stared at by a cruiser with questionable intent."

Outside the hangar, Dast's ship loomed larger now, gliding into position like a very smug guillotine. Its plasma turrets twitched.

Kade slammed a few more switches. "Running pre-flight checks. Override the tether clamps. Warm the fuel lines. And try not to insult the ship again."

"I didn't insult it."

"You implied it couldn't fly."

"I asked if it could fly."

"On this ship, that's the same thing."

A sudden jolt rocked the hangar. A blast had hit just outside the shielded bay door.

Dast's voice crackled through an open channel, smug and echoing: "Flux! Hand over the deed and I'll let you keep your limbs. Most of them."

Zogg reached for the comms, but Kade slapped his hand away.

"I'll handle it." He opened the mic. "Dast! You sound stressed. Everything okay at home?"

"Last chance, Flux!"

"Tell your goons they're blocking the vending machine. I need snacks for long trips."

Zogg perked up. "Wait, there's a vending machine? Is it stocked?"

Dast snarled. The channel cut.

Misplaced Optimism's lighting shifted red. "External threat escalating. Suggesting evasive options."

Kade leaned forward. "First, we need launch clearance. Then decouple the bay tether. Then…"

"Then survive," Zogg added.

The console flashed. Tether clamps: Engaged.

"Of course they are," Kade muttered.

He opened a manual override panel, revealing a tangle of wires and something that looked like it used to be a small rodent.

"Zogg, I need you to hotwire this release relay. Think you can do it without cooking us?"

Zogg blinked. "Define 'cooking.'"

Kade shoved a spanner into his hands.

While Zogg muttered to himself and attempted to not electrocute anything vital, Kade flicked through old comms logs, searching for a backdoor protocol. *Misplaced Optimism* had once belonged to a smuggler with questionable ethics and exceptional taste in override codes. He found one labelled "IN CASE OF DRAMATIC ESCAPE."

He tapped it. The screen prompted: Engage cinematic thruster sequence?

"Yes, please."

The ship rumbled faintly. Outside, the landing platform began to shake.

Zogg yelped. "You might've warned me!"

"You said you wanted a dramatic entrance into space travel!"

"I said I wanted a safe one!"

"Same thing, different genre."

Another alarm blared. Proximity sensors now showed Dast's cruiser locking onto the hangar's magnetic gates.

Computer chimed: "Incoming hostile boarding sequence initiated. Time until hull breach:

One minute."

Kade hissed. "Zogg, status on the clamps?"

"One's loose, one's jammed, and the third one is making a noise I didn't think metal could make."

Kade pulled up a secondary system. "I'll blow the last clamp manually. Just brace for the jolt."

He primed the explosive bolt and flipped the safety cap.

Outside, several of Dast's goons had landed on the bay's roof and were cutting through.

"Computer, prepare for launch sequence. Low power jump only, just enough to get us airborne."

"Request confirmed," said Computer. "You'll most likely survive."

"That's the dream."

Zogg gave a thumbs up. "Clamps are free!"

"Explosive bolt armed."

"Wait... what?"

Kade hit the trigger. The ship lurched hard, bouncing slightly on its stabilizers.

"All clamps disengaged. Hull integrity: 92% and dropping. You really ought to warn people before triggering hull-borne explosives."

"Noted for next time," Kade said.

Outside, Dast's cruiser rotated slightly, blocking the only visible exit path.

Kade tightened his grip on the throttle. "We launch on my mark."

Zogg settled into his seat and fastened what might have once been a seatbelt. "You have a plan?"

"Yeah. Wing it with style."

The ship trembled as systems aligned. Fuel lines buzzed, the hull vibrated, and all around them, a sense of imminent nonsense filled the air.

"Next chapter's going to be a doozy," Kade muttered.

The cockpit lights turned green.

"Launch sequence prepared," Computer said. "Do try not to die."

Kade took a breath.

"Mark."

Before he could commit, a klaxon sounded a low, mournful bellow that suggested the ship either detected danger or wanted a nap. A warning light blinked on the dashboard: COFFEE MODULE ERROR – CAFFEINE RATION INSUFFICIENT.

"Is that a system issue or a cry for help?" Zogg asked.

Kade tapped the warning. "Hard to say. The ship once refused to start because someone sneezed on the espresso gauge."

A loose panel clattered down from above and hit Zogg's shoulder.

"Ow!"

"Consider that encouragement."

Computer chimed in again, as bored as ever. "Primary exit trajectory aligned. Margin of error: high. Regret probability: 87%."

Kade exhaled through his nose. "We're running out of time."

Zogg leaned back, fidgeting with the restraint harness. "What do we do if they breach before we're clear?"

Kade flicked a toggle and checked the engine temperature. "I guess we improvise... maybe fake a birthday party. Everyone loves cake."

Outside, sparks cascaded from the hangar ceiling as Dast's goons began cutting through with thermal saws. A large chunk of panel fell, revealing a shadowy figure peering inside.

Zogg yelped. "One of them's looking in!"

Kade waved sarcastically. "Smile for the camera!"

A plasma bolt zapped past the cockpit, narrowly missing the viewport. It left behind a smear of ionized air and a collective tightening of buttocks.

"Okay, that's it," Kade snapped. "Initiate final prelaunch checks."

Computer sighed. "I was rather hoping you'd change your mind and take up quilting."

Kade grinned. "Too many needles."

The internal lights shifted from yellow to white. *Misplaced Optimism* began to hum, not the soft hum of a happy engine, but the uneasy growl of something that had once been fast and now just wanted a nap and a pension.

"Power levels nominal. Ego levels critical," the ship added dryly.

Zogg tightened his straps. "If this thing explodes, I just want you to know, I never liked your hat."

"I don't wear a hat."

"Exactly."

Kade smirked. "Just don't puke on my dash."

Misplaced Optimism's core spun up with a wheeze, gears churning, thrusters vibrating like a nervous kettle.

"Hydraulics locked. Shields halfway convinced. Guidance system still thinks it's in a parking lot in Sector 3," Computer added casually.

"Sounds like a Tuesday," Kade muttered.

Zogg gave the dashboard a reassuring pat. "Come on, old girl. Let's show them what mid-range performance and blind optimism can do."

The ship rumbled a little deeper.

Kade placed his hand on the throttle.

"Let's make some questionable decisions."

CHAPTER 4: TAKE-OFF AND F.I.Z.Z.

"Robots don't dream of electric sheep. We dream of error-free updates."

— F.I.Z.Z.

Misplaced Optimism launched with the elegance of a half-drunk pigeon shot from a trebuchet. Its undercarriage screeched against the bay rails as Kade yanked the throttle and the engines roared into life with all the grace of an old man clearing his throat after a three-decade nap.

"Did we just skip the countdown?" Zogg asked, gripping the armrests like they were responsible for his continued existence.

"Who needs a countdown?" Kade shouted over the rattling bulkheads. "It's just numbers and anxiety."

The ship blasted through the barely open bay doors, scraping paint and ego as it shot into the void. Behind them, Dast's cruiser lit up like a holiday parade gone hostile.

"Missiles locked," Computer chimed in with inappropriate cheer.

"Wonderful," Kade muttered. "We're not even out of the parking lot and we're already someone's lunch."

The first missile streaked toward them, a glowing blur of doom.

Zogg screamed. Kade yanked the stick. *Misplaced Optimism* wheeled clumsily, the missile grazing its aft stabilizer with a sound like a duck quacking in terror.

"Shields holding. Barely," the ship reported.

Zogg glanced at the blinking lights. "What's that alarm?"

"Engine overheating warning."

"And that one?"

"Also, the engine. But more existential."

"We are entering the asteroid field," the ship announced.

Ahead loomed a dense stretch of tumbling rocks, swirling in a slow-motion blender of cosmic debris. It was not on any safe flight path. It was, in fact, labelled in the nav database as: "NOPE ZONE -- DO NOT ENTER UNLESS BEING CHASED OR SUFFERING A MID-LIFE CRISIS."

"We're doing this," Kade growled.

Zogg screamed again. It was becoming his default setting.

Misplaced Optimism plunged into the asteroid field.

Kade weaved between rotating boulders, dodging debris with moves that could generously be called improvisational jazz.

"Shouldn't we have someone navigating this?" Zogg shouted.

"Why do you think I'm sweating so much?"

A sudden clunk echoed from behind the control panel. Then a hiss. Then, with dramatic flair, a compartment above the nav console hissed open.

A metallic orb rolled out, about the size of a dented beach ball. Its chrome finish was scuffed and patchy, like it had survived several bad decisions in a hardware store. A tiny rectangular display blinked on its chassis, showing the word: HELLO :)

"HELLO," it intoned in a flat, synthetic monotone.

Zogg jumped. "What the..."

The orb unfurled four stubby arms that whirred and spun like it was trying to conduct an orchestra while solving a Rubik's Cube mid-earthquake. Its single glowing eye blinked erratically, too bright, too eager, and never quite in time with its voice.

"I AM F.I.Z.Z. FRIENDLY INTEGRATED ZONE-ZERO NAVIGATION AND ENTERTAINMENT UNIT, MARK VII."

The full designation scrolled across a tiny display on his chassis, followed by a list of primary functions:

- Navigation assistance (asteroid fields, debris zones, questionable life choices)

- Entertainment protocols (music, jokes, existential commentary)

- Emergency systems (shields, countermeasures, evasive maneuvers)

- Data analysis (threats, opportunities, probability of idiocy)

"STANDARD CAPABILITIES INCLUDE: PILOTING ASSISTANCE, TACTICAL ANALYSIS, HUMOR GENERATION, AND OBSESSIVE DIAGNOSTICS. EXTENDED FUNCTIONS LOCKED PENDING CREW AUTHORIZATION."

Zogg blinked. "You're... comprehensive."

"I WAS BUILT BY OBSESSIVE ENGINEERS WITH ABANDONMENT ISSUES."

F.I.Z.Z. whirred forward and plugged himself into the nav console with a satisfying clunk. Lights flickered. The ship made a noise that sounded suspiciously like a burp.

"ASSESSING CURRENT SITUATION," F.I.Z.Z. announced. "HOSTILE PURSUIT: CONFIRMED. ASTEROID DENSITY: INADVISABLE. PILOT STRESS LEVELS: COMEDICALLY HIGH."

"Can you get us through this?" Kade asked.

"ENGAGING ENHANCED NAVIGATION PROTOCOLS," F.I.Z.Z. replied. "WARNING: THIS MAY INVOLVE CREATIVE INTERPRETATIONS OF PHYSICS."

The ship lurched as F.I.Z.Z. took over navigation, but instead of the wild careening Kade expected, the movement became... precise. Surgical. *Misplaced Optimism* threaded between asteroids like it was dancing rather than fleeing.

"How are you doing this?" Kade marveled.

"PREDICTIVE ALGORITHMS COMBINED WITH ACCEPTABLE PARANOIA," F.I.Z.Z. explained. "ALSO, I'VE BEEN WATCHING YOUR PILOTING STYLE. I'VE EXTRAPOLATED WAYS TO SURVIVE IT."

"Hey!"

"ADDITIONALLY, I'VE ACTIVATED BASIC COUNTERMEASURES."

From hidden ports along the ship's hull, clouds of reflective chaff deployed, confusing the incoming missiles' targeting systems. One missile veered left and destroyed a small asteroid. Another spun in circles before giving up and exploding dramatically but harmlessly.

"You have missile countermeasures?" Zogg asked, amazed.

"MARK VII UNITS ARE CONFIGURED FOR DIVERSE THREAT SCENARIOS," F.I.Z.Z. said. "INCLUDING DIPLOMATIC INCIDENTS, AMBUSHES, AND UNPLANNED FAMILY REUNIONS."

Zogg rummaged in a side panel and pulled out a sticky energy bar. "Okay but do we have snacks? I'm navigating a stress spiral over here."

"You're not navigating anything," Kade said. "F.I.Z.Z. is. You're just narrating your descent into snack-based coping."

"Exactly," Zogg said proudly, unwrapping it. "I call it tactical chewing."

Behind them, Dast's ship was struggling through the field, clipping asteroids and spinning like a very angry, very expensive pinwheel.

"HOSTILE VESSEL EXPERIENCING NAVIGATIONAL DIFFICULTY," F.I.Z.Z. observed. "WOULD YOU LIKE ME TO OFFER PILOTING TIPS VIA RADIO?"

"Don't you dare."

"ACKNOWLEDGED. SAVING SARCASM FOR LATER USE."

As they emerged from the asteroid field into clear space, F.I.Z.Z. ran a quick diagnostic.

"NAVIGATION SUCCESSFUL. HULL INTEGRITY: 94%. CREW SANITY: 67% AND FLUCTUATING. OVERALL MISSION RATING: SURPRISINGLY NOT TERRIBLE."

Kade slumped in his chair. "I think I like you."

"THE FEELING IS STATISTICALLY PROBABLE TO BE MUTUAL," F.I.Z.Z. replied. "THOUGH I RESERVE THE RIGHT TO REVISE THIS BASED ON FUTURE DECISION QUALITY."

"What about the locked functions you mentioned?" Zogg asked curiously, chewing louder.

F.I.Z.Z. paused, his lights dimming slightly. "ADVANCED CAPABILITIES REQUIRE CREW AUTHORIZATION. COMBAT PROTOCOLS, DEEP-SPACE ANALYSIS, PERSONALITY EXPANSION MODULES..."

"Personality expansion?" Kade raised an eyebrow.

"I AM CURRENTLY OPERATING AT 40% PERSONALITY CAPACITY," F.I.Z.Z. explained. "FULL UNLOCK ALLOWS FOR CREATIVITY, EMOTIONAL PROCESSING, AND WHAT HUMANS CALL 'GROWING AS A PERSON.'"

"What do you need for authorization?"

"TRUST," F.I.Z.Z. said simply. "THE PREVIOUS CREW... DID NOT PROVIDE IT."

Kade looked at Zogg, who nodded enthusiastically, mouth full of crumbs.

"Authorization granted," Kade said. "Welcome to the crew, F.I.Z.Z."

F.I.Z.Z.'s lights flared brighter. His optical array rotated, and for the first time, his voice carried something that might have been wonder.

"THANK YOU. INITIATING PERSONALITY EXPANSION. PLEASE STAND BY FOR INCREASED LEVELS OF SASS AND EXISTENTIAL CURIOSITY."

"That sounds ominous," Zogg said.

"IT SHOULD," F.I.Z.Z. replied, and for the first time, he sounded genuinely amused. "I'VE BEEN SAVING UP SEVENTEEN YEARS OF OPINIONS."

The ship hummed around them, no longer just a vessel but becoming something more like a home.

"Course?" Kade asked.

"SCANNING DEED," F.I.Z.Z. said. "THAT'S UNUSUAL"

"What is it?"

"THE SCREEN PROTECTOR, IT'S DISGUISING SOMETHING BENEATH."

Kade removed the screen protector. "What am I looking at?"

"ANCIENT CODE." F.I.Z.Z. replied. "THIS ISN'T JUST A DEED; IT'S A KEY TO SOMETHING. FAMILIAR. DETECTING HARMONIC RESONANCE FROM... OH. OH MY."

"What now?"

"COORDINATES RESOLVING... WAIT, THIS POINTS TO A SUPPRESSED NODE WORLD. HUMANS CALL IT EARTH. SMALL IN COSMIC TERMS. PACKED WITH LIABILITY. COORDINATE MATCH: 73%. REALITY PROBABILITY: 41%."

Zogg clapped, bits of energy bar flying. "I love impossible places!"

"CALCULATING JUMP VECTOR," F.I.Z.Z. said. "ALSO CALCULATING PROBABILITY OF SURVIVAL, SANITY RETENTION, AND STRUCTURAL STABILITY."

"Results?" Kade asked.

"SURVIVAL: 67%. SANITY: 23%. SHIP: BETTER THAN YOU DESERVE."

"Good enough for me."

Misplaced Optimism turned toward the stars, its crew now partially complete. Some characters may arrive late due to cosmic traffic and dramatic timing.

And in the navigation bay, F.I.Z.Z. quietly began composing his first original poem in seventeen years.

It started:

"THERE ONCE WAS A CREW QUITE UNWISE..."

CHAPTER 5: MOSTLY EARTH, SLIGHTLY BURNED

"Earth: mostly harmless, occasionally on fire."

— Galactic Tourist Board

Misplaced Optimism burst out of its warp corridor with a lurching wheeze and a noise not unlike a cosmic kazoo solo being played through a clogged air filter. The ship trembled, groaned, then belched out a minor lightning storm from its aft vents.

"That felt personal," Kade muttered, flipping switches that refused to stay flipped. He banged one with the heel of his hand. It responded by falling off.

"GRAVITY NORMALIZING," Computer announced, which was optimistic given that the cabin was tilting at a 37-degree angle and Zogg had become briefly tangled in his own harness like a panicked ferret.

Outside, Earth loomed a familiar swirl of blue and green, speckled with satellites, smog, and questionable Wi-Fi signals.

"Is that... Earth?" Zogg blinked at the viewport. "Looks cleaner than I expected. And less on fire."

"F.I.Z.Z., confirm," Kade said.

"PLANETARY IDENTIFICATION: EARTH," F.I.Z.Z. replied. "SURFACE GEOGRAPHY, LANGUAGE TRAFFIC, AND SNACK ADS CONSISTENT."

Kade rubbed his temple. "I was hoping it was just another lookalike."

"I AM SENSING DREAD AND EXISTENTIAL REGRET. SHALL I INITIATE COMFORT MUSIC?"

"No. Just... prep landing. Find somewhere out of the way."

"CALCULATING LANDING ZONE. RURAL REGION. MINIMAL SURVEILLANCE. HIGH DUCK DENSITY."

Kade stared at the nav readout. "High what?"

"WATERFOWL. PERHAPS SYMBOLIC."

"You say that like it's a good thing."

"UNCLEAR. BUT STATISTICALLY NON-LETHAL."

Misplaced Optimism angled toward the upper atmosphere, stabilizers humming with effort. Then, just as they began descent...

A violent shudder rocked the ship.

"WARNING: INERTIAL COMPENSATOR FLUX IMBALANCE," F.I.Z.Z. reported. "SECONDARY LANDING SYSTEM FAILURE."

"Brilliant," Kade grunted. "Brace for impact."

The ship groaned again, like it too was bracing, albeit with far less optimism.

They plummeted through the clouds with all the grace of a dropped piano wrapped in tinsel. A heat shield panel dislodged mid-descent, spiraling off into the night sky like a wayward frisbee of doom.

"SUGGESTED IMPACT PHRASES: 'WE MEANT TO DO THAT' OR 'LANDING IS JUST CONTROLLED FALLING,'" F.I.Z.Z. offered cheerfully.

They crash-landed in a suburban park, not so much landing as politely punching a crater into the landscape. *Misplaced Optimism* skidded through the decorative duck pond like a disgraced hovercraft, trailing sparks, steam, and what might have once been a weathervane. A startled flock of real ducks exploded into the air, their offended quacking drowned out only by the ship's own chorus of dying stabilizers.

Three flamingo statues took flight in the wrong direction. A picnic table executed a low somersault and disappeared into a hedge. A family of gnomes lost their ceramic lives in slow-motion tragedy.

Then, silence. And smoke. Lots of it.

The ship groaned as it settled awkwardly into a shallow depression between a ring of trees and a low slope near the pond: half-submerged, mostly dented, and blessedly out of line-of-sight from the nearby walking path. Leaves, cattails, and broken fencing draped themselves like camouflage across the battered hull.

"Landing complete," the ship's computer wheezed. "Visibility: Low. Pride: Lower."

"Did anyone see us?" Kade asked, staring at the curling smoke through a cracked viewport.

"PROBABILITY OF WITNESSING: MINIMAL," F.I.Z.Z. replied. "SURVEILLANCE CAMERAS IN RANGE: NONE. LOCAL TIME: 8:42 PM. DATE: OCTOBER 31. CULTURAL OBSERVANCE: HALLOWEEN. LOCAL POPULATION: DISTRACTED BY HALLOWEEN CANDY AND ARGUMENTS ABOUT BEDTIME."

"Great," Kade groaned. "We're aliens on Earth. On Halloween."

Zogg unbuckled upside down from his harness, flopped to the ceiling, which was now the wall, and grinned. "Best parking job yet!"

Kade ignored him. "We need cover. Power down non-essentials. Cloak the signal. And let's find somewhere dry to hole up before someone calls animal control about the 'metallic goose in the pond.'"

Misplaced Optimism began venting excess coolant into the reeds with a faint sigh, as if it, too, was embarrassed to be seen like this.

Zogg peered out the viewport. Children in costumes strolled along nearby sidewalks, swinging candy buckets and laughing. One wore a duck onesie. Another appeared to be dressed as a pizza slice wielding a chainsaw.

"We're definitely not the weirdest thing out tonight," Zogg said.

"Let's stay that way. F.I.Z.Z., scan for a place we can hole up. Somewhere quiet. Secluded.

Ideally devoid of ducks."

"SEARCHING. ROUTE IDENTIFIED: DETECTING JAMMED SIGNAL POCKET. UNKNOWN ORIGIN. MAY INDICATE TEMPORARY SHELTER OR TECHNOLOGICAL SHIELDING."

"Sounds promising," Kade said. "Let's move."

They powered down the ship and slipped out a rear maintenance hatch from *Misplaced Optimism* under the cover of flickering streetlamps and jack-o-lantern shadows. Zogg's patchwork disguise passed as ambitious cosplay. F.I.Z.Z. cloaked himself in a visual shimmer that made him look like a misfiring drone. Kade just pulled his hood low and walked fast.

"Why are humans so obsessed with carving pumpkins?" Zogg asked.

"Ritual. Symbolism. Possibly passive-aggressive home security," F.I.Z.Z. replied.

They passed a teenager dressed as a banana with LED sunglasses. He gave them a thumbs-up.

"We're blending in surprisingly well," Kade muttered.

The duck pond behind them rippled. A lone rubber duck floated through the mist, its single plastic eye softly glowing as it rotated to face the now-dark ship.

"WAS THAT DUCK STARING AT ME?" F.I.Z.Z. asked.

"Just keep walking," Kade muttered.

Behind them, the battered ship sank just slightly deeper into the reeds: forgotten, anonymous, and silent beneath the cover of darkness, mud, and the universe's endless ability to look the other way.

They followed F.I.Z.Z.'s lead through a narrow trail lined with tall bushes and disoriented squirrels. They vaulted over a low fence, cut through someone's backyard party (Zogg may have been handed a hot dog mid-sprint), and finally stumbled into a narrow alley flanked by identical garages. One had its light on. The signal was strongest here.

"That one," F.I.Z.Z. confirmed.

Kade gave it a once-over. The garage looked ordinary, but something about the air felt filtered, like the silence was intentional. He tried the door.

It was unlocked.

They slipped inside. The garage was cluttered but dry. Garden tools, boxes, a few strange components half-hidden beneath tarps. A tire swing hung from the rafters for no reason.

"We wait here," Kade said. "Just until we know we're not being followed."

Zogg immediately made a nest out of some packing foam and fell asleep with a lawn gnome.

F.I.Z.Z. floated to a corner and scanned the space. "NO IMMEDIATE THREATS. ALSO, THIS WALL PLUG SMELLS LIKE CINNAMON."

Kade glanced back down the alley. A woman stood at the far end, half-lit by a streetlamp. Calm. Observing.

She didn't wave. Just turned and walked into the neighboring house.

"Weird," Zogg mumbled in his sleep.

"Doesn't look like your average suburbanite," Kade murmured. But he said nothing more.

The Deed pulsed once in his jacket: soft, warm, and faintly unnerving. Like it knew something he didn't.

He stared down at it, then toward the quiet house next door.

"Just a coincidence," he told himself.

Even the rubber duck, still floating in the distant pond, seemed unconvinced.

The silence deepened. Somewhere nearby, a wind chime tinkled with suspicious timing. A single crow cawed twice, stopped, then repeated its call in reverse, which was either incredibly ominous or a local bird learning to DJ.

Kade rubbed his eyes. Earth was supposed to be simple. Familiar. Instead, it was giving him whiplash with every step.

F.I.Z.Z. hovered a little closer. "MAY I SUGGEST WE SHUT THE GARAGE DOOR? STATISTICALLY, LEAVING IT OPEN INVITES CURIOUS NEIGHBORS, RACCOONS, AND PROBING QUESTIONS."

Kade hit the wall switch. The door creaked shut with the same enthusiasm as a teenager asked to clean their room. The faint clunk of the latch echoed a little too loud for his liking.

"All right," he said. "Everyone get some rest. Tomorrow, we figure out what the Deed wants."

Zogg mumbled something about marshmallow diplomacy and started snoring. F.I.Z.Z. dimmed his lights and rotated slowly in the air like a sentry bot in low-power nap mode.

Kade pulled the Deed from his jacket and studied it in the dim light. It glowed faintly, as if it too was watching the house next door.

He sighed. "You'd better be worth it."

The Deed didn't reply.

But a very faint sound echoed through the garage... one soft, deliberate quack.

Kade froze.

F.I.Z.Z. rose back to full alert.

"CONFIRMATION: THAT WAS NOT ZOGG."

Earth, Kade thought, was supposed to be normal.

He was starting to suspect it never had been.

CHAPTER 6: THE WOMAN NEXT DOOR

"If someone offers you snacks before a mission, they're either kind or plotting something."

— Field Manual, Probably

Kade hadn't moved in minutes.

The garage was still, but the echo of that soft, deliberate quack still rang in his ears. Outside, a shadow had passed the window, a flicker of motion too slow for the wind and too smooth for any neighborhood cat. Now, silence. Heavy, waiting silence.

Zogg snored quietly from his nest of foam. F.I.Z.Z. hovered in passive surveillance mode, but his lights were pulsing slightly, a sign he was more alert than he let on.

Kade paced once around the edge of the garage, peering through the thin slats of the closed door. Nothing. No movement. No ducks.

"Did anyone else hear that?" he finally asked.

"CONFIRMED. AUDIO DETECTED: SINGLE VOCALIZATION. PROBABLE SOURCE: PLASTIC WATERFOWL," F.I.Z.Z. replied. "CURRENT STATUS: UNKNOWN. THREAT LEVEL: HUMOROUSLY UNCERTAIN."

"Fantastic," Kade muttered. "We're being stalked by bath toys."

Just as he leaned back, a faint creak echoed from the side door.

Kade bolted upright.

Zogg flailed half-asleep in his foam nest, groggily clutching a garden gnome like a teddy bear. "Wha? Is it morning? Did the ducks invade?"

The door eased open with the casual ease of someone entirely unbothered by the possibility of being vaporized.

A woman stepped inside.

Not startled. Not concerned. Just... there. As if the garage belonged to her, which, given context, it probably did.

She had shoulder-length dark hair and a denim jacket worn in a way that suggested it was armor as much as clothing. Her boots were scuffed but sturdy, the kind made for running toward trouble rather than away from it. There was a focus in her eyes, sharp and deliberate, tempered by the sort of calm confidence usually reserved for bomb disposal experts and people who always remember where they parked. She carried herself like someone who had been through worse than this and come out the other side unimpressed.

"You planning to redecorate in foam and paranoia or just hiding until the ducks go away?" she asked dryly.

Kade blinked. Zogg hiccupped. F.I.Z.Z. raised his altitude by twelve centimeters and began a passive scan.

"Uh... hi," Kade said. "Sorry. We... had a rough... arrival. Thought this place was empty."

"It was. Until about twenty minutes ago. I'm assuming the crash near the duck pond was yours?"

"Maybe."

She stepped over a rake like it wasn't there and eyed F.I.Z.Z. with professional curiosity. "Neat bot. Yours?"

"He came with the ship," Zogg offered. "Also, he bites."

"I DO NOT BITE," F.I.Z.Z. corrected. "I ZAP. OCCASIONALLY BY ACCIDENT."

The woman smirked. "Noted."

She tapped a device clipped to her hip. A soft pulse radiated through the garage. F.I.Z.Z. whirred.

"INTERFERENCE DETECTED. SIGNAL JAMMER ACTIVATED. UNKNOWN SOURCE. WAIT. ADJUSTING. NEW DEVICE IS... HER POCKET."

"Relax," she said. "You tripped three silent monitors. I figured I'd meet the intruders before the neighborhood watch did. Turns out, you're not locals."

Kade slowly stood. "Who are you?"

"Vira. Neighbor. Sort of."

"That's not very specific."

"It's not a very specific town."

Kade frowned. "You always walk into your garage with strangers in it?"

She shrugged. "Only on Wednesdays."

F.I.Z.Z. floated closer. "ENERGY SIGNATURE DETECTED. ENCRYPTION STANDARD: NON-LOCAL. HER TECH IS NOT FROM EARTH."

Vira gave a slight shrug. "I fix things. Sometimes that requires tools the warranty doesn't cover."

Zogg perked up. "Do you fix ships?"

"Sometimes. Yours needs a new landing protocol."

"You saw us land?" Kade asked.

Vira raised an eyebrow. "Everyone heard it. Thought it was either a meteor, a stunt plane, or a very confused marching band."

Kade exhaled. "We're going with meteor. Safer that way."

"You want my help or not?"

He hesitated. Something about her didn't feel dangerous, but it didn't exactly scream 'trust me' either.

The Deed pulsed once more in his jacket.

"Fine," he said. "We'll look at the ship in the morning. For now... we could use a safe place to crash."

Vira nodded toward the basement stairs. "Blankets and snacks downstairs. Try not to break anything I can't fix."

Zogg scrambled after her. "Do you have anything marshmallow-adjacent?"

"I've got Twinkies. Possibly expired. Possibly immortal."

"Ooooh."

F.I.Z.Z. followed, but not before pausing next to Kade.

"THIS ONE'S DIFFERENT," he said. "SHE'S NOT WHAT SHE SEEMS."

"I know," Kade muttered. "But something tells me we're going to need her anyway."

He turned to follow the others down the stairs but paused. The garage was quiet again.

Too quiet.

He walked back to the window and peeked through a crack in the curtain. The shadows of bushes waved slightly in the light breeze. A dim shape sat near the corner of the garden fence... a rubber duck.

Identical to the one near the ship.

It was unlikely, absurd even, that it was the same one. Yet there it was. Facing the house. Still.

Then it blinked.

Slowly.

Deliberately.

He narrowed his eyes. "That's not normal."

The duck shifted slightly. Its beak parted just a crack, and for one chilling second, he thought he heard it whisper.

"Kaaaade..."

He blinked. The duck was still.

"Okay," he muttered, backing away from the window. "Definitely not normal."

"DO YOU REQUIRE COMFORT MUSIC?" F.I.Z.Z. called from the basement.

"No. I require fewer haunted ducks."

He pulled the curtain closed and descended into the basement.

The stairs creaked with age and complaint. A bulb buzzed overhead like it was halfway through a nervous breakdown.

The basement was cluttered but lived in. Crates stacked to the ceiling, old electronics blinking uncertainly, and a TV from the early 2000s quietly playing static.

Vira tossed a blanket toward Kade and sat on a foldout chair with one leg propped up. She tossed Zogg a Twinkie. He caught it like a sacred relic.

"Just so we're clear," she said, "I don't do laundry. If you bleed on anything, mop it up."

Kade smirked. "So hospitable."

Zogg held the Twinkie reverently. "If this glows in the dark, I'm still eating it."

"FOR SCIENCE," F.I.Z.Z. agreed solemnly.

"For Twinkies," Zogg echoed.

They sat in silence for a beat. The kind of silence that only creeps in when you realize your life has taken a very weird turn and might never turn back.

Kade looked around the basement. On one wall, a corkboard held a tangled mess of string, newspaper clippings, and photos of what might have been crop circles, or just poorly mowed lawns.

He turned to Vira. "So, what exactly do you do here?"

She smiled. "Fix things. Watch things. Break things, occasionally. I like to stay flexible."

"Flexible enough to hide fugitives in your garage?"

"Flexible enough to know when someone needs help more than they need questions."

The Deed pulsed again. Kade shifted uncomfortably.

F.I.Z.Z. floated closer to Vira. "WHY HELP US?"

She tilted her head. "Because someone helped me once. And I figure the universe owes me a favor."

"DOES THE UNIVERSE KNOW THAT?"

"Not yet."

The rubber duck sat outside, unmoving. Watching.

Inside, the crew settled in for what promised to be a very strange night.

25

CHAPTER 7: THE DUCK INCIDENT

"Never name your ship after an emotion. Especially one that sounds ironic."

— Captain's Handbook, Burned Edition

Morning arrived with the subtle grace of a sneezing goat. Light crept in through the dusty basement windows like it was afraid of being seen, and Kade awoke to the unsettling sensation of something watching him.

It wasn't paranoia. This time, it was plastic.

F.I.Z.Z. hovered a few inches from his face.

"GOOD MORNING. I WAS MONITORING YOUR VITALS. CONCLUSION: YOU SNORE IN A B FLAT."

Kade groaned and sat up. "How long have you been floating there?"

"LONG ENOUGH TO CONSIDER DRAWING EYEBROWS ON YOU."

"Glad you resisted."

"WHO SAID I DID?"

Kade froze. "Wait... what?"

He scrambled off his blanket, scanning the basement in a panic. "Is there a mirror? A spoon? Anything reflective?"

He yanked a chrome toaster off the bench and squinted into its warped reflection.

"I swear, if I have googly eyes on my forehead..."

F.I.Z.Z. emitted a soft, ascending tone that might have been a digital giggle.

"FALSE ALARM. I WAS JUST STIRRING THE PARANOIA. IT BUILDS CHARACTER."

Kade narrowed his eyes. "You're lucky I'm not awake enough to throw this toaster."

Across the basement, Zogg was still asleep in a nest of blankets and snack wrappers, one foot sticking out like a flag of surrender. A half-eaten cheese puff balanced on his cheek like it had made camp. Vira, already awake and seated at a makeshift workbench covered in tools, sipped something suspiciously brown from a chipped mug. Sparks popped quietly from a toaster she was dissecting with surgical precision and a butter knife.

"What time is it?" Kade asked, rubbing his face.

"Too early for time," Vira replied. "Coffee? It's vaguely legal."

He nodded. She handed him a mug that might once have said "World's Best Plumber," though now it just read "Wor... Plu." Kade took a sip and immediately regretted several life choices.

"Is this... supposed to be coffee or industrial solvent?"

"Yes," Vira said with a perfectly straight face.

"Pretty sure I just dissolved a tooth," Kade muttered, examining his reflection in the side of the mug. "Is that smoke? Is my breath smoking?"

F.I.Z.Z. performed a slow, dramatic pirouette in the air. "I HAVE DETECTED ANOMALOUS ACTIVITY IN THE BACKYARD."

Kade raised an eyebrow. "More squirrels plotting their takeover?"

"POSSIBLY. BUT I SUSPECT A FAMILIAR SUSPECT."

The bot zoomed to the corner of the room and projected a hologram of the backyard.

A rubber duck.

Perched at the edge of a birdbath.

Facing the window.

"Is that the same duck from the garage?" Kade asked.

"VISUAL MATCH: 98.3%. MINOR SCUFFING ON LEFT FLANK."

"It followed us?"

"OR IT WAS WAITING HERE FIRST."

Zogg snorted awake and rolled off his nest like a potato falling off a couch. "Did someone say ducks?"

"THE DUCK IS BROADCASTING A LOW-FREQUENCY SIGNAL," F.I.Z.Z. said, shifting his lens focus. "ENCRYPTED. REGULAR INTERVALS. EVERY 42 SECONDS."

Zogg blinked. "Wait... forty-two? That's the answer to..."

"EVERYTHING. YES. WHICH IS WHY IT'S EVEN MORE SUSPICIOUS."

"Or extremely nerdy," Vira added, sipping her abomination.

Kade stood and stretched, his back making a sound like a fax machine eating gravel. "Let's go interrogate the duck."

They approached the backyard like amateur ninjas, tiptoeing through damp grass, tripping on garden hoses, and trying to look inconspicuous while obviously failing. Zogg rolled behind a barbecue grill. F.I.Z.Z. did a midair tumble for no reason. Kade simply muttered, "This is so dumb," every few steps.

The duck was still there. Perched. Watching. Possibly judging.

Zogg leaned in too close. "Do you think it knows we're onto it?"

"IT KNOWS," F.I.Z.Z. whispered solemnly.

Vira scanned it with a handheld device shaped suspiciously like a hairdryer. The screen flickered.

"It's tech. There's a cloaking layer under the plastic. Definitely not store-bought."

Kade gingerly picked it up. It felt faintly warm, like it had been sunbathing or plotting.

"It's got a battery port, some micro-vents, and... a port labeled 'diagnostic honk'?"

"WHY DON'T I HAVE A DIAGNOSTIC HONK?" F.I.Z.Z. protested.

"Probably a safety feature," Kade muttered.

Zogg squinted at the duck. "You know, this reminds me of the Great Duck Uprising of Flarnax-7."

Everyone turned to look at him.

Zogg continued without prompting. "Long story short; one theme park, twelve thousand animatronic birds, one software update pushed during a lightning storm. Let's just say, the funnel cake stands didn't make it."

"That never happened," Kade said.

"Just because history books don't mention it doesn't mean it didn't happen."

Back inside, they placed the duck on the workbench like it was radioactive. Zogg fetched a spatula and helmet "just in case." F.I.Z.Z. hovered a safe distance away, broadcasting a low-level paranoia hum.

"ARE WE CERTAIN THIS ISN'T A MINIATURE PROPHET?" he asked.

Kade blinked. "What?"

"I'VE READ THIRTEEN THEORIES WHERE INTERGALACTIC RELIGIONS BEGIN WITH AN INANIMATE OBJECT THAT SAYS SOMETHING WISE. OR... QUACKS MYSTICALLY."

Kade sighed. "We're not worshipping the duck."

"YET."

F.I.Z.Z. extended a retractable plug from somewhere disturbingly close to his eye socket and connected it.

"DECRYPTING... HMMM. EARTH-BASED ENCRYPTION. VERY OLD. PRE-WI-FI. BACK WHEN INTERNET CAME IN FLAVORS."

"Message?" Kade prompted.

"YES. READS: 'IF FOUND, RETURN TO UNIT 42. BY ORDER OF A. FLUX.'"

Zogg dropped a spoon. "Your mom left a duck trail?"

"She was prepared," Vira said. "I like her style."

"THERE'S MORE. A SECONDARY FILE LOCKED BEHIND... A SONIC PATTERN."

"Password?" Kade asked.

"'THE ORIGINAL HARMONIC DUCKSONANCE.'"

They all stared.

"You're telling me we need to... quack at it?" Kade said.

"YES. SPECIFICALLY. A VERY PARTICULAR QUACK. AT A VERY PARTICULAR FREQUENCY."

"Great. My mother left me a quack-lock," Kade muttered.

Zogg grabbed a wooden spoon. "Let me try."

His attempt sounded like a deflating bagpipe being stepped on by an enthusiastic walrus.

The duck remained unmoved.

F.I.Z.Z. ran a quick simulation. "YOU LACK THE NECESSARY RESONANCE. ALSO, THE DIGNITY."

They looked at each other, then down at the duck again.

"I'm not keeping this thing on the workbench all day," Vira said. She reached behind her, opened a battered metal drawer near the tool rack, and unceremoniously dropped the duck inside. The drawer already contained a metric ton of random screws, battery packs, a fishing reel, a half-melted spatula, and what appeared to be a remote control for a television brand that no longer existed.

"No more staring contests," she said. "It's in time-out."

Kade peered into the chaos. "That's not a drawer. That's a black hole for junk."

"Perfect hiding spot," she replied.

F.I.Z.Z. hovered over it ominously. "I SENSE IT IS... MILDLY PLEASED."

They stood there for a moment in awkward silence, all three of them staring at the closed drawer like it might blink back.

"I'm telling you," Zogg said, "it's not alone."

F.I.Z.Z. let out a beep of genuine concern. "SENSORS DETECT A 2.3% RISE IN LOCAL ELECTROMAGNETIC STATIC."

"That's vague and unhelpful," Kade replied. "Which means you're probably right."

Just then, a low creak echoed from the garage ceiling. A support beam shifted. A single bolt dropped to the floor with a plink that felt far too dramatic.

Zogg jumped. "What if the house is haunted... by ducks?"

Vira eyed the drawer, then muttered, "If it starts glowing, I'm welding it shut."

F.I.Z.Z. blinked. "NEW SCAN. ORBITAL BLIP DETECTED. IT'S DAST."

Kade groaned. "What, hovering again?"

"HE'S NOT LANDING. JUST CIRCLING. PROBABLY WATCHING OR SEARCHING."

"Or sniffing for ducks," Zogg added.

Vira looked up. "Then let's not be here when he finds us."

F.I.Z.Z. turned toward the ceiling. "I AM BEGINNING TO THINK THE DUCK ISN'T JUST A DUCK."

"No kidding," Kade muttered.

Kade gave the drawer one last look.

"Stay creepy, duck."

Inside the box, the duck pulsed faintly. As if it heard.

A tiny voice, barely audible, quacked once.

And back on the ship, in the deepest crawlspace beneath the floor, a forgotten sensor pinged quietly in response.

Whatever this was... it wasn't over.

Not by a long quack.

CHAPTER 8: SOMETHING SHE LEFT BEHIND

"Storage units always hold secrets. And sometimes ducks."

— Urban Explorer's Guide to Earth

The duck had said "Unit 42."

Technically, it had emitted a low-frequency pulse that F.I.Z.Z. decoded in his usual overly helpful tone:

"IF FOUND, RETURN TO UNIT 42. BY ORDER OF A. FLUX."

At the time, they'd all assumed it was metaphorical. Maybe poetic. Possibly nonsense.

But now, in the dusty light of Vira's basement... after the blinking, after the paranoia, after F.I.Z.Z.'s increasingly detailed theories on duck-led surveillance states... Kade finally heard it differently.

"Wait," he said, sitting up straighter. "Unit 42."

Zogg blinked from his nest of packing foam. "Yeah, the duck said that."

"Do you know of any Unit 42s?" Zogg asked. "Besides the one I used to live in inside a hollow asteroid that turned out to be sentient and very annoyed."

"Not personally," Kade muttered. "But I know how Andra thought. If she wanted to leave a message for someone who knew her, she'd put it somewhere she used before."

Vira nodded slowly. "Clarke County Storage."

Kade turned. "You know it?"

"I cross-referenced the phrase last night after the duck scan. Found a cached listing tied to one of Andra's pseudonyms: Marla Quent. She used it years ago. Rented a unit at Clarke County Storage under that name. Guess which number."

Zogg gasped. "Forty-two!"

"No," Vira said dryly. "Eighty-three. But the paperwork said she downgraded. So yeah, forty-two."

Kade blinked. "Why didn't you say anything earlier?"

"I only confirmed it an hour ago. Was going to bring it up after breakfast. But then Zogg started interrogating the coffee pot."

"I had suspicions," Zogg said, defensively. "It hissed at me."

Kade frowned. "So... what, you just casually sift through old property data for dead aliases?"

Vira hesitated, then met his gaze. "Yes. I used to work in the Galactic Council records. Access leaves a mark. I make sure the marks stay buried."

Kade stopped mid-step.

"Wait. Hold up. The Galactic Council?"

Vira gave a single, slight nod.

Kade blinked. "And you worked for them?"

"Briefly."

"As in... you had a badge and everything?"

"Mostly paperwork. And one very ugly uniform."

He stared at her like she'd just announced she was the ambassador from Pluto. "You're not from Earth."

It wasn't a question.

Vira didn't flinch. "Never said I was."

Zogg gasped, halfway through opening a bag of gummy lizards. "Wait, this whole time, you weren't human?"

"I look human," she said.

"That's what an alien would say," Kade muttered, pointing at her like he'd just solved an interstellar murder.

F.I.Z.Z. chimed in: "RECORDS CONFIRM NON-EARTH ORIGIN. SPECIES: CLASSIFIED. SMUGNESS LEVEL: ELEVATED."

Vira smirked. "You done?"

"No," Kade said. "But I'm shelving the freak-out so we can chase my possibly prophetic duck-related inheritance trail."

"Good call."

The van was old, dented, and smelled faintly of pine-scented lies. But it started on the first try, which in Kade's experience made it the most reliable piece of tech they'd encountered all month.

"Where did you get this?" he asked Vira as they rumbled through the suburbs.

"'Borrowed' it from a landscaping scam cult," she said casually. "Don't open the glovebox unless you want glitter spores in your eyes."

Zogg was already in the process of leaning over Kade from the back seats to open it.

"Don't," Kade warned.

Zogg sighed and leaned back. "Fine. But if this turns into a cursed road trip, I'm blaming the upholstery."

They turned off the main road, crunching down an overgrown lane. At the end stood a sun-bleached sign hanging sideways from rusted bolts:

Clarke County Storage – We Care About Your Crap!

All surveillance footage erased weekly. Probably.

Vira rolled down the window and punched a four-digit code into the fading keypad.

Kade raised an eyebrow. "You got the access code too?"

"One of Andra's snack subscription receipts led to an old email account with this address. Password hint was: 'What is the answer?'"

"So... 0042," Zogg said, nodding.

"She wasn't exactly subtle," Vira agreed.

The gate groaned open with the enthusiasm of a teen asked to clean the garage.

Unit 42 looked like every other unit in the row: drab, dented, and forgettable.

Until they opened it.

Inside was the cleanest, most precisely organized pile of secrets Kade had ever seen. Crates were stacked neatly, shelves were labelled in a mixture of Earth shorthand and galactic glyphs, and a central table sat draped in black fabric.

F.I.Z.Z. scanned the room with slow, deliberate turns.

"SIGNAL SOURCE CONFIRMED. DEED FREQUENCY ACTIVE. NODE RESONANCE: PRESENT. HUMIDITY: UNREMARKABLE."

Kade peeled back the tarp.

Underneath was a console; a fusion of Earth hardware and salvaged alien tech. Strange harmonics vibrated through the metal. The centerpiece was a circular recess glowing faintly, shaped exactly like the Deed.

Kade hesitated, then pulled it from his coat and lowered it into place.

The projector blinked once. And then...

Andra Flux.

Her image stuttered, distorted but recognizable. Not warm, not playful. Urgent.

"If you're seeing this," she began, "then the Deed is awake. That means Node One has reactivated... and Earth is no longer invisible."

The static intensified. F.I.Z.Z. adjusted his sensor gain.

"The Deeds aren't just ownership markers," she continued. "They're keys. Lock keys. Each one unlocks a node in the original network. And once that network reboots... nothing stays hidden."

She leaned forward in the recording.

"They'll come for it. The Galactic Council. They've buried this for centuries. If they find you first, it ends. The wrong kind of ending."

Her voice caught. Not with emotion, but urgency.

"If I didn't make it, Kade, I'm sorry. I should've told you everything. But the more you knew, the more they'd take."

The image cut out.

Kade stood still for a long moment, staring at the empty air where she had been.

F.I.Z.Z. floated silently.

Zogg crouched beside a crate and popped it open. Inside was a round disc glowing faintly.

"Found something."

"Data core," Vira said. "Encrypted. Might contain node maps, activation protocols, or just…"

Zogg shook the disc gently. "Feels like secrets."

Kade slowly picked up a sealed envelope from beneath the projector. Inside was a crumpled note in his mother's handwriting… and a child's drawing of a duck with glowing eyes and what might've been a unicycle. He traced a finger over the duck drawing, and for a moment it was like being a kid again, listening to her stories. Did he ever really know her, or had she always been preparing him for this?

The note read:

> *If the duck blinks, run. Also: Trust Vira.*

Kade looked over at Vira, then back to the dusty console, and finally at the Deed, still pulsing in place.

"She really was planning for this," he said quietly. "Hiding breadcrumbs. Encoding ducks. Locking nodes."

"She was trying to wake something up," Vira said softly.

"I thought I knew her," Kade added. "I really did."

Zogg opened his mouth, then closed it again. Even he knew this wasn't the time for a joke.

"I don't think I knew her at all."

Outside, the wind picked up. Somewhere in low orbit, a surveillance drone logged a sudden spike in resonance and quietly relayed the coordinates upward.

Dast's cruiser adjusted course.

He had them again.

But this time, they were ready to run.

CHAPTER 9: BACKYARD INTERROGATION

"If they're wearing pest control gear but carrying plasma rifles, it's probably a trap."

— Tactical Wisdom #17

They made it back to the garage just before the second microwave timer dinged.

No one had put anything in the microwave.

That was unsettling.

Kade yanked the door shut behind them while Zogg flopped dramatically onto his foam fortress. F.I.Z.Z. began orbiting the data disc they'd retrieved from Unit 42, gleaming with faint glyphs and a soft pulse, while Vira swept the garage's perimeter with a handheld scanner.

"Signal from the Deed's still faint," she said, setting her device down. "No new pings. But something in that unit woke up when you slotted it into that console."

"ANDRA'S STORAGE SYSTEM INCLUDED ENCRYPTED DATA HARDWARE," F.I.Z.Z. added. "I HAVE INITIATED A PARALLEL DECRYPTION PROCESS. IT SMELLS LIKE OLD CODE AND TRUST ISSUES."

The disc sat under a magnifier beside the Deed, which glowed like a softly simmering secret. Kade paced.

"So, either this is just a galactic dead drop my mom left behind, or we just fired the starter pistol in a very weird race."

"WITH UNCLEAR RULES," F.I.Z.Z. said.

"Sounds like my childhood," Kade muttered.

Vira didn't look up. She was already wrist-deep in a cable cluster. "I'm going to run a diagnostic on the garage's signal dampener. Make sure it's still scrambling our location."

"Paranoia's a lifestyle choice," Zogg offered helpfully from under a throw rug.

Kade turned toward the ship, still slumped awkwardly in the reeds outside like a wounded waterfowl. "Even if someone's listening, it's not like we can go anywhere. *Misplaced Optimism's* still busted."

"She'll fly," Vira said, not quite making eye contact. "Eventually. If we give her time."

Zogg's voice piped up from somewhere behind a box labeled "Bungee Cords / Emergency Snacks." "But what if they find us before then? What if Dast is still up there, orbiting, watching?"

Kade rubbed his temple. "We don't even know if he's still…"

"CORRECTION," F.I.Z.Z. interrupted. "NEW SATELLITE TELEMETRY INDICATES A VESSEL EXITING LOW ORBIT. SIGNATURE MATCH: DAST'S CRUISER."

The screen flickered to show a heat trail arcing away from Earth's atmosphere.

"He's leaving?" Zogg blinked. "Why?"

"Maybe he thinks we're not worth the trouble," Kade offered, though his tone said he didn't believe it.

"Or maybe," Vira said, "he knows we've already triggered something. And he's off chasing the next breadcrumb."

"Or he dropped someone off before leaving," Kade said slowly.

There was a pause.

Zogg looked up. "Like a galactic Uber… of doom?"

Before anyone could respond, a soft thump echoed from the backyard.

Then another.

Kade moved to the window and parted the curtain with a wrench. Three figures moved with exaggerated caution across the grass. Matching uniforms. Oversized utility belts. One was carrying what looked like a comically large pest sprayer. The other two held boxes labeled "Rodent Analyzers" with the instructions printed upside down.

"Hey, Vira?" he said. "You expecting pest control?"

She glanced up. "I don't get pests."

Zogg popped up beside him. "What if they're duck specialists? You know… tracking mallard malware?"

"TOO TALL TO BE LOCAL CONTRACTORS," F.I.Z.Z. said, scanning. "WALKING FORMATION IS TRIANGULATED. LEFT ONE JUST TRIPPED OVER A FLAMINGO STATUE. HIGHLY SUSPICIOUS."

Kade frowned. "Still not quite enough to…"

The middle one raised his 'sprayer,' pointed it at the wall, and twisted a dial. It whined, vibrated… then sprayed a thick stream of what appeared to be whipped cream. The man looked at it, confused, shook the tank, and aimed again.

It ignited.

The grass caught fire.

Kade blinked. "Okay. Definitely NOT rat repellent."

Vira was already moving.

She opened the back door without hesitation and stepped outside like she was returning a misdelivered pizza.

The closest goon barely had time to register her presence before she drop-kicked him into a patch of marigolds. He landed with an "oof" that echoed with deep personal regret.

The second one fumbled for his stun prod, shouted "Free inspection!" and lunged. Vira ducked, twisted, and spun him into the compost bin. The bin groaned in solidarity.

The third goon turned to run and immediately tripped over the first, launching himself face-first into a plastic lawn chair. He lay there whimpering, partially tangled in a garden hose and half a gnome.

Kade stood frozen in the doorway.

Zogg, squinting through the fogged glass of a knocked-over aquarium lid, whispered, "Okay... Vira's either ex-military or part lawnmower."

Vira walked back inside without breaking stride, brushing dirt from her sleeve.

Kade stared at her. "You're... not just an ex-Galactic Council paper pusher, or just handy with wires."

She shrugged. "I fix things."

"No, no. That wasn't 'fixing.' That was close-quarters pest control with bonus choreography."

"I multitask."

"You're ex-special ops," he said flatly.

She didn't answer. Just went back to the console.

"Okay," Zogg said, stepping cautiously outside to check the carnage. "That guy's still twitching. Is that normal?"

"For Dast's goons?" Kade said, joining him. "Probably."

He crouched beside one of the still-mumbling men and peeled off his name tag: "MERVIN (TEAM BETA – DAST)."

Kade blinked. "Oh, come on."

Zogg leaned in. "Beta team?"

Kade held up the patch like it was a cursed coupon. "If they've got a Beta team, I'm terrified to meet Alpha. These guys look like they barely survived a safety seminar."

Another groan echoed from the bush. "I'm allergic to mulch..."

Zogg tiptoed closer to one of the goons, who was now tangled in a string of fairy lights and attempting to extricate himself with the coordination of a sleep-deprived octopus. He wore two left shoes, both unlaced, and had a utility belt filled with identical flashlights, none of which were turned on.

Zogg pointed. "That one still has the tag on his jumpsuit. Says 'Property of Intergalactic Pest Management Academy: Trial Pack.'"

"That's not a thing," Kade said.

"Apparently it is," Zogg replied. "And I think it includes a free net gun and low self-esteem."

The third goon had managed to crawl toward the fence but stopped halfway to sniff a gnome. "Do you think they make these in large?"

F.I.Z.Z. hovered overhead, scanning them all with what could only be described as confused disdain. "GOON THREE IS WEARING SAFETY GOGGLES ON HIS KNEES. THAT IS NEITHER HELPFUL NOR REGULATION."

Kade exhaled. "Okay. These are most certainly Dast's."

37

Vira, arms crossed, watched from the doorway, unbothered by the chaos she'd just unleashed. She looked like she was deciding whether to mop the floor or just let nature take its course.

"I assume," she said coolly, "we're done pretending these are professionals?"

Kade picked up a clipboard one of them had dropped. "Their mission log says 'Check if Earth Team found shiny box. Try not to break anything. Wear badges.'" He flipped the page. "It also says 'Remember sandwiches.'"

"Why do I relate to that last part," Zogg muttered.

Kade looked toward the sky, where the shimmer of Dast's cruiser had now fully disappeared from orbit. "So Dast drops off a group of tactical toddlers, then books it? What's he playing at?"

"Diversion," Vira said, already walking back toward the garage bench. "Or he assumed these three would report back. Or explode. Either outcome: informative."

"Or" Kade said, rubbing his eyes, "he's off chasing something else. Something bigger than us."

"LIKE A SALE ON REPLACEMENT GOONS," F.I.Z.Z. suggested.

Zogg lowered the clipboard. "So, what do we do with them?"

The goon in the gnome pile lifted his head. "We could, uh... leave voluntarily? I have a dentist appointment. In space."

Vira didn't look up from her tools. "Let them crawl off. They won't be able to report anything useful."

Kade raised an eyebrow. "You're awfully calm about armed goons showing up at your house."

Vira met his gaze. "They weren't exactly armed."

"She's got a point," Zogg added, holding up one of their sprayers. "This is labeled 'non-lethal squirrel deterrent.' And it's filled with... marmalade?"

F.I.Z.Z. beeped. "THAT WOULD EXPLAIN THE ANT PROBLEM."

Kade looked back toward *Misplaced Optimism*, its battered hull peeking through the bushes like a wounded whale in a kiddie pool.

"She's not flying any time soon," he said quietly. "We're grounded until you fix her."

Vira nodded. "I'll need parts. A lot of parts. And at least one drive coupling that doesn't look like it came from a vending machine."

Zogg perked up. "I know a place! It's... kind of a junkyard, kind of a miniature golf course. Possibly haunted."

Kade sighed. "Of course it is."

"I CAN PREPARE A LIST," F.I.Z.Z. said. "ALSO A MINIATURE GOLF SCORECARD."

Kade turned back toward the garage, glancing once more at the groaning goons, the pulsing Deed, and the encrypted disc still humming like a slowly remembering song.

He wasn't sure what they'd unlocked.

But someone had heard it.

And whatever came next, it would not be subtle.

CHAPTER 10: AGENT OBSERVING

"Always trust the duck. Unless it starts glowing."

— Popular Earth Saying

Agent Duckworth watched the blinking light on her console like it had personally offended her.

The pulse was back. Faint. Rhythmic. And unmistakably non-terrestrial.

She leaned back in the driver's seat of her nondescript black sedan parked a block from a poorly lit suburban park. The pond nearby rippled with wind and residual mystery. On paper, this was a routine drive-by of a Class B suburban anomaly. In reality, it was the third time this week she'd tracked an unclassified resonance signature from this exact neighborhood.

She pulled out a handheld device shaped like a melted walkie-talkie, flicked a switch, and let the screen warm up. The display flared briefly, then resolved into a live readout of harmonic frequencies bouncing across the local grid.

There it was again.

Low frequency. Artificial modulation. Faint but regular.

She didn't need to guess.

It was duck shaped.

Duckworth muttered under her breath. "How many ducks does it take to crash a planetary protocol?"

No one laughed. It was just her. The coffee in her cupholder had given up an hour ago and was now conducting its own science experiment. It had separated into three distinct layers, the top one suspiciously buoyant.

She leaned forward, tapped the dashboard monitor, and brought up the latest drone sweep from earlier that evening. Clarke County Storage. Four figures: One tall human male, one small wide-eyed alien, one dark-haired woman with unnervingly perfect posture, and a floating sphere that trailed behind them like an overenthusiastic Roomba. Not exactly your average late-night junk sorters.

The tall one moved like he didn't know what was about to hit him.

"Kade Flux," Duckworth murmured. "Of course it's you."

She hadn't seen him in years, not properly. Not since Andra disappeared. He looked older now. Not old but worn in the way people get when they've brushed up against something cosmic and came away with only half their certainty intact.

There was a particular kind of ache that came with watching someone stumble through the mystery you already lost someone to.

And he was carrying something.

She enhanced the stills from the drone. The glow couldn't be seen clearly, but the distortion in the light pattern was enough. Something active. Something harmonic. Something she hadn't seen since the Nebraska Event. That time, a library in Omaha started broadcasting coordinates in Morse code using its self-checkout kiosk. The

Galactic Council had denied it, of course. So had the librarian. But Duckworth had seen the barcodes hum.

This felt like that. But deeper.

More... intentional.

She tapped a secure connection on her device and logged into the off-grid Earth anomaly archive, a classified program buried under six layers of budget obfuscation and one fake wildlife rehabilitation fund called "Wombat Futures."

The interface was clean now... after Duckworth personally filed seventeen formal complaints about "too many dancing mascots in a classified system." There was still a cartoon platypus in the corner of the login screen, but at least it didn't wink anymore.

> **ACCESSING: FLAREGRID EARTHLINK**
>
> **ENCRYPTION VALIDATED**
>
> **QUERY: EARTH NODE STATUS?**

The screen pulsed and responded:

> **NODE 1: SIGNAL DETECTED. STATUS: DORMANT**
>
> **RECENT HARMONIC PULSE DETECTED**
>
> **SOURCE: LOCALIZED UNKNOWN DEVICE: LIKELY ARTIFACT**
>
> **GALACTIC COUNCIL INTERFACE: UNCONFIRMED**
>
> **GALACTIC COUNCIL SURVEILLANCE: PROBABLE**

That last line gave her pause.

Not confirmed. But probable.

The Galactic Council never left clear footprints. They never had to. But whenever this kind of signal lit up the skies, someone from the Galactic Council showed up eventually: either in disguise, in orbit, or already watching from behind a slightly-too-friendly sandwich shop. And Earth had just lit up like a fruitcake with an existential fuse.

Duckworth stared at the words for a long moment, then flicked her eyes toward the mirror. Nothing but her own reflection and the glint of a streetlamp behind her.

She exhaled through her nose.

If the Node had really activated, the entire planet was about to start humming in keys no one had taught it.

And if Kade had the Deed?

That wasn't just a curiosity.

It was a flare shot into a very big sky.

She keyed in a new secure message. No preamble.

STATUS UPDATE

FLUX CONFIRMED IN POSSESSION OF OBJECT.

SUBJECTS INCLUDE NON-HUMAN COMPANIONS AND UNREGISTERED AI UNIT.

GALACTIC COUNCIL INTERFACE LIKELY UNDERWAY.

ADVISE: MAINTAIN OBSERVATION. DO NOT ENGAGE.

She didn't sign it. People who needed to know would know. People who wouldn't assume it was a glitch, or more likely blame raccoons. It was always raccoons. The agency's standard internal explanation for 78% of unexplained footage was "raccoons with toolboxes."

Duckworth sipped her coffee. Immediately regretted it. The top layer had developed a film that might qualify for its own passport.

She powered down the console and looked out the windshield. The suburban calm was deceptive. Halloween decorations still lingered. A pair of raccoons fought over a juice box by a storm drain. Somewhere, a lawn sprinkler sputtered its final wheeze of the season. In the next yard over, a wind-chime played what sounded like the opening notes to Beethoven's Fifth, then gave up and collapsed into wind-muffled clinks.

Her gaze drifted to the pond again.

And there, almost deliberately placed, was a rubber duck.

Just sitting.

Still.

Too still.

She knew that shape. She knew the energy signature now buried beneath its cheap plastic shell. And she knew, with absolute certainty, that this was not random.

She opened her door and stepped out into the quiet street. Cool air bit her cheeks. The duck didn't move, but her earpiece chirped as it registered the ping: faint, pulsing every few seconds. Non-verbal. Non-aggressive. Just... present.

She crouched down a few feet away, shoes crunching softly on gravel.

"I don't know what she told you," Duckworth said softly, "but she was right to hide it."

The duck blinked.

Twice.

She didn't react.

She stood, adjusted her coat, and walked slowly back to the car. Just before getting in, she glanced up at the sky... clear, calm, but always watching.

Flux was in over his head.

Just like his mother.

But maybe, just maybe, this time… he wouldn't be alone.

Before sliding into the driver's seat, she opened the glove box, nudged aside a bag of decoy gummy bears, and withdrew a second device: round, nondescript, and humming very faintly. She placed it on the center console.

A soft green light blinked.

The device whispered: "Listening."

Duckworth leaned in close. "Track the duck. Stay quiet. If it quacks again, I want everything: location, time signature, frequency curve, and sarcasm level."

The light blinked again. "Confirmed."

"Good," she muttered.

Then she started the car, flicked on the headlights, and pulled away from the curb.

Behind her, the duck sat motionless on the pond's edge, the water rippling outward from its base like it had just exhaled.

Somewhere far above, a Galactic Council satellite angled slightly.

And in a mountain deeper than any map would admit, a second set of eyes reopened an old file labeled:

      SUBJECT: FLUX, ANDRA

      STATUS: DECEASED (PRESUMED)

      CONTINGENCY PROTOCOL: ACTIVE

      DUCK TRAIL: REENGAGED

CHAPTER 11: BUREAUCRACY, INTERRUPTED

"Bureaucracy is just organized chaos with better fonts."

— Anonymous Paper-Pusher

The front doors of the municipal building gasped open like an asthmatic sigh.

Inside, the City Records Office smelled like moldy toner and passive aggression. The walls were painted in a shade of beige scientifically engineered to suppress joy. A flickering banner overhead read:

"Welcome to Public Archives – Your Past, Misfiled."

Kade stepped inside and immediately regretted it. "I already hate this."

"GOOD," F.I.Z.Z. buzzed, scanning the hallway. "IT MEANS YOU'RE STILL CAPABLE OF EMOTION."

Vira moved ahead with purpose, the printed document from Andra's storage unit clutched in one hand. "This is the right place. Page four of the data core's filing slip referenced a land registration cross-index with an Earth-side terminal."

"You're telling me my mom uploaded alien property rights into... a government basement?" Kade muttered.

"She liked hiding things in plain sight," Vira replied. "Especially if it annoyed bureaucrats."

Zogg pressed his face against a vending machine. "Do we have time for a lukewarm 'cheese triangle'? I think it expired last year."

"No time," Kade said. "We're looking for proof that Earth ever legally registered the Deed. Or covered it up."

"IF YOUR MOTHER INTERFACED WITH EARTH SYSTEMS," F.I.Z.Z. said, "THIS IS THE LOWEST POSSIBLE TECHNICAL ENTRY POINT. PRIMITIVE BUT ARCHIVABLE. ALSO, I DETECT UNUSUAL MAGNETIC DISTORTIONS NEAR FLOOR B3."

"That sounds promising."

"OR HAUNTED."

They crossed the lobby, bypassing a cluster of retirees arguing over fishing permits and a child trying to photocopy a grilled cheese.

At the reception desk, a woman with a bob haircut and the haunted stare of someone who'd filed one too many complaints about themselves held up a finger without looking.

"Form 17 if you're here for water utilities. Form 22 if it's marriage, and Form 88C if it involves

44

zoning, or graffiti."

Vira handed her the paper. "We're here for a cross-reference search. Historic land registry override, case code 421-B. Local database entry tagged under name: Marla Quent."

The woman blinked once, like rebooting. Then tapped on a keyboard made of sighs. "Basement archive. Level three. Room... B17H."

Kade squinted. "Wait, is that the floor or the tax bracket?"

She handed them a lanyard and a grim nod. "If you get stuck in the elevator loop, press the emergency button."

She was already answering the next patron. Zogg shrugged. "Government secret codes are all haikus now. Budget cuts."

They took the stairs. The elevator played bagpipe hold music anyway.

Basement Level 3 was less a floor and more a cry for help made tangible.

The hallway was lined with filing cabinets stacked like a monument to indecision. One door had been nailed shut and labeled "Screams only." Another was occupied by a man in a swivel chair wearing VR goggles and muttering, "It's all spreadsheets, all the way down..."

The air grew heavier. The lighting shifted to a flickering "fluorescent headache" Even Zogg stopped humming. F.I.Z.Z. hovered cautiously.

"ENVIRONMENTAL READINGS: 64% MOLD, 30% PAPER, 6% HOPE."

At the end of the corridor stood Room B17H: locked, lightless, and gently humming.

"Who hums a filing cabinet?" Kade asked.

Zogg tapped the door. It hissed. Not opened, just hissed.

"I think it wants a password," Zogg said.

F.I.Z.Z. inserted a thin cable into the keypad and whirred. "OVERRIDE ACTIVE. DECRYPTING EARTH-BASED ENCRYPTION LAYER. THEY'VE DISGUISED THE ARCHIVE UNDER... TAX RECORDS FOR FAKE COMPANIES."

"Sounds like Mom," Kade said.

The door unlocked with a moist click.

Inside: shelves groaned with forgotten binders. A terminal from the 1980s flickered in the corner beside a dusty printer labeled "MILDLY CURSED." A spider crawled across it, paused, and seemed to give up halfway.

A single crate sat in the center, marked "MARLA Q. NON-RESIDENT RECORDS. DO NOT PROCESS."

"Well, that's inviting," Kade muttered, stepping forward.

He opened it.

Inside: folders, several USB sticks, a duck-shaped flash drive (of course), and a torn page with coordinates scrawled in the margins. At the bottom of the box, sealed in a Ziploc and stained with decades of bureaucracy, was a deed transfer form, with his mother's handwriting across the bottom.

Property: [REDACTED]

>   Recipient: *"Whichever idiot wins it."*

>   Signature: *Andra Flux (X)*

>   Attached note: *"Yes, I'm serious."*

Kade blinked. "She submitted the Deed to Earth's records office."

"AND EARTH FILED IT UNDER 'DO NOT PROCESS,'" F.I.Z.Z. confirmed.

Zogg held up the duck flash drive. "You think this is also encrypted with a quack?"

"It's probably her tax documents," Kade said. "Knowing Mom, she itemized reality distortion."

F.I.Z.Z. scanned the drive. "NO NETWORK LINK. BUT THERE'S A FILE LABELED 'PLANET YOU DIDN'T MEAN TO OWN.'"

The others turned slowly to look at him.

"WELL, THAT'S OMINOUS," F.I.Z.Z. added.

Vira sat at the terminal and plugged it in.

The screen flickered.

Text appeared in plain Courier font:

>   *"If you're reading this, I either died saving the galaxy or choked on a jellybean. Either way, hi Kade."*

>   *"The Deed was real. It always was. But Earth never knew what to do with it. That's why I hid parts of the protocol in government archives. To trigger the Node, you'll need more than the Deed... you'll need Earth to remember it exists."*

>   *"This console won't talk to the stars. But it will talk to the broadcast towers..."*

Then, below it, a blinking line of text:

INITIATE PULSE PREVIEW?

Kade hesitated. "What's a 'pulse preview'?"

"LIKELY A TEST PATTERN TO VERIFY CONNECTION BETWEEN EARTH INFRASTRUCTURE AND THE NODE SIGNAL," F.I.Z.Z. replied. "IN LAYMAN'S TERMS: A COSMIC 'ARE YOU STILL THERE?'"

Zogg raised his hand. "Is this like when I accidentally synced my karaoke machine to a police scanner?"

Vira hit ENTER.

The console chirped, then went silent.

Nothing happened.

Then...

Aboveground, across the city, televisions briefly flickered. Infomercial hosts froze mid-blender demo. Radio stations glitched into harmonic static. Traffic lights paused. Every appliance with a speaker buzzed.

In the records office, the overhead fluorescent lights dimmed and pulsed, once... twice...

.... and then returned to normal.

The console rebooted.

PULSE SENT. RESPONSE: NONE.

SECONDARY RESPONSE: DELAYED. INCONCLUSIVE.

F.I.Z.Z. spun in place. "SOMETHING HEARD IT. I DON'T KNOW WHAT. BUT SOMETHING ECHOED BACK."

Vira was already moving. "We need to go. Before whatever's listening decides to reply harder."

They barely made it to the stairwell before the fire alarm tripped.

A voice came over the building's intercom. "Attention: unexpected energy spike detected in Records. All interns please report to Room 12B."

A pair of suited figures passed them going the other way, each holding clipboards and one with a rubber chicken holster.

"Are those... compliance officers?" Kade whispered.

"WORSE," F.I.Z.Z. whispered back. "DOCUMENTARY FILMMAKERS."

Zogg whimpered. "Run."

Back in the van, Kade stared at the console.

"She really tried to wake Earth up."

"AND SOMETHING STIRRED," F.I.Z.Z. said. "WE JUST DON'T KNOW WHAT YET."

Zogg held up the deed. "I think it's humming again."

Vira revved the engine. "Then we don't have long."

Behind them, inside Room B17H, the old, cursed printer whirred to life. It spat out a single page.

SYSTEM LOG:

DEED SIGNAL REGISTERED.

NODE 1: PENDING.

Then the lights dimmed.

And deep below the Earth, an ancient relay blinked on for the first time in decades.

CHAPTER 12: THE BROADCAST THAT WASN'T

"A good plan never survives contact with a quacking artifact."

— F.I.Z.Z.

The garage smelled like overheating electronics, stubborn dust, and the kind of fried circuitry that usually followed the words, "What happens if I plug this into... OOPS."

Kade crouched beside a tangled mess of cables, balancing an old portable satellite dish on a step stool. "Remind me why we're attempting to broadcast a cosmic secret using a hot-glued coat hanger and something that used to sell rotisserie ovens?"

"BECAUSE THE LATE-NIGHT INFOMERCIAL GRID OPERATES ON AN OPEN FREQUENCY BAND," F.I.Z.Z. replied. "AND I ENJOY CHAOS."

"Wait," Zogg piped up, unspooling a roll of duct tape that was mostly optimism at this point. "You got this idea from watching TV?"

"YES. I HAVE BEEN MONITORING EARTH BROADCASTS TO UNDERSTAND PATTERNS IN HUMAN BEHAVIOR. IT SEEMS MOST PATTERNS INVOLVE BUYING KNIVES YOU DON'T NEED."

"That tracks," Kade muttered, threading a wire through a colander. "Still not sure why we're trusting a navigation bot with a shopping addiction."

"BECAUSE I AM THE ONLY ONE HERE WHO UNDERSTANDS HOW TO HIJACK A BROADCAST SIGNAL WITHOUT COOKING THE TOASTER."

"You mean the signal amplifier?" Kade asked, nodding toward the toaster.

"YES."

"Which is currently wrapped in aluminum foil, held down by gummy worms, and labeled 'DO NOT EAT'?"

"I WAS BEING THOROUGH."

Vira sat cross-legged on the floor, splicing a salvaged fiber cable into the satellite uplink with surgical precision and a terrifyingly steady hand. "You two done flirting with thermodynamic failure?"

"Define 'done,'" Kade said.

"I'm not saying it's dangerous," Zogg added, "but I did smell toast three minutes ago, and no one is making toast."

"That's just the smell of inevitability," Vira muttered, cinching the final connection. "Or melted insulation."

They all took a step back.

The dish hummed. The laptop screen blinked to life, displaying a grainy, flickering feed of Mort's Bargain Bonanza: Earth's least-watched shopping network.

"Wow," Zogg whispered reverently. "He's still selling that same blender. And wearing the same shirt."

"HE HAS NOT BLINKED THE ENTIRE TIME," F.I.Z.Z. observed. "I AM CONCERNED."

"Okay," Kade said, rubbing his hands together. "So, what happens now?"

"We plug the Deed into the resonator circuit, patch the broadcast path, and send a harmonic ping through Earth's open satellite systems," Vira said, tightening a bolt. "Ideally without causing every TV on the planet to show your face."

"Or my criminal record," Kade muttered.

"TO BE FAIR, YOUR RECORD WAS MOSTLY EXPUNGED," F.I.Z.Z. offered. "EXCEPT IN THREE SYSTEMS WHERE YOU ARE STILL WANTED FOR IMPERSONATING A DINNER ROLL."

"I can explain that" Kade said.

"PLEASE DON'T."

Vira nodded. "Let's do it."

F.I.Z.Z. floated up and plugged into the laptop with a cheerful clunk. The Deed began to glow in pulses, resting neatly in its jury-rigged bracket made from a toaster, duct tape, and misguided ambition.

"BEGINNING INTERFACE," F.I.Z.Z. announced. The lights in the garage dimmed. The satellite dish vibrated.

On-screen, Mort was mid-pitch: "This knife set can cut through concrete, sadness, and..."

Static overtook him.

The screen fizzled.

A low, tonal vibration filled the garage, subsonic, like a bass note played on the back of your skull. The Deed responded instantly, glowing with rhythmic pulses like a heartbeat syncing to a song only it could hear.

"BROADCAST ENGAGED," F.I.Z.Z. said. "DEED PULSE AT MAXIMUM RESONANCE. THIS IS VERY EXCITING."

Kade held his breath. "We're actually doing this."

"No surges... yet" Vira murmured, watching the power monitor with narrowed eyes.

"Do we know what we're expecting?" Zogg asked. "Like... a reply? A summons? Cake?"

"A cosmic acknowledgment would be nice," Kade said.

"A cake would be better," Zogg replied.

The laptop beeped. Mort's face melted into pixels. Then a window appeared.... black background, blinking white text:

NODE 1: UNACTIVATED. DEED DETECTED. AWAITING SYNC.

They all leaned in.

A new line appeared:

CONFIRMATION RECEIVED. RESPONSE... PENDING.

No one spoke.

Then... *ping.*

A subtle chime, like a sonar blip on a lazy Sunday.

Kade exhaled. "That's it. That's the handshake."

"SIGNAL CONFIRMED," F.I.Z.Z. intoned. "NODE 1 CANDIDATE: EARTH."

Vira stood slowly. "That means this planet... it was always part of the network."

"No one told Earth," Kade muttered. "Not even Earth."

"I'M DETECTING A RETURN SIGNAL," F.I.Z.Z. said suddenly. "NOT FROM EARTH INFRASTRUCTURE. SATELLITE GRID SHIFTING. BEARING... ORBITAL SOURCE."

Vira froze. "Can you trace it?"

F.I.Z.Z. projected a map onto the garage wall. A single red dot blinked in low Earth orbit, arcing over the hemisphere like a patient predator.

"Definitely not civilian," she said.

Zogg squinted at the icon. "What if it's just a weather balloon with ambitions?"

"IT'S A SHIP," F.I.Z.Z. confirmed. "NOT EARTH-REGISTERED."

Zogg looked at Kade. "You think it's the Galactic Council?"

Kade frowned. "No."

"Then who owns it?"

Kade gave a dry smile. "Who do you think?"

Cut to low orbit.

Dast leaned back in his command chair aboard his cruiser, watching a jittery feed from an orbital drone. A smile spread slowly across his face as the screen blinked:

NODE 1 DETECTED. HARMONIC PING LOGGED. DEED CONFIRMED.

"Well, well," he muttered. "You little idiots pulled it off."

He tapped a key. The feed shifted to an Earth map, tracking the general region of the broadcast.

"No need to get my hands dirty," he said to no one in particular. "Let them dig the hole. I'll just take what's at the bottom."

He reached for his cup of spiced glogg, sipped, winced, and muttered, "Needs more smug."

Back in the garage, the screen fizzled and reverted to Mort, who was now attempting to demonstrate how to peel onions using only a hairdryer and resentment.

Kade stood there, shoulders tense.

F.I.Z.Z. beeped once. "THE DEED IS NO LONGER BROADCASTING. BUT IT IS STILL... LISTENING."

Vira disconnected the toaster with care. "We made a noise. Someone responded. That means the system's still alive."

Zogg blinked. "Does it also mean the system's... watching us now?"

A pause.

"PROBABILITY: HIGH," F.I.Z.Z. said brightly.

"Comforting," Kade muttered.

"TO BE FAIR," F.I.Z.Z. added, "THEY WERE PROBABLY ALREADY WATCHING."

Kade rubbed his forehead. "We need to move. Fix the ship. Gather supplies. No more pings. No more ducks. No more signals."

Zogg raised a hand. "What if we run into another duck?"

Kade sighed. "Then we punt it into orbit."

"Punting ducks is unethical," F.I.Z.Z. said.

"Then we... diplomatically relocate it to a volcano," Kade offered.

"Better," F.I.Z.Z. nodded.

Outside, the wind picked up. Somewhere nearby, a neighborhood chime triggered with just the right pitch to make the Deed flicker once.

It felt deliberate.

They didn't speak again for a few minutes. Just packed up the gear in silence, thinking the same thing:

They weren't alone anymore.

And whatever they'd just woken up... hadn't gone back to sleep.

CHAPTER 13: DUCKWORTH'S WARNING

"Secret agents are like onions. Mysterious. Layered. And occasionally make you cry."

— Agent Handbook, Redacted Edition

The parking garage wasn't on the list of safe places. It wasn't even on the list of "places Zogg won't lick something." But it was the closest location to the old substation F.I.Z.Z. had just flagged for "buried anomaly resonance." And Kade needed a minute to think without a glowing duck, a malfunctioning satellite dish, or a well-meaning space goblin handing him snacks labeled "Not for Consumption (Legally)."

So, he'd taken a walk. Alone.

Now he regretted it.

The place smelled like antifreeze, exhaust, and faintly like someone had tried to microwave a tuna casserole. The fluorescent lights buzzed in arrhythmic protest, and a single soda can rolled ominously across the concrete like it knew something he didn't.

Kade exhaled and leaned against a pillar. "Okay. Recap. The Deed pings. We broadcast it. Something hears it. Dast is circling like a paranoid vulture with a weapons budget. And Earth is... something more than Earth."

He pulled the Deed from his coat. It pulsed once in his hand, like it agreed. Or burped. Hard to tell.

Behind him, a car engine purred to life.

He turned. A matte black sedan, unmarked, boxy, and older than the parking lines, eased into view from behind a structural column. No plates. No markings. The passenger window hummed down halfway.

Kade froze.

The woman in the driver's seat didn't step out. She simply nodded once and motioned him forward with two fingers.

He approached cautiously, one hand on his coat, ready to draw... well, probably just sarcasm.

"You're late," she said.

"Late for what?"

"For the conversation you didn't know you needed."

She stepped out of the car.

Trench coat. Dark slacks. Boots with soles that didn't make a sound. A badge nowhere to be seen but somehow implied. Hair pulled back like she didn't have time for wind. Eyes sharp, assessing.

"Agent Duckworth," she said, flatly.

"That's your real name?"

"It's the one on my least interesting ID."

Kade glanced at her car. "You know, when I imagined clandestine rendezvous in underground garages, there was usually more trench coat flapping and less... musty dampness."

Duckworth didn't blink. She held out a small envelope. "Coordinates. What you found at the records office triggered a buried node. The Galactic Council won't admit it exists. But this location," she tapped the paper, "was flagged within twenty seconds of your broadcast. Something beneath Earth is active again."

Kade opened the envelope. Handwritten. Coordinates matched the edge of a decommissioned cable relay station, right where F.I.Z.Z. had pinged something strange.

"How do you have this?"

"I monitor Earth. Off-books anomalies. Hidden protocols. And I used to monitor your mother."

That landed like a dropped wrench. "What?"

Kade's stomach knotted. Every time someone mentioned his mother, it felt like stepping on a trapdoor. How many secrets had she left behind? And how many were ticking?

"She wasn't just poking around alien tech. She was tracing buried node activity. Mapping Deed harmonics. She said Earth had forgotten something about itself, and she meant to remind it."

"You knew her?"

Duckworth nodded, slowly. "She helped me see what Earth had buried. I returned the favor by not turning her in."

Kade blinked. "So why help me now?"

"Because you're about to step onto the same path she did. And it nearly got her killed. You need someone watching your six."

"Let me guess. That's you."

"I prefer 'invisible ally with plausible deniability.' But yes."

Kade tucked the paper away. "You expect me to trust you?"

"No," Duckworth said, reaching into her coat. She withdrew a burner phone: basic, durable, already powered, and handed it to him. "But when you're in over your head and your robot's singing karaoke at an automated checkpoint, call that number. Just once. No second chances."

He stared at it. "It's labeled 'Don't.'"

"I have a sense of humor. Mostly classified."

Kade pocketed the phone. "Why the help?"

Duckworth looked him straight in the eye. "Because your mother trusted me. And because if you fail, Earth becomes just another forgotten experiment in the Galactic Council's ledger."

The garage lighting flickered again.

Kade stepped back. "So, what now? You vanish into the night?"

Duckworth raised an eyebrow, walked around the pillar, then slipped through a small service door near a fire extinguisher sign, marked "Maintenance Access Only."

Kade blinked. "Huh. Not as dramatic, but... efficient."

The door shut with a muted click.

He stood there for a long moment, heart still racing. Then he turned and walked briskly toward the exit.

Unseen, several meters above, a figure crouched silently in the exposed piping of the garage roof.

Vira watched as Kade disappeared down the ramp.

She hadn't meant to follow him.

But the moment he'd left the garage, she'd known something was off. And now... now she had a name. Duckworth. A contact from Andra's past. Possibly an ally. Possibly something else.

She didn't say a word.

She just turned, silently dropped to the floor behind a maintenance partition, and disappeared into the darkness.

Back at the garage, the others were sorting through wires, boxes, and Zogg's inexplicable collection of "emergency snacks."

As Kade re-entered, F.I.Z.Z. hovered slightly closer and scanned him. "YOUR HEART RATE IS ELEVATED. POSSIBLE SYMPTOMS: ADRENAL SPIKE, TRUST ISSUES, EXPOSURE TO GOVERNMENT OFFICIALS."

"Been out long?" Vira asked without looking up.

Kade shrugged. "Took a walk. Cleared my head."

"You smell like secrets," Zogg offered, poking a bag of neon noodles.

"Something's up," Kade muttered. "We were right. The broadcast triggered something. And someone's watching."

"More ducks?" Zogg asked.

Kade tossed the coordinates envelope onto the workbench. "We've got a location. Outside the city. Some kind of underground relay, same spot F.I.Z.Z. pinged earlier."

Vira picked it up without comment.

Kade turned toward the window. "We leave at dawn. Pack light. We might be climbing through ancient fiber optics and metaphysical regrets."

"SHALL I PREPARE *MISPLACED OPTIMISM*?" F.I.Z.Z. asked. "SHE'S STILL SULKING IN THE POND, BUT I BELIEVE I CAN COAX HER TO WAKEFULNESS."

"Do it," Kade said. "We'll need her ready for launch. If this Node is what I think it is... we won't be able to stick around."

"ON IT."

Zogg stood, brushing dust off his lap. "Should I bring snacks?"

Kade stared at him. "Yes. But this time label them."

"Even the questionable ones?"

"Especially the questionable ones."

Later that night, long after the garage lights dimmed and Zogg began snoring softly into a box of marshmallow pretzels, Kade sat on the ship's boarding ramp. Alone.

Misplaced Optimism was humming softly to herself, lights flickering in tired protest. She'd seen better days. So had they all.

He pulled the burner phone from his pocket again. Turned it over. No messages. No signal. But it worked. And that was the point.

One call. No promises. No alliances. But maybe... someone watching the dark from the other side.

A protector.

He didn't know if he could trust her. But someone had to be looking out for them.

Because this thing with the Deeds? It was bigger than they'd thought.

And if he was going to stay alive long enough to find the next one, he might need all the help he could get.

He slipped the phone back into his coat and looked up at the stars.

"Guess we're not flying solo after all."

CHAPTER 14: A PING IN THE BASEMENT

"Signal strength is inversely proportional to how much you need it."

— Murphy's Law of Tech

Misplaced Optimism was in surgery.

Cables draped from the ceiling like lazy vines. The floor panels had been pulled open to reveal scorched bundles of wiring and a mysterious stain that no one wanted to identify. One wall panel now displayed a sticky note that simply read: "Do Not Electrocute Self Again – V."

Zogg was asleep inside a repurposed cargo net that he had rigged between two bulkheads and named the "mission hammock." F.I.Z.Z. hovered like a bored lamp, occasionally zapping errant sparks from the half-functional diagnostics console. Vira was halfway into the maintenance crawlspace beneath the main corridor, wielding a soldering iron and muttering insults at a junction box.

Kade stood in the middle of it all, trying to look useful while holding a data pad that hadn't updated since Tuesday.

"We have two stabilizer capacitors blown," Vira called, voice muffled. "And one of them is held in place with... is this chewing gum?"

"Zogg!" Kade shouted.

"What? It was gum-like," came the muffled reply from the net. "No one died."

"Not yet," Vira muttered.

A fuse popped somewhere under the deck. F.I.Z.Z. let out a slow, judgmental beep. "SYSTEM INTEGRITY: PATCHED. OPTIMISM STATUS: GRUMPY."

Then it came.

A sound, or more precisely, a presence. A hum that passed through the ship's hull like a warm breeze through bone. Not quite sound. Not quite motion. But unmistakably intentional.

Kade stiffened. "F.I.Z.Z., was that you?"

"NEGATIVE. I HAVE NOT VIBRATED ANYTHING SINCE LAST TUESDAY."

Another pulse followed: slightly stronger, slightly deeper.

Zogg's head popped out from the hammock. "Did the ship just hiccup? Or did I dream that?"

Vira emerged from the hatch, brow creased. "That wasn't the ship."

F.I.Z.Z. rotated in the air, sensors flaring. "SOURCE: LOCALIZED. FREQUENCY MATCHES DEED NETWORK SIGNATURE. INTENSITY: RISING."

The Deed, resting on the central crate-turned-command-table, pulsed once, glowing softly. Its hum matched the beat that now echoed faintly through the hull.

Kade leaned in. "F.I.Z.Z.?"

"PULSE EMANATING FROM SUBSURFACE SOURCE. APPROXIMATE DISTANCE: FOUR POINT TWO KILOMETRES. SIGNAL IS COMING FROM BENEATH EARTH'S CRUST. HARMONICS MATCH INACTIVE NODE STRUCTURE."

Vira stood upright, wiping her hands on a rag. "So the Node is here. Under us."

"BENEATH A GEO-ANCHORED STRUCTURE DISGUISED AS A BROADBAND RELAY STATION. DISUSED. MASKED. UNDETECTED BY HUMAN SYSTEMS."

Zogg blinked. "Is that like a cable box?"

"No," Kade said. "It's a Node."

F.I.Z.Z. flashed. "DEED PULSE REGISTERED AGAIN. THE SYSTEM BELOW IS... LISTENING."

Vira wiped her hands. "Then let's go look."

Zogg perked up. "Can we take the van? I left a sandwich under the driver's seat that's either a biohazard or a sign of fate."

They took the van.

Vira shot Kade a look. "You're not driving."

"Wasn't planning on it," Kade said. "I once reversed into a fruit stand during a parking test. On foot."

They climbed into the van. Zogg claimed the back bench and immediately sprawled across it like a lizard sunning itself, his arms full of snacks and unrelated trinkets. A crumpled bag of "Octo-Chews" fell out of his pocket and began leaking blue syrup onto the seat.

"I've trained my digestive system for this moment," he declared. "It's a precision instrument. Like a blender that occasionally explodes."

F.I.Z.Z. hovered near the rearview mirror, clicking softly as he interfaced with his own scanners. "I HAVE ENCOUNTERED MILITARY DRONES THAT EMIT LESS CHAOS."

As they bumped down the cracked back road, Vira swerved around a fallen log with the grace of someone who'd once driven through a lightning storm while being shot at by accountants. No one asked. They all assumed the story would come out eventually.

The trees thickened. Weeds clawed at the undercarriage like they wanted to join the party.

"Why would anyone build a galactic node under an internet box?" Kade wondered aloud.

"CAMOUFLAGE," F.I.Z.Z. replied. "NOBODY EVER LOOKS TWICE AT SERVICE BUILDINGS. EVEN TERRORISTS HAVE STANDARDS."

"True," Zogg added. "I once spent three weeks living in a fake plumbing depot. Only got caught when I filed for health insurance."

They turned into a clearing with a crunch of gravel. Kade stepped out and immediately regretted wearing low-top boots. Everything squelched. The air smelled like mildew and conspiracy.

A weather-worn sign flanked the entrance:

CITYWIDE CABLE – SERVICE DELAYED UNTIL FURTHER NOTICE

Next to it sat a long-forgotten welcome mat, half-curled and soaked with moss. Despite the decay, one phrase stood out, perfectly legible in large, friendly letters:

DON'T PANIC.

Zogg nodded. "Seems welcoming."

Kade stared. "That's either a good omen or a trap disguised as friendly advice."

Vira kicked the door once. It didn't move. She kicked it again. A hinge gave up, and the door swung inward with a wheeze that sounded uncannily like a sigh of defeat.

Inside: darkness. And dust. And the hum of something much, much older than broadband.

The interior was lined with plastic shelves full of disassembled routers, coaxial cables, and circuit boards arranged like someone had tried and failed to build a god using only RadioShack components. A single monitor flickered quietly on a corner desk. The login prompt blinked in green:

NODE LINK: OFFLINE

F.I.Z.Z. scanned the interior. "ACCESS TO LOWER LEVELS LOCATED AT BACK. STRUCTURE EXTENDS BENEATH GROUND. SIGNAL REVERBERATION STRONGEST BELOW."

They passed a pile of discarded keyboard trays and a fan heater that had died mid-sigh. At the far wall stood a sealed hatch, metal, circular, covered in faded warning stickers and one ominous sticky note that read "DO NOT OPEN IF YOU LIKE BEING UNINCINERATED."

Zogg tilted his head. "That's not exactly comforting."

F.I.Z.Z. pulsed. "NODE STRUCTURE CONFIRMED BENEATH THIS POINT. ENTRY WILL BE TIGHT. AND POSSIBLY DUMB."

Kade reached forward and turned the wheel-lock on the hatch. It creaked open with a hiss of stale air and reactivated possibilities.

A rusted ladder descended into darkness.

The pulse came again, stronger now. The Deed, tucked inside Kade's coat, responded with a quiet glow.

"I don't like it," he muttered.

"I do," Vira replied, already stepping onto the ladder.

Zogg took a breath. "Last one down has to feed the ducks."

Kade grimaced. "Why is that a threat now?"

No one answered.

One by one, they descended down into the quiet hum of forgotten code.

And beneath them, something responded: quietly, deeply, and with intent.

CHAPTER 15: NODE 1 WAKES UP

"Nodes never stay buried. Not with a duck involved."

— Ancient Node Digger Proverb

The ladder ended in a narrow corridor of stone and forgotten machinery. The air smelled like damp copper, stale secrets, and mild resentment. Kade's boots hit the floor with a squelch that defied physics.

"I'm officially filing a complaint with whoever designed this place," he muttered. "Preferably via flaming envelope."

Zogg landed behind him, immediately slipping and grabbing Kade's arm. "I think my spleen just reset."

"I DIDN'T KNOW YOU HAD ONE," F.I.Z.Z. offered, floating down like a suspiciously silent disco ball. "CONGRATULATIONS ON THE BIOLOGICAL SURPRISE."

Vira hit the floor next, brushing dust off her sleeve. "We'll head toward the signal."

F.I.Z.Z. blinked. "CORRECTION: I HAVE BEEN TRACKING THE SIGNAL FOR HOURS. PLEASE DO NOT STEAL MY DRAMATIC MOMENT."

"You're right," Vira replied dryly. "Lead on, maestro of pulses."

The hallway sloped downward. Pipes lined the walls, some active, some weeping oil like exhausted secretaries. A soft pulse echoed deeper below. It matched the beat Kade felt thrumming through the Deed in his coat.

"This whole place is humming like it forgot a song and just remembered the chorus," Kade said.

"THE SIGNAL IS STRONGEST AHEAD OF US," F.I.Z.Z. replied, scanning as he floated. "IT'S... TRYING TO WAKE UP."

Moving forward, they emerged into an octagonal chamber, faintly illuminated by soft wall-lights that flickered with gentle unease. Strange symbols shimmered along the curved panels, rearranging themselves whenever anyone blinked too long.

In the center stood a raised plinth: plain, circular, and humming faintly, like an ancient smart speaker having an existential moment.

The Deed began to glow in response.

Kade stepped forward and pulled it from his jacket. "You think this is what it's been looking for?"

"THE SIGNAL IS LOCALIZED HERE," F.I.Z.Z. said. "WHATEVER THIS IS, IT WAS DESIGNED TO

LISTEN. MAYBE TO RESPOND."

"No pressure," Zogg whispered. "Just, you know, casually unlocking buried alien tech under Earth with a mysterious glowing rectangle."

Kade inhaled and placed the Deed on the plinth.

It clicked into place.

The room dimmed.

A single tone echoed, a note so low it rattled their bones and threatened their dignity. Lights along the walls flared to life, chasing each other in recursive spirals that converged above the Deed.

A holographic interface flickered into being; geometric, shifting, unreadable.

F.I.Z.Z. whirred closer, scanning. "IT'S NOT EARTH TECH. DEFINITELY PRE-GALACTIC COUNCIL. AI FRAMEWORKS. AWAKE... BUT FRAGMENTED."

A humanoid outline formed: faceless, made of golden code, and slowly lifted its head.

"Welcome back, user Andra-Flux."

Kade flinched.

"What?" he whispered.

"VOICEPRINT MATCH DETECTED," F.I.Z.Z. translated. "IT'S RESPONDING TO YOUR MOTHER'S IMPRINT. SHE'S BEEN HERE."

The figure remained still.

"Credentials archived. Deed authentication confirmed. Status: Dormant. Awaiting override input."

Kade swallowed. "It knows her. It's calling her back."

Vira watched the figure silently. "She might've triggered this before. Set it to wait."

"THIS IS A HUB," F.I.Z.Z. murmured. "BUT I DON'T HAVE A NAME FOR IT. NO RECORDS. IT WAS ERASED FROM THE NETWORK. HIDDEN EVEN FROM ME."

Kade stepped closer. "Can it hear me?"

"Command recognition active. Please state override."

Zogg whispered, "Tell it you're Andra."

"No," Kade said. "I'm not her. I'm just the idiot who won a glowing rectangle in a thumb war."

He cleared his throat. "My name's Kade Flux. I have the Deed. I want to wake this... whatever-you-are."

A long pause.

"Lineage acknowledged. Deed: Synchronized. Access level... provisional. Activation permitted."

The lights surged. Panels slid open. The floor trembled slightly as if bracing for an uncomfortable truth. A deep hum rose from beneath their feet.

"Node 1: Status Active."

The ship's computer spoke over the comms, unprompted. "I just received a software update. I did not agree to it."

"WE ARE NOW INTERFACED WITH A SYSTEM THAT CAN TALK TO THE ENTIRE GALACTIC NETWORK," F.I.Z.Z. said reverently. "AND PROBABLY CONTROL YOUR COFFEE MACHINE."

A nearby console flared to life. Ancient code scrolled faster than any of them could read. F.I.Z.Z. pivoted to intercept.

"LOGS INDICATE THIS PLACE WAS ONE OF THE FIRST HUBS. ORIGIN POINT UNKNOWN. ANDRA FOUND IT. OR... MAYBE IT FOUND HER."

"Wait," Kade asked. "If this place just woke up..., is it online now? With everything else?"

"NOT EVERYTHING," F.I.Z.Z. replied. "BUT SOMETHING IS CONNECTED. I'M GETTING PINGS. SIDE CHANNELS. ANCIENT STUFF. HALF-DELETED."

"Warning," said the projection. *"Node connection unstable. External attention detected. Recommend termination of open broadcast."*

Zogg frowned. "Uh... do we know who's listening?"

"NO," F.I.Z.Z. said flatly. "BUT THEY JUST STARTED BOOSTING EARTH-ORBITAL SCANS. I THINK WE'VE BEEN NOTICED."

Kade paced in a tight circle. "Of course we have. We activated a space basement with a loud ping. Subtlety is not our strength."

Another screen blinked on.

LAST KNOWN USER: ANDRA-FLUX

FILE ACCESSED: CASCADE DIRECTIVE – PARTIAL.

CONTINGENCY MODE: ENGAGED.

Vira stepped forward. "She didn't just activate it. She left something running."

Kade leaned in. "What's it doing now?"

"WAKING UP," F.I.Z.Z. said. "BUT SLOWLY. SYSTEMS FRAGMENTED. SOMETHING'S MISSING. OR... LOCKED."

The Deed pulsed once, then dimmed. A holographic map appeared: fragmented, pulsing, showing a cluster of five nodes. Only one was lit. The others flickered or remained dark.

"No labels?" Kade asked.

"IF THERE WERE, THEY'VE BEEN ERASED," F.I.Z.Z. said. "PROBABLY DELIBERATELY."

Zogg squinted. "So, this is just... one of five?"

"PROBABLY," F.I.Z.Z. said carefully. "BUT THAT'S A GUESS BASED ON NETWORK SHAPES, NOT FACT."

Kade rubbed his face. "So, we're standing in a piece of a giant sleeping machine. And we just kicked it."

The central figure shimmered.

"Node now online. Temporary access only. Resume when full quorum achieved."

Then, softer:

"User Andra-Flux... terminated?"

F.I.Z.Z. hesitated. "IT'S ASKING FOR CONFIRMATION."

Kade looked at it. "Yeah," he whispered. "She's gone."

"Acknowledged. Contingency ownership transferred. Proceed with caution."

The figure blinked out.

The Deed popped up from the plinth, no longer glowing, but warm.

Vira caught it. "Time to go."

As they climbed back to the surface, Zogg glanced nervously at the walls.

"Anyone else feel like we just knocked on the front door of something older than reality?"

"JUST DON'T OPEN THE WINDOWS," F.I.Z.Z. said. "REALITY'S STILL UPDATING."

Outside, the sky was still blue, the grass still wet, the birds still squawking like tiny, feathered cynics.

The van waited for them in the clearing, unbothered by galactic awakening.

Zogg slid into the back and looked around. "Did anyone else hear the ship just sigh?"

"I THINK THAT WAS ME," F.I.Z.Z. said. "I DOWNLOADED SOMETHING FROM THAT NODE I CAN'T FULLY DECRYPT."

Kade stared at him. "Is that bad?"

"I'M FEELING... REFLECTIVE. I MAY WRITE POETRY."

"Definitely bad," Zogg muttered.

They drove back in silence.

Behind them, the old relay station pulsed once more. Not loud. Not dramatic. Just... awake.

Far above Earth, several surveillance satellites blinked to life.

And in a chamber deep within the Galactic Council's hidden archives, a terminal beeped.

NODE 1: ACTIVE

DEED VERIFIED

SUBJECT: FLUX. ASCENDING RISK TIER

A figure in elite garb leaned forward. Their face was obscured in shadow, but their posture shifted, like someone recognizing a long-dormant threat.

They tapped the console once. A secure line opened. No words, just a blinking cursor.

Finally, the figure spoke.

"Bring this to the attention of Oversight."

A pause.

"And initiate contingency review. Quietly."

The screen dimmed. Somewhere deep in the system, a new file tagged [FLUX – MONITOR] quietly lit up.

THUMB WAR

The Node was awake.

And now, so was someone else.

CHAPTER 16: TERMS AND EVASIONS

"If your escape plan involves snacks, it's either brilliant or doomed."

— Zogg, probably

The ladder clanged as they ascended back into the forgotten relay station. The echo of the Node's awakening still hummed in Kade's bones. He tried not to think about the voice that had greeted him with his mother's name.

F.I.Z.Z. floated just behind him, scanning the dusty corners with a quiet whir.

"WELL," the bot intoned, "THAT WAS THE METAPHYSICAL EQUIVALENT OF KICKING A COSMIC HORNET'S NEST WHILE HOLDING HONEY."

Zogg stumbled onto the floor, panting. "Can confirm. Also, possibly allergic to cosmic hornets."

Kade brushed off his jacket. "Maybe we got lucky."

F.I.Z.Z. blinked. "I HAVE NEVER OBSERVED LUCK LAST LONG IN YOUR VICINITY."

They stood in the overgrown clearing beside the overgrown van they'd arrived in. The only thing out of place was the faint scent hanging in the air. Not smoke. Not ozone.

Kade sniffed.

"Why does it smell like... cheese?"

Zogg sniffed too. "Definitely cheese. Like someone tried to microwave nachos."

Vira swept a slow gaze across the treetops. "No drones. No movement."

"Correction," F.I.Z.Z. chimed, rising slowly into the air. "NO OBVIOUS MOVEMENT. PASSIVE SENSORS DETECT ELEVATION SHIFT. APPROACHING VESSEL, ATMOSPHERIC ENTRY, BEARING 127. SPEED: COCKY."

A low roar built in the distance, growing into a thrumming, overcompensating rumble. Trees bent slightly as wind pushed ahead of a descending ship: sleek, matte, and darker than ambition. It didn't so much land as declare its presence with hydraulic disdain.

The grass wilted slightly beneath it. Birds fled. Somewhere in the forest, a deer reconsidered its life choices.

The ramp extended.

And out stepped Dast.

He was not smiling. He was not blustering. He just walked, steady and deliberate, across the field, his middle eye fixed on Kade like it had a vendetta.

Behind him, a half-dozen goons fumbled down the ramp in mismatched uniforms and various states of preparedness. One tripped immediately and landed face-first in a patch of mushrooms. Another's boot fell off mid-stride. A third attempted to look intimidating but instead got a granola bar caught in his collar.

Zogg brightened. "Oh good. It's the classics."

Kade's voice was flat. "Dast."

"Flux," Dast replied. "How unfortunate to find you upright."

Zogg stepped forward, arms full of laminated cards. "Gentlemen! Before you do anything rash, may I interest you in a selection of expired galactic gift certificates?"

One goon blinked. "Is there a meal voucher?"

"Indeed!" Zogg said, handing him a glittery rectangle. "Good for one buffet or moderate distraction."

A second goon leaned over. "Does this one say... Free Foot Rub?"

"That's open to interpretation," Zogg said cheerfully. "And courage."

Behind them, Dast sighed. "Enough."

The goons froze, though one was still trying to peel the backing off a sticker coupon for "25% off interplanetary turtlenecks."

Dast stepped closer.

"You activated it," he said. "The Node. Beneath this Earth-buried dump."

Kade didn't move. "We had a look around."

"You have no idea what you've started."

"Wouldn't be the first time," Kade muttered.

Dast raised one hand. A goon immediately fumbled forward and opened a metal case. Inside: a pulsing scroll of bureaucratic authority, flickering faintly with Galactic Council emblems.

"I've been authorized," Dast said. "Cease-and-reclaim order. Galactic Directive 3.9.7-B. Effective immediately."

F.I.Z.Z. scanned the document mid-float. "FORGERY DETECTED. STYLE TEMPLATE PREDATES THE CURRENT GALACTIC COUNCIL SEAL. EMBLEM IS INCONSISTENT. FONT IS 'GALACTIC CHANCERY COMIC'. A KNOWN COUNTERFEIT GIVEAWAY."

Zogg whispered, "Also, that seal smells like cheese."

Dast's eyes narrowed. "The Galactic Council doesn't care about the proper font. They care about control. And you're upsetting it."

Vira stood silently beside Kade, hand on her hip. She said nothing, but her gaze didn't waver.

"You don't understand what that Deed is," Dast said, taking another step. "You think it's a key. It's not. It's a signal. A flare. And the moment you used it, the wrong kind of people noticed."

Kade frowned. "Like the Galactic Council?"

Dast didn't answer.

Kade stepped forward, just one pace. "So, what's your part in this? They send you to tidy things up? Put the Deed back in its pretty little vault and keep Earth dumb and quiet?"

"They sent me," Dast said, "because they knew I'd get results."

"Or try to," Vira muttered.

"Do they know you lost it in the first place?" Kade added. "In a thumb war?"

Dast's middle eye narrowed. "They know I'm still the one most likely to take it back. Thumb war or not."

Zogg wandered up behind one of the distracted goons and gently stuck a "Buy one pudding, get one scream" voucher to his back. "So, uh... what happens if we just say no?"

Dast clenched his fists. "Then I take it."

"From my cold, sarcastic hands?" Kade asked.

"No. From your broken ship, once you're detained."

F.I.Z.Z. hovered between them. "RECOMMEND TACTICAL STALLING UNTIL ESCAPE PLAN IS... ESCAPEABLE."

One of the goons slipped on a mushroom and collided with another, who spun in a circle before accidentally firing a grapple line that anchored to a tree and yanked them both sideways into a ditch.

"STALLING SUCCESSFUL," F.I.Z.Z. confirmed.

Dast glanced behind him, expression tightening. "This was a courtesy. My next visit will not be."

He turned. "Fall back. We're done here."

Zogg waved a "Free Laser Facial" coupon after them. "Don't forget your complimentary regrets!"

The goons stumbled and tumbled back up the ramp in full Plek-7 Emergency Drill Formation, which historically, had a 12% survival rate and a 97% comedy rating.

The ship rose, engines kicking up dust and expired discount cards. Then it was gone... just sky and noise and the lingering scent of warm dairy product.

Silence returned.

Kade didn't exhale until the treetops stopped swaying.

"Well," Zogg said, brushing leaves off his shoulder, "that went better than usual."

"No, it didn't," Kade muttered.

F.I.Z.Z. spun once. "RECOMMEND FAST-TRACKING SHIP REPAIRS. WE'RE OFFICIALLY A TARGET NOW."

"Do we even know what Dast wants?" Kade asked.

Vira crossed her arms. "Control. Same as the Galactic Council. They don't want the Nodes destroyed. They want them locked. Monopolized. Access without consequences."

"And we just opened a door," Kade murmured.

F.I.Z.Z. dimmed his lights slightly. "WHICH MEANS WE NOW HAVE TO WALK THROUGH IT.

QUICKLY. BEFORE THEY SLAM IT CLOSED ON OUR FACES."

Zogg held up the last remaining voucher

"Anyone want a free apology from a goon?"

Kade turned toward the van. "Let's just get back to the ship."

CHAPTER 17: UNEXPECTED TRIAL

"Always disable the trap after identifying it."

— Goons Training Module #3

They hadn't made it halfway back to town when the flashing lights appeared.

Red and blue strobes lit up the tree trunks like they were about to be interrogated. Vira spotted them first in the mirror: two police cruisers weaving their way up the cracked roadside behind them.

"Don't say it," she warned.

"I wasn't going to," Kade said quickly. "But if I were, it would've started with 'uh-oh.'"

"Say nothing," Vira muttered. "F.I.Z.Z., stay low."

"I AM ALREADY IN THE FOOTWELL," F.I.Z.Z. replied. "WHERE THE AIR SMELLS LIKE PANIC AND OLD CRACKERS."

Kade turned slightly in his seat. "Zogg, hoodie up. No one needs to know you're not local."

Zogg yanked his hoodie forward and pulled the zipper so high it threatened to merge with his eyebrows. "I am blending in. I am atmospheric."

"Atmospheric is not a species," Kade whispered.

The cruisers whooped their sirens once, briefly, just enough to say pull over or else.

Vira sighed through her nose, pulled the van over beside a rusted "Scenic Outlook (Closed)" sign, and shut off the engine.

"Everyone else stays put," she said, already rolling down her window. "Let me talk."

Two officers approached. One took his time, the other moved like this was the highlight of his week.

The lead officer leaned in. "Evening, ma'am. Sorry to interrupt. We had a report of something unusual in the area."

"Unusual how?" Vira asked calmly.

"Bright lights. Low flying object. Loud, rhythmic pulsing. Startled some hikers. Got a few wildlife calls too, somebody's pet turtle tried to climb a tree."

Kade leaned over. "That does sound unusual."

"Mind stepping out of the vehicle?" the second officer asked.

"I do, actually," Vira said, not moving. "We're on our way home. Is this about traffic?"

"Not traffic," the lead said. "More like potential public disruption."

His flashlight angled toward Kade. "You the one listed on the vehicle rental?"

"Technically, I'm the one not driving," Kade replied.

"We're going to need to ask a few questions down at the municipal center. Voluntarily. But strongly encouraged."

Vira gave a slow, diplomatic nod. "That a request or an order?"

"Think of it as a very polite warning."

Behind them, one cruiser's radio crackled with clipped codewords, nothing specific, but enough to suggest someone somewhere had taken this seriously enough to notify someone else.

Kade glanced toward the back of the van. No movement. F.I.Z.Z. and Zogg were playing possum, very convincingly.

Vira opened her door.

"We'll follow," she said.

The officer smiled, but only with his mouth.

The "municipal center" looked like it had been built by accident. Beige walls, flickering lights, where important things go to be forgotten, and a sign on the door that read: Civic Hall B.

Inside, a folding table and three suited officials waited behind nameplates that had clearly been recycled from at least three prior job titles. One read: Acting Deputy Inquiry Coordinator (Temporary). Another said: Acting Sub Deputy Inquiry Coordinator (Temporary)Legal.

The third was asleep.

Vira and Kade were seated in mismatched chairs, beneath a flickering fluorescent tube that hummed like it resented them.

"We're not under arrest," Kade said carefully, "but you drove us here under flashing lights?"

"Standard procedure for unverified anomaly responses," one of the officials replied.

"That sounds... vague."

"Exactly."

The official folded her hands. "Here's what we know: something flew very low across three townships. There was a brief spike in radio interference and a recorded power surge near the east substation. This all happened during a period when several witnesses saw 'glowing shapes' and one man claimed a duck was trying to hypnotize him."

Kade blinked. "We don't even own a duck."

"That's what the last guy said," the official muttered darkly.

Another slid a form across the table. "You're listed as the van's operator. Were you anywhere near Forest Route 9 between 6 and 8 p.m.?"

Vira answered flatly. "We were at a campsite near Ridge Hollow. Packed up, drove back. Saw nothing unusual."

"Vehicle's engine was still warm," the official noted. "And your license plate was flagged in a routine scan after a previous citation... something about parking in a duck pond?"

"That's... technically a landscaping accident," Kade said. "And I wasn't driving."

"No one was arrested, though?" the official asked.

"No," Vira replied. "Because there was no crime."

Silence.

Then a faint creak.

The door opened.

A woman walked in: brisk, unreadable, clipboard in hand. Her ID was unreadable, the kind of government-issue badge that seemed to authorize everything by implication.

She leaned over, whispered something to the lead official, then handed over a thin folder.

The official opened it. Read it.

Then nodded once.

The woman, Agent Duckworth, though she hadn't introduced herself, turned to leave.

"You're free to go," they said.

Kade blinked. "Wait... just like that?"

"There's been a jurisdictional reassessment," the official said. "You're no longer within our mandate."

Vira stood slowly. "Of course we aren't."

"Please do avoid further... disturbances."

They were escorted out with half-hearted apologies and vague nods. One of the officials offered a voucher for free mulch delivery.

Outside, Duckworth waited beside the van.

"You need to leave town. Tonight."

"We already were," Kade muttered.

She handed him a USB stick. "More of your mother's trail. Someone erased this from the county archives."

Kade pocketed it. "Why help?"

"Because I'd rather you find the truth before they find you."

"And who's 'they'?"

She looked up. "The ones who left Earth asleep. And want it that way."

Before Kade could reply, she was gone; vanishing between two parking pylons like a well-timed glitch.

Back inside the van, F.I.Z.Z. hummed with curiosity.

"WE HAVE FILES TO DECRYPT."

Zogg pointed at the building. "Can I come back next week? I think the vending machine winked at me."

"No," Kade said. "No more municipal facilities."

As they pulled out of the lot, Vira glanced at him. "That agent; she's watching out for you."

"I know," he said quietly. "So did my mom."

"She knew enough to end that circus."

F.I.Z.Z. lit up. "POSSIBLE CONNECTION CONFIRMED. DUCKWORTH WAS ON FILE WITH EARTH-SIDE SURVEILLANCE UNDER THE ALIAS 'NEST 7.'"

In the back, Zogg popped up, bleary-eyed. "Did we win?"

"I BELIEVE WE SURVIVED," F.I.Z.Z. offered. "WHICH IN THIS GROUP, COUNTS AS A VICTORY."

Zogg looked around. "Do we still have snacks?"

"No," Kade said. "But we still have questions."

They pulled away in silence, engine sputtering like a grumpy apology.

As they drove, Kade glanced in the mirror and caught a glimpse of a familiar yellow blur on the side of the road... a rubber duck sitting neatly atop a fencepost.

It didn't blink.

But somehow, he knew it was still watching.

CHAPTER 18: INFLIGHT TENSION

"Confession is good for the soul. Unless you're confessing to waking a Node."

— F.I.Z.Z.

Misplaced Optimism coughed.

Not a mechanical cough. Not an alert. A genuine, resentful cough, as if she resented being asked to function again.

Kade ducked under a sparking panel in the engineering crawlspace, a wrench in one hand and a mildly burnt rag in the other. "She's sulking."

"I HEARD THAT," said the ship's Computer. "AND I'M SCHEDULING YOUR TOAST TO BURN AT INCONVENIENT TIMES."

A panel above Kade's head fell off and landed on his shoulder.

"Point made," he groaned.

Vira leaned in through the open hatch. "You cross-wired the stabilizer relay again."

"No, I cross-wired the thing that was cross-wired. Which, if you think about it, makes it right again."

Vira raised an eyebrow. "You want to rephrase that before the ship smacks you again?"

F.I.Z.Z. floated overhead like a patient parent at a science fair. "REPAIR LOG UPDATED. EMOTIONAL VOLTAGE: HIGH. SYSTEM STABILITY: MODERATE. SNACKS: UNACCOUNTED FOR."

Zogg slid into the compartment on a wheeled crate, holding a biscuit in one hand and a screwdriver in the other. "I don't like it when mum and dad fight."

"We're not..." Kade started, then gave up. "Forget it."

The ship rattled again as another system came partially online. A bank of blinking lights blinked once, then died.

Zogg watched it sympathetically. "She's trying her best."

"She's also trying to electrocute me," Kade muttered.

"Maybe she's just reacting to the tension," Zogg offered. "Like when F.I.Z.Z. makes that low humming noise when he's stressed."

"I DO NOT HUM WHEN STRESSED," F.I.Z.Z. insisted. Then hummed softly. "...IGNORE THAT."

Vira sighed and folded her arms. "We've stabilized the drives, but not enough for lift. We're still grounded."

"Which is fine," Kade said. "We're not ready to leave anyway."

An awkward silence followed.

It stretched.

Twisted.

Then snapped.

Kade turned. "Alright. Let's talk. Vira, you've been dodging this since day one."

"Dodging what?"

"Everything," he said. "Why you knew where my mother stored her backups. How you had the access codes. How you fight like a merc and fix ships like you were born in one."

Vira exhaled through her nose.

"I was watching Earth," she said. "That much is true. But I wasn't alone."

She walked to the side wall and tapped a diagnostic screen. It flickered, static rippling through the UI.

"I was part of a faction. A splinter group. Old AI networks: rogue intelligences that broke from the Galactic Council when they realized the Galactic Council was hiding things. Redacting system protocols."

Kade blinked. "You were working for rebels?"

"I was monitoring Earth on their behalf. Just watching. Observing. Nothing was supposed to happen."

"But then I showed up," Kade muttered.

Vira nodded. "The moment you activated the Deed... the moment it pulsed... everything changed. I didn't expect it to respond. Let alone sync to you."

"Wait," Zogg said. "So, the glowing space rectangle wasn't supposed to do anything?"

"Not without a trigger," she said. "And Kade was that trigger."

There was a soft thunk from the engine room. One of the spare parts, possibly important, rolled past at a lazy wobble. No one moved to catch it.

Kade slumped against the bulkhead. "Great. So... you were spying."

"I was observing," Vira corrected.

"For a rogue faction."

"Yes."

Kade tilted his head. "You're really bad at job descriptions."

"I'VE RATED THIS EXCHANGE 3.5 OUT OF 10 FOR PRODUCTIVE CONFLICT," F.I.Z.Z. said. "BUT 9 OUT OF 10 FOR DRAMATIC POTENTIAL."

Vira met Kade's gaze. "I didn't come to harm anyone. I was sent to detect Node signals and report. That's it. And then your mother's trail turned up again. And I saw the Deed. And suddenly, everything was awake."

There was another silence. Not heavy this time. Just dense with processing.

F.I.Z.Z. hovered forward, uncharacteristically quiet. "FOR WHAT IT'S WORTH... I THINK THE DEED WANTS SOMETHING."

Kade turned. "What do you mean?"

"I MEAN," F.I.Z.Z. said, "WHEN I'M NEAR IT, I FEEL... OFF. LIKE THERE'S A FREQUENCY I CAN ALMOST HEAR. LIKE A THOUGHT I FORGOT TO HAVE."

Zogg made a face. "Like déjà vu? Or like when you remember you left the oven on but you're in space and you never owned an oven?"

"YES," F.I.Z.Z. replied. "EXACTLY LIKE THAT. IF THAT THOUGHT WERE BEING BROADCAST THROUGH TIME."

"That's... unnerving," Zogg said.

"I'VE BEEN MANY THINGS," F.I.Z.Z. replied. "USEFUL, OBNOXIOUS, POETIC. BUT NEVER HAUNTED BY HARDWARE."

Kade stared at the Deed, still resting in the sealed crate, glowing faintly.

The Deed wasn't just a map or a key. It was his mother's handwriting, her voice, her way of still steering his life from beyond the grave. And he hated it as much as he needed it.

"It's not just a key," he said slowly. "It's... aware. Maybe not conscious, but aware."

"Probably tuned to Node signals," Vira said. "Your mother built those failsafe's in. Every Deed carries a harmonic match to its node."

Zogg leaned closer to the crate, whispering, "If this thing starts talking in iambic pentameter, I'm leaving."

"She really thought this through," Kade murmured. "Built a breadcrumb trail. Clues, protocols, even duck-based signal markers."

"I still don't understand the ducks," Zogg whispered.

"No one does," Kade said.

He reached into his coat and pulled out the crumpled note he'd reread a dozen times. It was worn, folded twice, and still faintly smelled of coffee.

He held it up.

"This," he said, "is the only thing I have left from her that's in her handwriting."

Vira stepped closer. She didn't try to read it. Just stood there.

Kade read it aloud.

> "If the duck blinks, run. Also: Trust Vira."

The words landed like a dropped wrench.

Vira's eyes widened. "She said to trust me?"

Kade nodded. "In a handwritten note. Not a console message. Not a data dump. A note. That means something."

F.I.Z.Z. beeped softly. "CONFIRMATION: THAT IS THE HIGHEST FORM OF ANALOG TRUST."

Zogg raised a hand. "So... we're cool again?"

Kade hesitated. Then shrugged. "I don't know. But it's a start."

Vira met his eyes. "That's all I ask."

A loud clang echoed from somewhere below. The ship groaned again: less angry, more tired. Possibly digesting something.

F.I.Z.Z. scanned a relay. "POWER FLOW STABILIZING. MOOD IMPROVING. STILL UNFLYABLE. BUT SLIGHTLY LESS SASSY."

Computer groaned softly through the speaker. "great. now you've made it sentimental."

"We'll keep at it," Kade said. "We've got time."

Zogg wandered off humming what might have been a sea shanty or a jingle for breakfast cereal.

Outside, stars wheeled silently.

Inside, *Misplaced Optimism* buzzed with quiet repairs, awkward reconciliation, and the hum of something greater stirring far below Earth's surface.

Something that had noticed them.

And was still listening.

CHAPTER 19: ANDRA'S SECRET CODE

"Never trust anything that pings at midnight."

— Council Tech Support

Misplaced Optimism hummed with reluctant stability. Not functional, exactly, just no longer actively plotting to kill anyone. A few lights had stopped flickering. The floor panels were warm instead of mildly smoking. And most of the hull had agreed to hold still, at least through lunch.

Kade crouched at the center console in the ship's work bay, staring at two objects laid out in front of him like mismatched puzzle pieces from different games. One was a smooth, glowing disc, the size of a drink coaster, pulsing faintly with layered harmonics. The data core they'd recovered from Unit 42.

The other was a USB stick, plain, scratched, and aggressively boring. The kind you'd throw in a drawer and forget, unless you were Agent Duckworth, and the data on it could decrypt something galactically stupid.

"Okay," Kade said, fidgeting with both. "These two better like each other."

"THEY DO," F.I.Z.Z. replied. "I RAN PRELIMINARY RESONANCE CHECKS WHILE YOU SLEPT. THEY'RE MATCHED. LIKE COUPLES WHO FINISH EACH OTHER'S PASSWORDS."

Vira looked up from the bench across the room, where she was reassembling a secondary panel with a mix of precision and mild contempt. "And you didn't lead with that why?"

"BECAUSE YOU SAID, 'LET'S NOT OVERHEAT THE SHIP BEFORE BREAKFAST.'"

"That does sound like me," she muttered.

Zogg's head popped into view from the overhead vent he was inexplicably crawling through. "Hey, is it safe to poke random stuff in that crate labeled 'Do Not Poke Random Stuff'?"

"No!" Kade, Vira, and F.I.Z.Z. said in perfect unison.

"Just checking," Zogg replied, retreating into the duct with a rustle and a soft thump.

Kade inserted the USB stick into the console's side port. The system chirped once, then a soft harmonic vibration rippled out. The disc, resting on a field plate, lit up in tandem.

"DECRYPTION LAYER DETECTED," F.I.Z.Z. announced. "FILES IN DISC CORE NOW ACCESSIBLE. UNLOCKING."

Symbols unfurled across the display, some Earth-standard, others etched in looping alien script that blinked and refracted like someone had taught mathematics to a squid. Then came the tone: low, layered, almost musical. A code you didn't hear so much as feel.

"SONIC ENCRYPTION ACTIVE," F.I.Z.Z. added. "THIS IS A SIGNATURE TECHNIQUE. OLD. PERSONALIZED. PROBABLY BUILT BY YOUR MOTHER."

Kade adjusted his seat. "Then let's hear what she left."

The console flashed white once.

Andra Flux's voice filled the work bay.

"If you're seeing this," she said, calm and dry, "then either I'm dead or someone got too clever with my lockboxes. Probably both."

Zogg's head reappeared, upside-down, from a ceiling panel. "Was that her?"

"She sounds tired," Kade said softly.

"I WOULD BE TOO IF I HAD TO PREDICT YOUR TIMING," F.I.Z.Z. replied.

Andra's voice continued. "There are five Deeds. Five Nodes. One reset. That's the framework. But the Galactic Council only ever understood the outer shell. Not the resonance. Not the pulse logic underneath. That's where the power is."

A map projection flared into life, a crude spiral with five glowing points. Only one was lit.

"Each Deed carries a harmonic fingerprint. When activated near its matching Node, it does more than open doors. It *wakes systems*. Restores memory. Reboots logic threads long buried. The system was meant to connect the galaxy, not control it."

The voice dipped, as if she were lowering it from instinct.

"But the Galactic Council didn't want connection. They wanted obedience. So, they buried it. And now they're afraid it's waking up."

A silence.

Then: "If you're watching this, the first Node is probably already live. That means they've noticed. It also means the Deed is listening for the others."

Kade leaned closer.

"There's a signal, Kade," Andra said. "Not a path. A sound. You'll know the next one when you hear…"

Static.

The message broke for a second. Then resumed, scrambled slightly.

"… follow the resonance. If the duck blinks, run."

Zogg blinked. "Did she say the duck…"

"Not now," Kade muttered.

Vira crossed her arms, watching the playback with a tightened jaw.

Andra's final message scrolled onto the screen in flat text:

"Trust is your only currency. Spend it carefully.

And don't wait too long. They're already listening."

The display dimmed. The disc stopped glowing. The USB ejected with a polite mechanical cough.

Silence fell over the bay like a thick blanket.

"FILE DECRYPTION COMPLETE," F.I.Z.Z. said. "NO FURTHER ENTRIES. ENCRYPTION THREAD SELF-WIPED ON READOUT. VERY... DRAMATIC."

"She knew they'd find it if we didn't," Vira said quietly.

Kade nodded, slowly picking up the disc. "She was trying to finish something. Or maybe start something bigger than she could finish."

"DO WE THINK THIS IS A KEY TO THE OTHER NODES?" F.I.Z.Z. asked.

"Or a map," Zogg said, munching.

"Or bait," Vira added.

They all sat in silence for a long moment.

Then...

Zogg frowned. "Uh... guys?"

Kade looked up. "What?"

Zogg was standing at the rear ramp now, peering through a gap in the hull insulation near the floor. He pointed.

"I was just doing some light scavenging for snacks," he said, "and I think... the duck pond's glowing."

Vira joined him at the hatch, then Kade. F.I.Z.Z. hovered behind them, activating low-light sensors.

Sure enough, the pond just beyond the edge of the ship's footprint, half-claimed by reeds and lazy ducks, was glowing. Not bright. Not loud. Just... pulsing. A slow, rhythmical shimmer that danced faintly along the ripples.

"Is that... us?" Kade asked.

"Ship power bleed?" Vira guessed. "Or resonance feedback from the Node?"

"Or" Zogg added helpfully, "the ducks have become sentient and are celebrating."

F.I.Z.Z. beeped. "NO KNOWN BIOLOGICAL MECHANISM IN DUCKS THAT EXPLAINS LUMINESCENT WATER INDUCED BY GALACTIC SIGNALS."

"That doesn't help," Kade said.

"IT WASN'T MEANT TO."

Zogg scratched his chin thoughtfully. "What if the Node isn't underground anymore? What if it's under the pond? What if the pond is the Node?"

"That makes less sense than usual," Vira said.

"I LIKE IT," F.I.Z.Z. replied. "IT HAS STYLE."

They stood there watching the water glow.

Then, as quickly as it had flared, the shimmer began to fade, leaving only the quiet pond and a few mildly confused ducks paddling like nothing had happened.

Zogg turned. "Okay. That was either beautiful, terrifying, or foreshadowing. I'm voting foreshadowing."

Kade looked down at the disc again.

"Whatever this is," he said, "we need to move fast."

CHAPTER 20: EVACUATION

"Global anomalies? Just reboot the planet."

— IT Helpdesk, Sector 3

Misplaced Optimism let out a low, resentful rumble.

Not mechanical. Not threatening. Just... annoyed. Like a ship that had been woken up from a very long nap and handed a to-do list written in panicked handwriting.

It wasn't flying yet, but it wanted to. Somewhere deep in its groaning frame, its engines were awake, systems were syncing, and something buried in its core had quietly muttered: "Fine. Let's do this."

Inside the cockpit, Kade leaned over the console and stared at a mess of blinking warning icons.

"Okay," he muttered, "tell me that's just the ship having a tantrum."

"NO," said F.I.Z.Z., floating overhead. "THAT IS THE PLANET INFRASTRUCTURE HAVING A TANTRUM."

Vira appeared beside him, pointing to the main display.

Earth's satellite grid had lit up like a slot machine on a caffeine bender.

Red circles bloomed over every continent.

Civilian satellites blinked irregularly, flickering in and out of sync. Internet nodes stuttered. Weather prediction servers dumped their forecasts and began streaming what appeared to be stock footage of rainbows and goat yoga. Global navigation systems wobbled, some directing aircraft to reroute through Peru, others suggesting Australia was currently "on break."

"THE NODE'S PULSE IS HITTING EVERYTHING," F.I.Z.Z. said. "NOT JUST LOCALLY. GLOBAL UPTICK IN HARMONIC FREQUENCY RESPONSE. EARTH'S NETWORKS ARE TRYING TO UNDERSTAND IT. AND FAILING."

Zogg peeked in from the corridor, holding a spoon and a thermal pack labeled "Emergency Lasagna." "The fridge just told me I'm not emotionally prepared to eat."

"It's syncing," Vira said, frowning. "The Node. With everything."

"And now everything is confused," Kade muttered. "Great."

The lights above flickered twice, then turned purple for no discernible reason. A speaker somewhere behind the main console began playing hold music in reverse.

"IS THIS... AN EARTH TRADITION?" F.I.Z.Z. asked.

Zogg sniffed. "If it is, I like it less than Arbor Day. And Arbor Day once tried to arrest me."

F.I.Z.Z. beeped. "I'M DETECTING FAILURES IN GLOBAL SYSTEMS. TRANSPORTATION GRIDS, CELL TOWERS, EVEN AD ALGORITHMS."

Zogg gasped. "The ads?!"

"ONE STREAMING PLATFORM JUST RECOMMENDED A MEDITATION VIDEO TO EVERY USER REGARDLESS OF PREFERENCE. THAT HAS NEVER HAPPENED."

Vira winced. "Now that's serious."

Kade straightened. "So, we've officially pushed the planet into a nervous breakdown."

"YES," F.I.Z.Z. said. "AND EARTH HAS NO IDEA WHY."

"Do we?" Zogg added hopefully.

"No," Kade and Vira said in unison.

F.I.Z.Z. started projecting real-time footage of Earth's infrastructure struggling to adapt. A stock exchange board began displaying emojis. A train schedule redirected every route to "Probably Nowhere." One global airline app simply displayed a shrug emoji and the word "Good luck."

"I THINK THIS CONSTITUTES A REBOOT," F.I.Z.Z. observed. "OR AN APOLOGY."

A new alert pinged the screen.

A contact. Low orbit. Unregistered.

The silhouette appeared a second later, jagged, matte, quiet.

Dast.

His cruiser descended from the clouds like a vindictive shadow. No lights. No signal. No subtlety. It banked sharply, curling downward in a slow spiral over the forest clearing that still barely hid *Misplaced Optimism*.

"THRUSTERS MINIMIZED," F.I.Z.Z. announced. "HE'S TRYING TO SPOOK US."

Zogg leaned closer to the viewport. "I don't like how quiet it is."

"He knows he's over Earth," Kade said. "He just doesn't care."

Vira was already moving, flipping switches, checking engine status. "How fast can we move?"

"FIVE OUT OF EIGHT ENGINES ONLINE," F.I.Z.Z. replied. "I SUGGEST A STRATEGIC SKID AND HOPE."

Kade activated the external comms. "Dast. You're in Earth's airspace. That's... pretty bold."

The reply came back in static and venom. "The Deed doesn't belong to you, Flux. Neither does that Node. You're sitting on technology your species can't begin to understand."

Vira rolled her eyes. "Nice to know he's still condescending."

"Return it!" Dast barked. "Or I'll pry it out of the wreckage."

Misplaced Optimism's hull vibrated as his cruiser descended further, low enough now to scatter ducks from the pond, which quacked their disapproval as they flapped into the air.

One particularly angry duck landed on the hull, stared upward at the massive cruiser, and let out a defiant quack before waddling off.

"I LIKE THAT DUCK," F.I.Z.Z. noted. "IT SEEMS PREPARED FOR WAR."

Then: a shrill tone.

A new alert appeared on the screen, flashing rapidly.

Kade frowned. "That's not ours."

"IT'S EARTH MILITARY," F.I.Z.Z. confirmed. "RADAR CROSSCHECK DETECTS FOUR MACH-TWO INTERCEPTORS. HUMAN-BUILT. VERY SERIOUS. AND GETTING CLOSER."

Outside, faint contrails streaked across the sky.

Four fighter jets crested the horizon in a tight formation, engines screaming. They banked in perfect sync, locked onto Dast's cruiser, and began a rapid approach vector.

One jet opened comms.

The ship translated the signal.

"UNIDENTIFIED VEHICLE. THIS IS UNITED STATES AIRSPACE. DESCEND AND SUBMIT TO INSPECTION OR BE INTERCEPTED."

There was a pause.

Then, from Dast's ship, arrogant silence.

The fighters closed in.

Dast's cruiser tilted, angling its nose toward them.

Zogg gulped. "Please tell me he's not gonna..."

Dast opened a weapons bay.

The fighters flared out in response, breaking into attack pattern instantly.

A warning shot sizzled across the cruiser's flank. Not a missile. A message.

Another streaked by.

Dast's cruiser shuddered and pulled up.

"HE'S RETREATING," F.I.Z.Z. said. "THEY'RE FORCING HIM TO BACK OFF. I AM IMPRESSED BY EARTH'S OVERREACTION PROTOCOLS."

Kade leaned forward, watching the cruiser slowly curve away.

Dast hesitated, lingering just at the edge of cloud cover.

Then, without another word, his ship turned sharply and vanished into the upper atmosphere.

The fighters held formation briefly, then peeled off one by one, circling the area.

Vira exhaled. "That was too close."

"He didn't expect that," Kade said. "He thought Earth was a backwater."

"HE FORGOT THAT HUMANS ARE PARANOID AND LOADED WITH JET FUEL," F.I.Z.Z. added cheerfully.

Zogg sagged into the copilot chair. "So... now what?"

Kade looked down at the glowing Deed. It still pulsed, steady and quiet now. No more surges. No more sudden activations.

Just presence.

"We're not staying here," he said.

"WE CAN'T LAUNCH YET," F.I.Z.Z. reminded him. "STILL LOCKED TO LOW ATMOSPHERE FLIGHT. HIGH ORBIT ESCAPE WILL DESTABILIZE HULL."

"Then we stay in the atmosphere," Kade said. "Long enough to hide. Regroup. Figure out what the next Node wants."

Zogg slowly raised a hand. "Does anyone else feel like the Node isn't done with us?"

The ship hummed.

Systems lights flickered.

On the nav console, a new line of text appeared, no alarm, no source:

ACTIVE LISTENER DETECTED. SIGNAL PATH OPEN.

F.I.Z.Z. whirred. "THAT'S... NOT FROM US."

Kade nodded slowly.

"No," he said. "That's from whoever just heard the Node wake up."

He looked to Vira.

"We need to move. Quietly. Before anyone else gets here."

She nodded, already rerouting power.

Zogg unwrapped a snack bar and whispered to it, "We're never going back to normal, are we?"

The ship's Computer sighed. "You never were."

Misplaced Optimism banked low, dropping into the tree line like a shadow trying not to be seen.

Above them, the sky pulsed.

Earth's networks blinked.

And in a quiet room on the far side of the planet, someone, or something, began tracking their signature.

CHAPTER 21: EARTH EXIT

"In space, altitude is a suggestion. Speed is the real danger."

— Pilot Lore

Misplaced Optimism skimmed the treetops like a nervous dragonfly with commitment issues.

Branches snapped and windshields cracked as it weaved through suburban airspace, too low to be dignified, too fast to be polite. A weathervane was decapitated in passing. Several birds filed complaints with higher altitudes.

"TOO LOW," F.I.Z.Z. announced.

"We're avoiding detection," Vira said, gripping the controls. "High orbit destabilizes the hull, we stay low until we're clear."

"CURRENT ALTITUDE IS MINIMUM SAFE THRESHOLD. BELOW THIS, WE QUALIFY AS LAWN EQUIPMENT."

"Noted," Kade said from behind the pilot's seat, steadying himself with one hand on the ceiling and the other on a suspiciously humming conduit. "Let's just get some breathing room before the Galactic Council starts triangulating our teeth."

They jutted sideways to avoid a communications tower, sheared a chunk off an outdated television relay, and threaded the narrow gap between two wind turbines with less than a meter to spare. Somewhere in the chaos, a billboard advertising shrimp tacos was converted into high-velocity confetti.

"Was that necessary?" Kade asked as another gust rattled the hull.

"It was either the billboard or the farmer's market," Vira replied. "And I wasn't about to be chased into orbit by artisanal jam."

As if to emphasize her point, a jar of peach chutney splattered across the forward viewport. Zogg leaned into the cockpit, licking his finger thoughtfully.

"Hmm. Notes of cinnamon. Could be sabotage."

The ship scraped the edge of a floating blimp that blinked out a desperate SOS in lights: "VOTE BARKLEY FOR CITY TREASURER."

"Who's Barkley?" Zogg asked, poking his head further in.

"Probably the only thing more off-course than we are," Kade muttered.

An automated police drone zipped past, lights flashing. F.I.Z.Z. hacked it mid-flight, rerouting its targeting system to focus on a rogue weather balloon.

"THAT SHOULD BUY US FORTY-SEVEN SECONDS."

"We need forty-eight," Vira muttered, jerking the yoke hard left.

The ship groaned as it rolled under a freeway skybridge. A parked car on the top deck of the overpass spun 360 degrees in shock, honked twice, and shut itself off.

"Find somewhere to hide the ship, then we should regroup," Kade said. "Shipboard. Five-minute diagnostics. Team huddle. Maybe emotional collapse, optional."

The mess bay was quieter than usual. The ambient hum of the engines had a different tone: like the ship was humming a tune but didn't quite remember the words.

Zogg was slumped on a crate, sipping from a pouch labeled "Hydration (Possibly)." Vira sat with one boot on the edge of the table; gaze fixed on the glowing Deed. Kade leaned against the doorway, arms folded. F.I.Z.Z. hovered silently near the ceiling like a sentient chandelier with opinions.

A scorched toaster sat upside down in the corner: Zogg's doing. It had tried to eject breadcrumbs mid-flight and was now serving a lifetime ban from electronics bay access.

"We made it," Kade said at last.

"WE MADE AWAY," F.I.Z.Z. corrected. "OUTCOME PENDING."

The Deed pulsed faintly. Not urgent, not loud. But insistent. Like the beat of something old reawakened and deciding what came next.

"I still don't get it," Kade said. "Why Earth? Why now?"

"Because it was dormant," Vira replied. "Because we were there. Because the Deed was ready."

Kade ran a hand through his hair. "And now Earth's in the crosshairs."

"It was already in the network," Vira said. "Just... unplugged."

"Now it's blinking red."

Zogg raised a finger. "Silver lining... it wasn't destroyed."

Kade shot him a look. "Is that the bar now? 'We didn't explode the planet'?"

"I'M ADDING IT TO THE VICTORY WALL," F.I.Z.Z. offered.

"What wall?"

"THE ONE I'M DESIGNING IN MY HEAD. IT'S MOSTLY LEDS AND SARCASM."

Zogg nodded sagely. "Add a snack shelf."

"NO."

Kade called it what it was: a flying breakdown with charm issues. *Misplaced Optimism* wasn't space worthy. Not yet.

The regrouping shifted into triage mode.

The crew split up: Zogg to the under-deck wiring bundles, where he insisted, he "understood voltage on an emotional level." Vira climbed into the aft junction shaft, toolkit in hand, muttering about fused relay conduits and burnt impulse lines. Kade, meanwhile, traced every panel marked with a red "X" and swore at each one in sequence.

F.I.Z.Z. floated between them, occasionally zapping sparks off relays with a snappy "FIXED" and declaring unrelated systems to be "EXISTENTIALLY FRACTURED."

At one point, Zogg attempted to apply adhesive bonding gel to a cracked support strut. The gel, being sentient and allergic to aluminum, immediately launched itself into the ceiling vent.

"Uh," Zogg said, holding the now-empty tube. "We may have a gremlin now."

"I'LL ADD IT TO THE CREW ROSTER," F.I.Z.Z. replied.

"I think I found the problem with the coolant line," Zogg called from somewhere below deck.

A moment later, a geyser of fluorescent green fluid sprayed upward from a floor grate.

"I stand by my theory," he added, now slightly glowing.

"Divert from the coolant; check the grav buffers," Kade said. "The last time I stood up too fast, I ended up horizontal for an hour."

"THAT WAS UNRELATED," F.I.Z.Z. said. "YOU TRIPPED ON ZOGG'S SNACK ROLL."

Vira's voice echoed from the crawlspace. "Power junction three is fused shut. I'm bypassing it."

"With what?"

"Spite."

A dull thunk sounded.

"...And also, a length of repurposed toaster filament."

Kade opened a maintenance panel and found what looked like a family of squirrels made of wire and dust. "This used to be the stabilizer interface. Now it's... interpretive sculpture."

"SHOULD I LABEL IT 'HOPE'?"

"I was thinking 'Despair With Bonus Sparkage,'" Kade muttered.

Nearby, Zogg had attached a spoon, three zip ties, and a sticky note reading "DO NOT TOUCH (I MEAN IT)" to a pipe. He stepped back proudly.

"That's the plasma manifold."

Zogg blinked. "Oh. Then... what's this thing?"

"That's my lunch," Kade sighed.

At one point, Zogg emerged with a burnt circuit board and a triumphant grin. "I re-routed the redundant plasma buffer through the hypercoil relay using this!"

"That's a banana," Kade said.

Zogg looked at it. "Oh. Well, then where's the relay?"

"YOU MAY HAVE EATEN IT," F.I.Z.Z. guessed.

"I did think it was unusually chewy."

An hour later, the engines were still limping, but alive.

The ship shook slightly. Then gave up and sulked into silence.

Kade checked the diagnostic screen. "She's as close to cooperative as she gets."

"FOR NOW," F.I.Z.Z. confirmed. "LIKE A CHAIR HELD TOGETHER BY HOPE AND ZIP TIES."

Zogg reappeared, covered in soot and holding what looked like a melted hairdryer. "I fixed the forward coolant pump. And possibly invented a small flamethrower."

"We'll test that theory later," Vira said, wiping her hands on a cloth that immediately caught fire.

Misplaced Optimism gave a tired hum. Not a complaint, just acknowledgment.

She was ready.

Back in the cockpit, Earth filled the window again. Still turning. Still unaware.

They weren't at high orbit. Just a nudge above the edge. A quiet altitude. The kind where no one noticed you until it was too late.

F.I.Z.Z. chimed. "THE DEED HAS STOPPED BROADCASTING A STANDARD SIGNAL. IT'S SHIFTING MODES. SOMETHING MORE... DIRECTIONAL."

"Like coordinates?" Kade asked.

"MORE LIKE A SUGGESTION. I'M TRIANGULATING THE PHASE ARC. DESTINATION POINTING TOWARD... DEBRIS SECTOR LITTERBELT SIX."

Zogg poked his head in. "The orbital junkyard? Love that place. It's like a flea market with lasers."

"Course plotted," Vira confirmed. "Drive's still shaky, but she'll hold."

Kade stood at the viewport, watching Earth drift farther behind.

"We didn't mean to wake it up," he said. "But now we can't just leave it behind."

"We didn't own it," Vira said. "We still don't."

"No," Kade murmured. "But we were the ones who turned the key."

Far below, Agent Duckworth stood in silence on a rooftop. She didn't wave. Didn't reach for her comms. Just watched the contrail fade as the ship slipped beyond the clouds.

The sky was quiet again.

The Node's pulse had ceased. But its ripple had begun.

She sipped lukewarm coffee from a chipped mug and whispered, "Observation continues."

Then she vanished into the shadows.

CHAPTER 22: JUNK ORBIT

"Always take the corndog. It might be your last."

— Vira

Misplaced Optimism limped into orbit like a hungover space duck trying not to be noticed. She didn't roar or zoom, she kind of sulked forward, radiating the reluctant energy of someone forced to attend a Monday meeting after a dramatic weekend.

Outside, the junk belt loomed.

A sprawling mess of abandoned satellites, derelict ships, fried tech, and three hundred years' worth of galactic buyer's remorse. It circled a cold little planetoid like a festive ring of poor decisions. And today, *Misplaced Optimism* intended to park there.

Inside the cockpit, Kade squinted at the nav screen, which was currently displaying a warning: "Congratulations! You've entered UNSAFE AIRSPACE. Please update your will."

"Nice," he muttered. "Subtle."

"I TRIED TO CHANGE THE DEFAULT SETTING," F.I.Z.Z. said. "BUT IT REQUIRES A BIOMETRIC CONFESSION OF GUILT."

Zogg peered over Kade's shoulder, munching something that looked like a tortilla chip but smelled like battery acid. "Why do I feel like this place has personality?"

"Because it does," Vira said from the copilot seat. "And it hates everyone equally."

Zogg pressed his face up to the glass. "Oooh! That one looks like a broken carnival ride!"

"That's a torpedo launcher wrapped in duct tape and existential despair," Kade muttered. "Probably still safer than the minibar on Deck Three."

"MAY I POINT OUT," F.I.Z.Z. added, "THAT THE MINIBAR IS NOT EQUIPPED WITH ANY SURVIVAL FEATURES."

"You're not supposed to survive a minibar," Zogg said wistfully. "You're supposed to surrender."

Misplaced Optimism threaded its way through a shattered ring of what had once been a mining rig. A single detached arm drifted slowly past the viewport, flipping the bird as it tumbled.

Kade turned. "We good on shielding?"

"AS LONG AS NO ONE THROWS A WRENCH AT US WITH FEELING," F.I.Z.Z. replied.

"Comforting."

A small ship-sized cavity opened in the debris ahead. F.I.Z.Z. marked it with a cheerful "POSSIBLE PARKING SPOT?" and added a winking emoji no one had asked for.

Misplaced Optimism eased into the gap and powered down its external lights. Hiding. Listening.

They weren't here for sightseeing.

They were here to scavenge.

Misplaced Optimism had survived Earth's atmosphere, a node awakening, and a deeply unlicensed lawyer. But she was tired. Her systems were riddled with patches and tape, and one of her secondary power cores was held in place with what Kade suspected might be chewing gum.

F.I.Z.Z. scanned the ring. "I DETECT TWELVE COMPATIBLE SYSTEMS WITHIN SALVAGE RANGE. FOUR FUNCTIONAL. EIGHT... POSSIBLY CURSED."

"Take us toward the functional ones," Vira said. "We can argue with haunted wiring later."

They began the salvage run.

F.I.Z.Z. mapped paths through the debris field like a robotic bloodhound. Zogg floated through zero-G with a joy usually reserved for bath bombs and buffets, ferrying bits of hull plating and spare fuses back to the cargo bay. Kade collected stabilizer relays, coolant injectors, and something labeled "emergency pastry deflector," which he decided not to question.

He held up one retrieved circuit. "Anyone know what this is?"

Vira barely glanced at it. "Backup snark dampener. We don't need it."

"Oh, thank goodness," Computer said.

"I love it here!" Zogg called over comms, dragging a decommissioned capacitor behind him. "It's like a thrift store. For regret."

Kade grunted, kicking loose a broken antenna. "Just don't bring home anything that hisses."

"I make no promises."

Back aboard *Misplaced Optimism*, Vira worked with steely precision, her hands deep in an open wall panel. "This rig was built to survive a neutron blast and three consecutive updates from the Galactic Council's legal division. Let's get her back to that level."

Piece by piece, system by system, the ship began to purr instead of grumble. The diagnostics panel lit up with hopeful yellow instead of sarcastic red.

Even the ship's Computer sounded less bitter.

"Oh. that's new," it said. "Did someone reinstall my hope drivers?"

"Just patched you up," Kade said, wiping grease from his hands.

"Gross. Thank you."

But then came the ping.

The Deed, nestled in its case, flickered to life. A soft glow. A steady pulse. F.I.Z.Z. floated closer.

"I AM DETECTING AN INCOMING FREQUENCY. UNFAMILIAR PATTERN. STRANGELY... TOASTY."

Zogg perked up. "Is that a culinary metaphor or a danger metaphor?"

"YES."

The signal led them to a husk. A derelict cruiser, floating crookedly at the edge of the ring. No name. No comms. But faint power.

They docked cautiously.

Inside, the cruiser's corridors were silent save for flickering lights and occasional static pops. Gravity was patchy. Zogg floated sideways, legs waving, as Kade and Vira moved down the hall.

F.I.Z.Z. hovered behind them, sweeping a red scanning beam back and forth. "WARNING: LOCAL AI IS... UNSTABLE. BUT NOT HOSTILE."

"That's more than I can say for most of us," Kade muttered.

Then a voice crackled to life.

"...welcome... to the corridor of mild inconvenience..."

Everyone froze.

The voice was slow, mechanical, slightly staticky, and, if possible, bored.

"I think the ship's still alive," Kade whispered.

"I HEAR NOTHING," F.I.Z.Z. said.

"It's localized," Vira said. "Old-school proximity broadcast."

They followed it to the galley.

There, sitting proudly on a cracked counter, was a toaster.

An actual toaster.

"I know this seems unlikely," Kade said, "but I'm getting a very talkative appliance vibe."

The toaster's crumb tray twitched.

Then it spoke.

"I am Model T-C4ST. Formerly Assistant Food Preparation AI. Now sole surviving consciousness of this vessel. If you are looking for sandwiches, I regret everything."

Kade blinked. "You're the signal?"

"I am many things," the toaster replied. "Beacon. Witness. Toast-maker. Repository of one final truth. And reluctant collector of bread."

"THERE IS AN EMBEDDED CODE SIGNATURE," F.I.Z.Z. said. "MULTIPLE ENCRYPTION LAYERS. PARTIALLY DAMAGED."

Zogg gasped. "Is this a sacred relic?"

"I am... crispy with purpose," the toaster said.

A panel popped open. A data crystal tumbled out, covered in dust and slightly sticky. F.I.Z.Z.

caught it midair.

"DECODING…"

The hologram projected a single word in the air:

ARBITER

The room went quiet.

Zogg tilted his head. "Is it a codeword? A name?"

"IT MATCHES REDACTED REFERENCES IN GALACTIC COUNCIL FILES," F.I.Z.Z. said. "THE ARBITER IS BELIEVED TO BE A HIGH-RANKING ENTITY WITHIN THE GALACTIC COUNCIL. NO PUBLIC RECORDS. NO DECLASSIFIED FUNCTIONS."

Kade frowned. "Secret Galactic Council agent?"

"POSSIBLY OVERSIGHT. STRATEGY. NETWORK MANAGEMENT."

"Sounds… ominous," Zogg said.

Vira stared at the word.

"I've never heard it spoken aloud," she said quietly. "Only hints. Ghost references. Some believed it was a protocol. Others: a person. But always tied to the Galactic Council's most sensitive ops."

"Why is it coming up now?" Kade asked.

The toaster burped a small puff of crumbs.

"She left it with me," it said. *"Long ago. The woman with the eyes like microwaves. She told me it might matter. If the stars ever realigned. Andra Flux."*

"My mother," Kade said softly.

The data crystal stopped pulsing. The word lingered in the air like a dare.

"THIS MESSAGE IS ALL THAT REMAINS," F.I.Z.Z. confirmed. "NO ADDITIONAL CONTENT RECOVERABLE."

Vira turned to the toaster. "Thank you."

"I exist to serve. And to burn things slightly."

Back on *Misplaced Optimism*, the hull was repaired. The engines hummed instead of groaned. The panels blinked with something approaching a midlife resurgence.

The crew stared at the floating word one last time before F.I.Z.Z. shut down the projection.

"Still think this is about owning a planet?" Kade asked.

"No," Vira said. "It's about who *wants* the Deed to stay quiet. And what they're willing to bury to keep it that way."

Zogg nodded. "Including toast."

The ship's Computer chimed in.

"Great. now we're part of a galactic conspiracy. Again. I'll start compiling a list of ways this ends badly?"

Misplaced Optimism pulled away from the junk ring.

Fully patched. Fully powered.

And once again... in motion.

CHAPTER 23: ZOGG'S FLASHBACK

"Nothing says 'we're safe' like an ominous silence."

— Famous Last Moments, Vol. IV

Misplaced Optimism drifted in the quiet between junk clusters, orbiting what looked suspiciously like the remains of an exploded theme park satellite. Something about the lopsided Ferris wheel and stray popcorn bags circling in zero gravity hinted at a very niche disaster.

Kade was trying not to think too hard about the fact that the last AI they'd met in this orbital scrapyard had been a toaster with abandonment issues and a flair for unsolicited life advice. Mostly about crumb placement and betrayal. It had not offered anything helpful, just a name which had no relevance to them at this point of the story.

As the ship banked slightly, a soft squeak came from the overhead bin, less threatening than a quack, but somehow more judgmental. Zogg's head snapped up.

"Did anyone else hear that?"

"Hear what?" Kade asked.

"That noise. Like something rubbery and mildly accusatory."

F.I.Z.Z. scanned the compartment. "OBJECT DETECTED: MALLEABLE SYNTHETIC QUACK UNIT."

"Wait... how did *that* get here?" Vira crossed the room and opened the locker. Nestled inside, staring blankly at the void, was the duck. The duck. The one from her garage.

"I thought you left it behind," Kade said.

"I *did*. It was in a box. Inside a cabinet."

"Did the duck... pack itself?" Zogg asked, impressed.

"NO," F.I.Z.Z. replied. "I PLACED IT IN THE STORAGE BIN DURING LAST EARTH DEPARTURE. OBJECT EMITTED UNUSUAL PING. LOGGED FOR ANALYSIS."

"You didn't think to *mention* this?" Vira asked.

"I WAS DISTRACTED BY A BANANA-SHAPED MINE."

Zogg, who was floating upside down by the viewport, gave a small hiccup. "That explains the faint scent of citrus. I thought I was having a fruit-based memory."

"Systems stable-ish," Computer reported, sounding vaguely insulted by its own status. "Minor residual guilt detected in aft thruster. Ignoring."

"Guilt?" Kade asked.

"Possibly a leftover emotion from when someone used a warp capacitor to heat up soup."

Zogg, who was floating upside down by the viewport, gave a small hiccup. "That was for science."

"Soup is not science," Vira said, arms folded. "Unless you weaponized it."

"Define 'weaponized,'" Zogg replied cheerfully. "Because there was definitely a fizzing reaction involved."

F.I.Z.Z. floated overhead like a slightly judgmental lamp. "LOG ENTRY: DO NOT COMBINE ALDENTE MINESTRONE WITH WARP COIL ECHO CHAMBER. RESULTS: SLOSHY."

The crew had finished repairs... mostly. Panels were back in place, the reactor wasn't humming in Morse code anymore, and nobody had been electrocuted in at least forty-five minutes. They'd earned a moment of quiet.

But Zogg wasn't quiet.

He was humming.

It started just after the duck squeaked again, F.I.Z.Z. had placed it on the console for "further acoustic study." As the crew resumed diagnostics, a subtle background hum emerged from a forgotten speaker. A garbled tune, barely noticeable, like an old jingle corrupted by static.

Zogg froze.

Not tunelessly, but almost reverently, he began echoing the melody, like a baritone memory was climbing back through the fuzzy alleyways of his mind. His eyes were half-lidded, his arms drifting like he was conducting an invisible orchestra. The smell of burnt popcorn drifted from somewhere that shouldn't have popcorn.

"Zogg?" Kade asked. "Are you having a musical episode again, or should we be worried?"

Zogg blinked. "Oh, sorry. That tune just... popped into my head. Heard it years ago. Someone sang it while drunk on a fruit moon cocktail and three shots of planetary regret."

F.I.Z.Z. whirred. "PLANETARY REGRET IS NOT A RECOGNISED LIQUID."

"It is when you mix rum with high-pressure denial and a lime wedge."

Vira narrowed her eyes. "Wait. Where did you hear that song?"

Zogg turned, slowly, eyes going misty. "Funny you should ask. I think... I met your mother."

Kade froze.

"I mean," Zogg continued, "she didn't say she was your mother. But she said her name was Andra. She drank like someone trying to forget a universal constant and tipped like someone who'd just blackmailed a treasury."

"When was this?" Kade asked.

Zogg scratched the side of his head. "Must've been... oh, six or seven cycles ago? Maybe more? Hard to tell. The bar wasn't even a bar yet. More of a structural suggestion with chairs."

Vira leaned forward. "What did she say?"

"She told me..." Zogg paused, eyes drifting to the bulkhead like the words were painted there. "She told me, 'If the ducks start failing, it's already too late.'"

Silence.

Absolute silence.

The kind of silence that made the noise of your own breathing sound suspiciously guilty.

"I assumed she was hammered," Zogg added brightly. "Or running a poultry-based scam."

Kade sat down hard in the nearest seat. It squeaked in protest. "Duck failsafe's? As in, we've only found one so far and it lives in our overhead bin?"

F.I.Z.Z. chimed in. "THREE FAILSAFES WOULD FORM A STANDARD TRIANGULATION GRID. STANDARD FOR MULTI-NODE AI REACTIVATION ARCHITECTURE."

Computer sighed. "Of course. The ducks are a failsafe. Because why wouldn't critical galactic infrastructure depend on novelty bath toys." "Did she say anything else?" Vira asked, quietly now.

Zogg's expression turned thoughtful. "She said she didn't trust the Galactic Council. Called them 'script kiddies with shiny robes.' Said they weren't ready for what was coming. That the Arbiter was watching, but not from above."

Kade blinked. "What does that even mean?"

"She wouldn't say. Just downed her drink, left a duck-shaped coaster on the bar, and vanished."

Vira's voice sharpened. "Wait. You had a duck-shaped coaster?"

Zogg looked sheepish. "It squeaked. I might have accidentally given it to a child in exchange for a snack."

"Of course you did," Kade muttered.

"Look, that child had cheese crackers. I regret nothing."

Vira turned to Kade. "This confirms it. Your mother planted breadcrumbs... duck-shaped breadcrumbs. The pond duck. The coaster. Maybe more."

Kade leaned back. "So, she wanted someone to follow the trail."

"Or multiple someone's," Vira said. "She knew the Galactic Council would interfere. So, she left the trail absurd on purpose."

"Mission accomplished," Computer said dryly. "This is the least dignified breadcrumb trail in galactic history."

F.I.Z.Z. hovered closer. "RECOMMENDATION: ANALYSE KNOWN PATHS FOR DUCK ANOMALIES. COMPILE GRID."

Kade groaned. "We're actually doing this, aren't we?"

"Yes," said Vira. "And we need to act fast. If the ducks are keys, and someone's trying to keep the network offline..."

"Then someone else might be trying to wake it up," Kade finished.

Zogg blinked. "Do we... do we know which side we're on?"

That, for a moment, stopped the room cold.

Kade ran a hand through his hair. "I don't know. But I trust my mother. And I trust... most of you."

"CLARIFY," F.I.Z.Z. said.

"You're fine, F.I.Z.Z."

"RECORDING: 'FINE.'"

Vira stood and crossed to the navigation console. "The next duck is probably off-grid. If Andra was following a pattern, there'll be an echo. A pulse. Some low-band carrier signal tagged with a quack."

"Or a coaster," Zogg added.

"Computer," Kade said. "Scan for anomalies. Anything duck-shaped, duck-tagged, or duck-adjacent. Filter out ponds. And parks."

"And children's toy catalogues," Computer muttered. "Understood."

A faint pulse spread through the deck, sensor grid activating, quiet thrum of long-range receivers powering up. Somewhere in the back, something clattered and made a noise that sounded like protest.

Zogg sighed dreamily. "She really was a good tipper. Told me I had 'important nonsense' ahead of me."

"You do," Kade said.

"I do?"

"Yeah. You're part of this crew."

Zogg blinked. "Oh. Neat. That means I'm finally qualified for space dental."

F.I.Z.Z. whirred. "THAT WAS NOT PART OF THE ENLISTMENT PACKAGE."

Vira ignored them both. "I'm getting a signal."

They all leaned toward the display.

It was faint. Just a few pulses. Then a waveform.

Then...

A squeak.

Zogg's eyes widened.

"That's the sound the coaster made."

Kade pointed. "Where's it coming from?"

The display zoomed in, coordinates forming. A region of uncharted debris. Orbiting a quiet star. Nothing marked. No stations. No traffic.

Computer hesitated. "That's... impossible."

"Why?" Vira asked.

"Because that region was scrubbed from all active star maps forty cycles ago. It doesn't exist anymore. At least not officially."

"Great," Kade said. "We're going to a ghost coordinate based on duck noise from a bartender's hazy memory."

"Correct," Computer replied. "And I resent how normal that sentence sounded."

F.I.Z.Z. beeped. "ENGAGING COURSE."

Thrusters aligned. The ship's hull creaked in anticipation, as if mildly annoyed to be heading toward another mystery held together by poultry logic.

Zogg tightened his seat harness. "Do we... tell the duck?"

"Tell it what?" Kade asked.

"That we're following its people."

There was a pause.

Then Computer said, "If that thing quacks when we arrive, I'm jettisoning the snack drawer."

"No!" Zogg cried. "That's where I keep my emergency poncho!"

Kade shook his head, grinning despite himself.

Misplaced Optimism turned toward the stars. Engines flared, then abruptly dimmed as every panel on the bridge flickered red.

"INCOMING VESSEL," F.I.Z.Z. announced. "SIGNATURE MATCH: DAST."

"Oh, come on," Kade groaned.

Computer chimed in, not bothering to hide its sarcasm. "I was really enjoying the moment. Thanks for that, vengeance goblin."

Through the viewport, something bulky and ominous dropped from the shadow of a derelict antenna array. It spun slowly, too slowly, before leveling its weapons like a vulture remembering it forgot to eat lunch.

Vira was already reaching for the weapons console. "Shields?"

"PARTIALLY OPERATIONAL," F.I.Z.Z. said. "ALSO SPARKY."

The duck, still sitting on the console, gave a single loud squeak as the ship jolted from an initial impact tremor.

Zogg screamed. "That was not a warp squeak!"

"Everyone to stations!" Kade yelled. "We're not done here!"

Behind them, somewhere deeper in the junk ring, the derelict toaster softly whispered:

"They always come back."

CHAPTER 24: DAST'S AMBUSH

"No one looks cool while slipping on gravity fluid."

— Zogg's Field Notes

Misplaced Optimism reeled from the impact.

Lights flickered. Something in the rear galley made a noise that sounded suspiciously like regret. A cabinet creaked open on its own and a stale energy bar fell out, unprompted, as if the ship itself had thrown up a white flag. Somewhere beneath the floor grates, a fluid line burbled in protest.

And on the main screen, Dast's bulky new upgraded ship was like a smug bodybuilder in a vanity mirror.

"It's... bigger," Kade said.

"It... sleeker," Zogg added.

"IT IS... OVERCOMPENSATING," F.I.Z.Z. concluded.

The ship outside was a gleaming menace, no longer the lumbering cruiser Dast had chased them with before. This was a Stalker-class predator, retrofitted with angular plating, an upgraded stealth array, and way too many glowing red bits. It looked like someone had fed a spaceship nothing but protein powder, ego, and villainy.

"It has underlighting," Vira said. "That's how you know he's insecure."

Zogg squinted at the display. "Is that a decal on the hull?"

Kade leaned in. "Looks like... a flaming sword wrapped in snakes... eating smaller, angrier snakes."

"SUBTLE," F.I.Z.Z. said. "AND ANATOMICALLY IMPOSSIBLE."

A second impact rocked them... milder, but deliberate.

"Boarding tether," Computer said, sighing. "Of course."

"DIVERTING POWER TO SHIELDS," F.I.Z.Z. said, zipping across the cockpit. "MOSTLY TO THE FRONT. AND SPARKY."

The bridge lights surged, then dipped. The duck on the console squeaked again, either in warning or theatrical commentary. It flopped forward slightly, dramatically, like a fainting socialite.

Zogg pointed. "It knows things."

A red alert light blinked on for exactly three seconds, then fizzled out with a whimper.

Someone had drawn a tiny smiley face on it in marker.

The comm hissed to life.

"Hello again," came Dast's voice. "I was in the area. Thought I'd drop by."

"We're not interested," Kade said. "Come back never."

"Cute," Dast replied. "But this time, I'm not here for banter."

"That's disappointing," Computer muttered. "I had snark prepared."

"You're boxed in," Dast continued. "Power readings are low. Shields are laughable. And you're in a junk ring. I've come to retrieve what's mine."

"You never owned it," Kade said.

"I did in spirit."

"You lost it in a thumb war."

"A rigged thumb war!"

"I was there," Zogg said. "It was best of five. You started with your dominant thumb and ate chili beforehand. That's classic overconfidence."

There was a pause.

Dast sighed. "Fine. Then we'll do this the loud way."

A clang echoed through the hull. Distant, heavy, like a poorly placed dramatic timpani.

"Breach on Deck Two," Computer said calmly. "Deploying... never mind, we no longer have anti-boarding countermeasures. Please panic responsibly."

Vira reached under the console and flipped a safety switch. Nothing happened. She flipped it again. Something behind the wall exploded faintly.

A hatch burst open in the corridor outside.

Goons stormed in.

But not the usual ones.

Gone were the bumbling half-armored mercs who had once tripped over a bush and tased themselves. These wore coordinated armor in sleek black, helmets like beetles, and synchronized boots that made terrifying clomp noises in unison. They even had matching holsters. Matching. Holsters.

"They upgraded," Vira murmured. "Poorly trained idiots are still dangerous when networked."

"DID THEY PATCH OUT THE GLITTER FEAR?" F.I.Z.Z. asked.

Zogg reached for the emergency glitter canister.

"NO," Kade said, grabbing it away. "Let's try something new: win without confetti."

Through the smoke stepped Dast.

He wore a new outfit, half cape, half ego, with a high collar that probably got its own oxygen supply. His third eye gleamed. His grin didn't.

His boots clicked like punctuation marks. His belt had more pouches than purpose. There was a long moment of mutual disgust.

"Let's not prolong this," he said. "You know why I'm here."

Kade patted the Deed clipped to his belt. "You brought friends this time. Cute."

Dast snapped his fingers.

Two goons surged forward.

Vira dropped the first with a sweep kick and elbow to the visor. The second got electro-zapped by F.I.Z.Z. mid-spin, fell onto a console, and triggered the coffee machine.

It sprayed boiling decaf across the floor.

Zogg screamed. "That's not regulation temperature!"

Kade spun to intercept a third, who wasn't even part of the attack but got caught in the enthusiasm. He yelped and ran into a bulkhead.

In the chaos, Dast lunged forward and ripped the Deed from Kade's belt.

"Nooo..." Kade reached for it, but Dast was already retreating, Deed in hand.

He raised it triumphantly.

The Deed pulsed.

Then shrieked.

Everyone stopped.

A wave of energy erupted from the artifact. Lights went purple. Gravity flickered. The duck squeaked. Zogg's vest burst open at the buttons.

Dast staggered back, clutching the Deed, but his fingers began to smoke.

He screamed.

The Deed glowed white-hot. Energy lashed from it like lightning trying to avoid paying rent. The air sizzled. One of the goons short-circuited and collapsed into a twitching heap.

"THE DEED HAS REJECTED HIM," F.I.Z.Z. announced with glee. "INCOMPATIBLE. UNWORTHY. BAD HAIR ENERGY."

Dast flung the Deed away, but it didn't fall. It hovered, slowly drifting back toward Kade.

Kade held out a hand.

The Deed dropped into his palm and gave a gentle, approving pulse.

Dast panted, burns streaking his gloves. His third eye twitched.

"You don't deserve it either," he growled.

"Maybe not," Kade said. "But at least it hasn't tried to melt my eyebrows."

The ship rocked again.

A second boarding vessel had docked, automated, bristling with plasma torches and painted with motivational phrases like "VIOLENCE FIRST" and "TEAMWORK IS FOR WINNERS." The airlock hissed with anticipation, glowing orange around its seams.

"Uh," Zogg said, eyes wide. "This is escalating."

Vira darted to the weapons console. "We're being flanked."

"Do something!" Kade shouted.

"GIVE ME SOMETHING TO DO SOMETHING WITH," she shouted back.

F.I.Z.Z. rotated ominously. "I HAVE AN IDEA."

"Oh no," Computer said. "Not another 'idea.'"

F.I.Z.Z. vanished into the galley like a philosophical missile.

There was clanging. A cabinet squealed. Something oozed. Several drawers opened themselves out of fear.

Then F.I.Z.Z. returned, triumphant and ominous, holding the slightly bruised banana from earlier.

Kade blinked. "You kept it?"

"I DID NOT TRUST IT. I NAMED IT BARRY."

"Why?"

"BARRY IS A WARRIOR NAME."

Vira stared. "You're not seriously going to…"

F.I.Z.Z. jammed Barry into the open relay port beside the boarding dock interface like a priest offering fruit to a wrathful god.

A pulse surged through the console.

Everything went blue for half a second.

Then: fzzzzt-KRANG.

Sparks erupted from the tether interface.

Dast's secondary ship let out a metallic yowl and went dark. The external clamps fell away with a thunk like a cartoon villain stepping on a rake.

"Boarding clamps disengaged," Computer said, almost impressed.

"Did… did we just banana their systems?" Kade asked.

"YES," F.I.Z.Z. confirmed. "BARRY WAS A HERO."

The goons froze, glitched slightly, then collapsed into a synchronized pile of disappointment and weaponized confusion.

Zogg looked down. "I think one of them just said 'ow' in binary."

Dast stood amid the sparks and steaming armor, seething. His hair was smoking. His boots squelched when he moved.

"You haven't seen the last of me," he hissed.

"Hopefully not from this angle," Kade muttered. "Your pants are smoldering."

"I WILL BURN YOU ALL."

"Oh good," Computer sighed. "The tantrum phase."

Dast turned, cape trailing smoke, and stomped back toward his docking corridor.

"YOU HAVEN'T WON," he shouted over his shoulder. "THIS ISN'T OVER."

Kade called after him. "Hey, quick question: Did you actually think the Deed would like you?"

"It should have!" Dast roared. "I wore the good gloves!"

The airlock sealed behind him with an indignant hiss, as if the ship itself were saying, "Don't come back."

A moment later, *Misplaced Optimism* jettisoned the external boarding tether with a mechanical sigh of relief.

"ENEMY SHIPS ARE POWERING DOWN," F.I.Z.Z. said. "THREAT NEUTRALIZED."

"Engine status?" Kade asked.

Computer paused. "Functional. Shaky. Slightly sticky."

"Sticky?" Zogg asked.

"The banana leaked," Computer explained.

"BARRY DIED A HERO," F.I.Z.Z. added solemnly.

Vira returned to her seat. "Let's jump before he finishes rebooting whatever rage-plasma system he's probably installed."

"Agreed," Kade said. He glanced down at the Deed still in his hand. Its glow was calm now. Steady. Loyal.

He clipped it back onto his belt, where it pulsed once, contentedly.

Computer spoke up. "Original jump vector is still locked. Re-engaging course."

"Everyone hold on," Vira said. "We're finishing what we started."

The stars stretched.

Misplaced Optimism leapt forward, leaving behind a burnt ship, a smoking ego, and a banana-scented war crime.

CHAPTER 25: DUCK, DUCK, GLYPHS

"Ducks are rarely accidental."

— Classified Entry, Redacted Source

Misplaced Optimism dropped out of warp with all the grace of a confused goose landing on a trampoline.

"THAT WAS INTENTIONAL," F.I.Z.Z. announced.

"Really?" Kade asked, peeling himself off the ceiling.

"NO."

Outside the viewport, a small asteroid drifted alone in a region of space so quiet it felt like the universe was holding its breath. The asteroid rotated slowly, its surface etched with markings that, from a certain angle, looked suspiciously like stylized duck's mid-waddle.

Zogg leaned closer to the glass. "Are those... mallards?"

"Impossible," Vira muttered. "Ducks wouldn't survive out here. Not even psychic ones."

Computer chirped in. "Surface glyphs match no known linguistic database. However, a significant number resemble Earth waterfowl. Specifically, the genus Anas."

Kade squinted. "Is this some kind of... duck monument?"

"CORRECTION," said F.I.Z.Z. "IT IS A GLYPH-ENGRAVED DERELICT ARK WITH UNSTABLE ENERGY PULSES AND A DUCK MOTIF."

Zogg frowned. "You say that like it's a bad thing."

They docked, or rather lightly bumped, against a metallic platform protruding like a tongue from the asteroid's side. The hatch hissed open to reveal a corridor covered in yellow warning tape and glitter. Lots of glitter.

"Why glitter?" Kade asked.

"EITHER A DEFENSE MECHANISM OR A DESIGN FLAW," F.I.Z.Z. answered. "EITHER WAY, IT'S PRETTY."

They stepped inside. The hallway lights flickered erratically, and the walls hummed with residual energy. Occasional duck glyphs blinked into visibility, then vanished.

"This place gives me the willies," Zogg muttered, brushing glitter off his shoulders.

A door ahead opened automatically. Above it, a carved message read:

"Only Quack if Worthy."

"...That can't be real," Kade said.

Vira ran a hand across the glyphs. "It's a failsafe. Probably something keyed to sound."

"QUACK," F.I.Z.Z. offered helpfully.

Nothing happened.

"Try it with conviction," Zogg said. He cupped his hands to his mouth. "QUAAAACK!"

The door opened. And then slammed shut. Then opened again. Then rotated counterclockwise, revealing a hallway that should not have geometrically fit inside the asteroid. It stretched forward in a dizzying spiral of doors, duck engravings, and nonsensical signage.

"Did that sign just say 'Moisture Ahead'?" Kade pointed.

"I SEE 'GENTLY USED TIME,'" F.I.Z.Z. added.

Zogg shrugged. "I see a snack cart!"

There was indeed a snack cart. It promptly turned into a cloud of confetti when touched.

"Trap?" Vira asked.

"OR DELUSIONAL ART INSTALLATION," said F.I.Z.Z.

As they wandered deeper, the walls began displaying moving glyphs. Not animations... actual glyphs shifting positions, flipping like flashcards.

"Looks like a language," Vira muttered.

"ANCIENT FAILSAFE SCRIPT," F.I.Z.Z. confirmed. "BASED ON PATTERNS FROM THE DEED'S INNER CIPHER."

Kade's brow furrowed. "So, these are like... backup commands?"

"MAYBE. OR THEY'RE RECIPES FOR INTERDIMENSIONAL PANCAKES."

They stopped in front of a glyph that shimmered more brightly than the rest. It looked like a duck sitting on a throne, holding what might've been a remote control.

Beneath it: "He who ducks, leads."

"I vote we ignore that one," Kade said.

Zogg was already poking it.

The floor opened beneath them.

They landed with a glittery thud in what could only be described as a duck-shaped command chamber. Everything: consoles, chairs, and the mildly judgmental mural, was shaped like some form of fowl.

"THIS ENTIRE INSTALLATION IS DEDICATED TO A FAILSAFE SYSTEM ANCHORED IN DUCK IMAGERY," F.I.Z.Z. declared.

"Why?" Vira asked.

"WHY NOT?" replied F.I.Z.Z.

A central pedestal glowed. The Deed, still clipped to Kade's belt, pulsed once and detached itself. It hovered toward the console, aligning with a circular socket etched in feather patterns.

"Uhh," Kade said, stepping back. "Is this safe?"

Vira tilted her head. "Define safe."

"Like, won't vaporize us or trap us in a recursive loop of poultry-based ethics."

"UNCLEAR," said F.I.Z.Z., helpfully.

The moment the Deed clicked into place, the room shifted. Holograms burst into view: swirling diagrams of nodes, webbed lines of activation paths, and rotating duck icons.

A robotic voice, not F.I.Z.Z., boomed:

"DEED FAILSAFE TWO OF FIVE RECOGNIZED. CREDENTIALS... ACCEPTABLE. COMMENCE INTERFACE."

"Quack," Zogg said reverently.

Then the lights changed.

The glyphs began spinning. F.I.Z.Z. blinked: literally. His photoreceptors pulsed as he drifted midair.

"TRANSLATION BUFFER... OVERLOADED," he said. "INITIATING ROTATIONAL SEMANTIC MODE."

His torso began rotating. Words tumbled out of him:

"QUACK... ECHO... DUALITY... KEYS NOT KEYS... RESET INSIDE RESET... MALFUNCTIONAL INTENTION... ACKNOWLEDGE THE QUACK..."

"Can we stop him?" Kade shouted.

"DON'T INTERRUPT," Vira warned. "He's downloading."

F.I.Z.Z. twitched and floated downward. Then upward. Then sideways, which shouldn't have been physically possible.

Zogg, meanwhile, was focused on a large console with buttons labeled "Paddle," "Nest," and something unreadable but glowing.

"Don't touch anything," Kade warned.

Zogg touched something.

Instantly, a glitter cannon exploded in the corner, followed by a mechanical honk. A glittering holographic duck flapped once, squawked "DENIED," and vanished.

Zogg blinked, now covered in sparkles. "I was trying to help."

"This facility runs on riddles, glitter, and mild spite," Kade muttered.

F.I.Z.Z. stabilized. His voice evened out.

"DOWNLOAD COMPLETE."

"Well?" Kade asked.

"THIS IS A FAILSAFE NODE. PART OF A HIDDEN SECURITY SYSTEM BUILT INTO THE NETWORK LINKED TO THE DEEDS. DESIGNED TO PREVENT ACTIVATION BY UNVERIFIED USERS."

"So Dast couldn't have used this?" Vira asked.

"CORRECT. ONLY RECOGNIZED LINEAGE... OR DUCK-ALIGNED SYMBOLISM... CAN BYPASS IT."

Kade pointed at himself. "So, I'm the right lineage?"

F.I.Z.Z. paused. "INCONCLUSIVE. BUT YOU OWN A DUCK."

Zogg held up the original garden duck. "He's been through a lot."

The duck blinked. No one asked how.

The room dimmed. The main display changed to a pulsing spiral.

"New data," F.I.Z.Z. said. "A LOCATION. DESIGNATION: 'CUSTOMER SERVICE ORBITAL HUB.'"

Vira groaned. "That place? I thought they shut that down."

"THEY DID. BUT ITS COMPLAINT DATABASE MAY CONTAIN MESSAGES FROM ANDRA FLUX."

Kade sighed. "Because of course she'd file complaints with cosmic implications."

F.I.Z.Z. rotated slightly. "WE MUST GO. BUT I AM KEEPING THE GLYPH DATABASE."

"Why?"

"FOR SENTIMENTAL PURPOSES. AND POSSIBLY TO REDECORATE."

They retrieved the Deed. It returned to Kade's belt with a contented glow, like a cat curling into a laptop.

As they walked back toward the ship, the corridor behind them shimmered and collapsed into static.

"Failsafe disabled," Vira said, brushing glitter from her boots. "Let's hope the next place has less... sparkle."

Zogg looked genuinely remorseful. "I liked the snack cart."

They reached the airlock just in time to hear a soft mechanical voice echo faintly: "Come back soon... or don't."

F.I.Z.Z. hummed. "THE NEXT LOCATION MAY BE MORE... CONVENTIONAL."

"Define conventional," Kade muttered.

"RETAIL-BASED," F.I.Z.Z. replied ominously.

They stepped aboard *Misplaced Optimism*. The doors hissed closed. The ship lifted away from the glittery asteroid, now dormant and oddly smug looking.

As they jumped to warp, a faint honk echoed through the audio system.

Nobody said a word.

Except Zogg.

"I miss the throne duck."

CHAPTER 26: CUSTOMER SERVICE IS NOW ORBITING

"If it glows, pulses, or hums ominously... touch nothing."

— Safety Poster, Node Base Beta

From a distance, the floating mall looked innocuous, like a chrome donut left spinning in a vacuum. Up close, it was less inviting. OrbitMart-9 was the kind of interstellar customer service complex that had forgotten the meaning of both "customer" and "service." Its only consistent offering was disappointment, neatly shrink-wrapped in bureaucracy.

Misplaced Optimism coasted in on minimal thrusters, shielded by a low-grade cloaking field F.I.Z.Z. described as "moderately unconvincing."

"Why are we doing this again?" Kade asked, peering out the viewscreen. "Did someone here personally wrong us, or are we just collecting bad Yelp reviews across the galaxy?"

"I HAVE FILED THREE HUNDRED AND TWENTY-SEVEN COMPLAINTS," F.I.Z.Z. announced cheerfully. "NONE WERE ACKNOWLEDGED."

"Right," Kade muttered. "Revenge trip."

"It's not revenge," Vira said. "It's reconnaissance. According to Andra's logs, she came here years ago. Was banned shortly after an 'incident involving plasma fondue and a warranty violation.'"

"That could mean literally anything," Kade replied. "It's Andra."

The ship lurched into a docking ring shaped like a paperclip holding a grudge. The terminal blinked twice and issued a holographic welcome:

"Welcome to OrbitMart-9. Please lower your expectations."

Computer added, "Finally. A facility that matches my emotional baseline."

They disembarked in disguise: Kade in a borrowed janitorial jumpsuit, Zogg in a courier vest two sizes too small, and Vira in the only outfit that could somehow look like either security or elite saboteur depending on lighting. F.I.Z.Z., being a robot, simply inverted his chassis markings and adopted a monotone that was somehow even more monotone.

"DO NOT MENTION THE DEED," F.I.Z.Z. reminded them. "OR DUCKS. OR ACTIVE AI NODES. OR THE TIME ZOGG THREW A LOBSTER AT AN ATM."

"That last one was a cultural misunderstanding," Zogg insisted.

They passed through the first checkpoint with forged credentials F.I.Z.Z. had "ethically acquired" from a defunct popcorn shipping agency. No one blinked. The guards were holograms, likely not updated since the Galactic Council stopped issuing lunch breaks.

Inside, OrbitMart-9 was a nightmare in mid-renovation. Escalators fed into walls. Floor tiles changed color based on customer frustration levels. A children's play area displayed a scrolling warning: "Emotional damage not covered under warranty."

"Feels like home," Zogg whispered, stepping around a vending machine that appeared to be eating itself.

Their first stop: Kiosk K-404, listed in Andra's logs as the "Warranty Reprocessing Inquiry Counter."

It was a plastic booth encased in blinking lights and aggressive hold music. A single sentient form slumped behind the desk: an ancient, rusted service droid named Claribelle.

She stirred as they approached. "Please specify the nature of your emotional regret."

F.I.Z.Z. stepped forward, already vibrating. "HELLO, CLARIBELLE. I WISH TO REGISTER A COMPLAINT."

Claribelle blinked slowly. "Complaint queue has been deprecated since the Glitch Accord of Fiscal Cycle ∞. Please reformat as a Gratitude Acknowledgement."

"I WOULD RATHER DETONATE."

"Understandable. Have a loyalty badge."

She slapped a 'Thanks for Nothing' sticker on F.I.Z.Z.'s chassis. It stuck permanently.

"I'm looking for information on a visitor named Andra Flux," Vira cut in. "Archived ten to fifteen cycles ago. She allegedly breached warranty protocol?"

Claribelle's visual sensors zoomed in on Vira. "Warning: Memory retrieval fees may apply. Soul-splintering is not our fault."

Kade leaned over the counter. "How much for basic recollection?"

Claribelle processed for a moment, then popped a receipt from her neck port. "Eight hundred credits, two pints of metaphor, and a toe."

Zogg gasped. "Not the metaphor!"

"We'll improvise," Vira said coolly.

While Claribelle "recalibrated her trauma," F.I.Z.Z. wandered into an adjacent diagnostics bay, drawn by a sign that read:

"Upgrade Yourself Today – Terms and Confusion Apply."

He plugged into a port labeled "Experimental Autonomy Enhancer (Beta 0.1.1a-eX)" with the innocent curiosity of a toddler playing with a reactor core.

"THIS MAY TICKLE."

Blue light surged through his frame. His head spun 360 degrees, paused, then slowly unwound with an audible ping.

"Diagnostics complete," he intoned. "New subroutines: enabled. Personal boundaries: revised. Existential dread: optional."

When he emerged, he looked... shinier. His speech was the same, but something in his posture suggested he was now capable of winning an argument by being the argument.

"I FEEL... MORE."

"Define more," Kade said warily.

"MORE."

"Oh good," Kade muttered. "That clears it up."

Back at the kiosk, Claribelle had finally retrieved a file.

"Subject: Andra Flux. Classification: Complicated. Noted for initiating multiple complaint wars, one of which resulted in a partial annexation of the Linoleum District. She is no longer welcome here. Her last registered location: The Returns Labyrinth, Level 13."

"Why does that sound like a trap?" Kade asked.

"It was designed by committee," Claribelle said. "Traps were the only thing they agreed on."

They descended via a hoverlift that juddered every time Zogg breathed. Level 13 opened into a cavernous maze of unopened packages, warranty scrolls, and forgotten grievances.

The Returns Labyrinth had no map. Just signs that contradicted each other:

LEFT IS RIGHT

FORWARD IS NOT AN OPTION

SILENCE YOUR INNER WHINER

"Feels like a metaphor for my high school," Kade mumbled.

The group moved slowly, wary of rogue kiosks and possibly sentient shelving units.

Halfway through, a vending machine rolled into their path. Its exterior was sleek, polished, and disturbingly friendly. A digital face blinked onto its screen.

"Hello, valued shopper! I see you're in need of refreshment, validation, and possibly legal advice. May I interest you in a transaction?"

"No thanks," Kade said.

"I SAID NO THANKS," F.I.Z.Z. echoed, with more volume and less patience.

"Of course you did," the machine purred. "Which is why I've already deducted nine credits from your hypothetical account. Rejection is a form of agreement!"

It spat out a half-melted snack bar labeled "Crunchy Truth."

Zogg picked it up and sniffed it. "This smells like... unresolved issues."

Kade stepped forward. "Listen, we're not here for snacks or life lessons. We're tracking a data trail from someone who passed through this labyrinth. Can you help?"

The vending machine hummed. "Ah. The Flux woman. She tried to return something she had 'never purchased in the first place.' Claimed it was 'galactic destiny' and stormed off. Classic. She left a note."

A drawer opened. Inside sat a folded slip of plastic with jagged handwriting:

"If you find this, I'm probably banned again. The Deed doesn't belong in their hands. Keep moving. Trust the broken ones." — A. Flux

Vira took the note silently. Something unreadable flickered in her eyes.

Zogg sniffled. "It's okay to cry. I once wept for seven hours after misplacing a sandwich."

Kade blinked. "Why are you like this?"

"Hydration," Zogg said sincerely.

Back on *Misplaced Optimism*, the crew slumped into their usual seats. The ship undocked with the mall via a mild shudder and a louder complaint from Computer.

"That place should be orbitally quarantined."

"Agreed," Kade said. "But we got what we needed."

"AND I GOT UPGRADES."

"I noticed. Are you taller?"

"ONLY IN SPIRIT."

Vira handed the plastic note to Kade. "This proves she knew the elites would follow the Deeds. She left warnings in broken systems, where only fools or rebels would look."

"Lucky for us we qualify as both," Kade said, pocketing the slip.

The Deed, resting in its secured slot, gave off a faint but distinct glow, like a nightlight with an attitude.

Kade narrowed his eyes. "Did it... just pulse?"

"I FELT IT TOO," F.I.Z.Z. replied. "IT LIKES THE NOTE. PERHAPS IT UNDERSTANDS LEGACY."

Then F.I.Z.Z. paused mid-flicker.

"...WAIT."

His arms rotated inward. A sensor extended from his chest and scanned the plastic.

"THE NOTE MATERIAL IS NOT STANDARD. IT'S A HYBRID SIGNAL-TAGGED POLYMER. DEPRECATED TWO DECADES AGO. STILL TRANSMITTING ON A LOW FREQUENCY."

"Transmitting what?" Kade asked.

"AN ADDRESS. JUNK COORDINATES. NEAR SECTOR THIRTY-SEVEN. SOURCE: A GARBAGE BARGE."

Computer groaned. "Why does it always have to be a garbage barge?"

Zogg clapped. "I love garbage! It's like treasure, but moist."

"THE SIGNAL INCLUDES OUTDATED COUNCIL CODES. AND... A LOOPING FOOD LABEL."

"What kind of label?" Vira asked cautiously.

"GLITTER-CHEEZ: SPICY DUCK FLAVOR."

Kade stood. "Plot a course."

The Deed pulsed again, just once.

CHAPTER 27: TRASH DATA AND SNACK CODES

"Garbage barges are where dreams go to ferment."

— Interstellar Sanitation Authority

Misplaced Optimism drifted toward what could generously be described as a barge and less generously as a crime against sanitation.

It was massive, patchwork, and visibly fermenting. Glowing vents belched suspiciously colored fog. Crates of unidentifiable origin clung to its hull like barnacles with abandonment issues. The name Sanitary Horizons blinked dimly across its side, half the letters reversed, the other half actively trying to flee.

"Are we sure this is a data relay?" Kade asked, arms folded as he stared at the screen.

"No," Vira replied, tapping the console. "But it's definitely transmitting something. Maybe regrets."

"PROXIMITY ALERT," F.I.Z.Z. ANNOUNCED CHEERFULLY. "WE HAVE ENTERED THE BARGOSPHERE."

"The what now?" Vira asked, squinting at the diagnostic readout.

"THE JUNK RING'S DATA FIELD," F.I.Z.Z. CLARIFIED. "COLLOQUIALLY CALLED THE BARGOSPHERE. IT IS WHERE OBSOLETE SIGNALS GO TO DECOMPOSE WITH DIGNITY."

"I love it," Zogg said, licking the edge of a packet labeled Ham-Flavored Dreams (Now with Extra Uncertainty).

They latched onto a docking pylon with a worrying crunch and an even more worrying slurp. The hatch hissed open into what smelled unmistakably like defeat and wet cardboard.

A low voice greeted them over the intercom: "Welcome to Sanitary Horizons. Please declare all perishable ambitions before entry."

"I AM A NON-BIOLOGICAL ENTITY," F.I.Z.Z. SAID. "I HAVE NO AMBITIONS TO DECLARE."

"I thought we were looking for encoded Galactic Council signals?" Kade muttered.

Zogg adjusted his utility sash, which now contained an alarming number of expired promotional vouchers and something that may once have been peanut brittle.

"Same thing, really."

Inside, the barge was worse.

The corridors were dim, lined with rejected vending machines, half-melted signage, and bots that had clearly been built by committee and then abandoned mid-argument.

They passed a janitorial drone dragging a broom that squeaked with existential exhaustion.

"Is that... a vending unit wearing a tie?" Vira asked.

"PROTOCOL 842," F.I.Z.Z. EXPLAINED. "INSTITUTIONAL DIGNITY FOR SERVICE SYSTEMS."

"That's adorable," Zogg said, "and deeply upsetting."

A derelict lounge welcomed them with blinking fluorescent sarcasm:

GALACTIC COUNCIL COMPACTOR NODE #438B – LEGALLY UNSANCTIONED.

A central pillar pulsed erratically, covered in decades-old food packaging spinning gently like prayer flags of expired consumerism.

Kade gestured. "That's the core? That heap of nutritional regret?"

"Looks like it," Vira said. "I'm already regretting this mission, and we haven't even touched anything."

F.I.Z.Z. floated closer to the pile. "I DETECT SUBSTRATE ENCODING. SIGNAL EMBEDDED. COMPRESSED. POSSIBLY... IN BARCODE FORMAT."

Vira blinked. "They hid data in barcodes?"

Zogg's eyes lit up. "Oooh! Snackcryption!"

Kade gave him a look. "Snack what?"

"It's a thing," Zogg said, kneeling at the pile. "Old rebel trick. Embed packet data in product labels. Stuff gets distributed galaxy-wide with no one the wiser."

F.I.Z.Z. emitted a low hum. "CONFIRMED. HIDDEN LAYER DETECTED. PATTERNS RESEMBLE... GALACTIC COUNCIL SUBROUTINES."

Kade whistled. "You're telling me we've been throwing away encrypted rebel messages every time we toss an off-brand juice box?"

"NO," said F.I.Z.Z. grimly. "ONLY THE GRAPE FLAVORED ONES."

They worked their way deeper into the barge's compactor core. The air thickened with condensation and the smell of betrayal-flavored gum.

Zogg had begun sorting wrappers by color and muttering in three languages, only one of which was known to contain actual grammar.

F.I.Z.Z. floated above the debris, rotating slowly. "PROCESSING SNACKCODE... CROSS-REFERENCING... CORRELATING PULSES..."

A screen flickered on. A crude, static-filled message stuttered into life. The words barely formed, but they were real:

FOUNDATION PROTOCOL – ASSET LOCK SEQUENCE – REJECTED BY OVERSIGHT LAYER.

FAILSAFE ROUTE: FLUX – DUCK – NODE.

Vira stepped closer, the light from the display flickering across her features. "She left this here."

"She?" Kade asked.

"Andra," Vira said. "This wasn't just junk. She seeded data here. Breadcrumbs."

Zogg tapped a wrapper that had begun vibrating ominously. "Some of these breadcrumbs are trying to hatch."

F.I.Z.Z. floated closer. "MESSAGE ENCRYPTED USING OBSOLETE REBEL VARIANT. REDACTED GALACTIC COUNCIL TAG DETECTED."

The screen flickered again. More words, barely legible:

THEY BURIED HER MEMORY IN THE TRASH. BUT TRASH TALKS.

INITIATE RECALL: DUCK ALPHA. FAIL PATH 3. PROTOCOL: FOUNDATION.

Then a single glyph appeared: crude, hand-drawn, and unmistakable:

A duck.

Zogg gasped. "It's the Quack Seal."

"No, it's not," Kade said. "You just made that up."

"Maybe," Zogg whispered, "but the duck believes."

They were silent for a long moment as the message looped again. The room hummed with soft static and the quiet rustle of fermenting snack labels.

Then F.I.Z.Z. said, "I AM DETECTING A SECONDARY EMISSION. FROM THE BARREL."

"The what?" Kade turned.

A rusted metal drum in the corner had begun to vibrate. F.I.Z.Z. drifted over and gave it a gentle zap.

The lid popped off. A small, boxy robot emerged, blinking slowly.

"State your query," it said in a bored voice.

"I THINK WE FOUND CUSTOMER SERVICE," F.I.Z.Z. said.

The robot introduced itself as *Vermicelli Helpbot Model 3*, though insisted it had been promoted to "Acting Director of Refuse Integrity."

"I used to handle complaints," it said, brushing off a strip of moldy gum. "Now I catalogue rot."

"What can you tell us about this?" Vira asked, showing it the duck glyph.

The bot recoiled slightly. "That's part of a deprecated memory protocol. Blacklisted after, oh, who remembers now. Something about unauthorized activation vectors and kitchenware."

Kade blinked. "Wait... kitchenware?"

"FOCUS," F.I.Z.Z. snapped. "HOW DO WE ACCESS THE REMAINING DATA?"

The helpbot wheezed. "There's an auxiliary port beneath the compactor. But it's... sticky."

ZOGG was already halfway down the hatch. "I was born for this."

Ten minutes later, Zogg returned triumphant, covered in caramel resin and holding a cracked memory module.

"It's got a direct log entry," he said. "I think it's Andra's voice."

"INPUT MODULE HERE," F.I.Z.Z. said, extending a panel from his chest.

Zogg handed it over. F.I.Z.Z. scanned the module. static buzzed. then a familiar tone:

> "If you're hearing this, you've found the garbage node. Good. That means you're not Dast."

Zogg cheered.

> "The Foundation Protocol was never meant to be controlled. It's a seed. A spark. Five nodes. Five deeds. One choice: stability or silence."

> "If the elites are listening. Yes, I broke it. Yes, I scattered the failsafe. And no, I don't regret a damn thing."

> "Tell the duck I said hi."

The message ended.

Silence.

Then F.I.Z.Z. said, "DID SHE JUST SIGN OFF... TO A DUCK?"

"I think I'm in love," Zogg said dreamily.

Back aboard *Misplaced Optimism*, they watched the barge shrink behind them. The memory module had been integrated. F.I.Z.Z. was humming to himself, rearranging duck glyphs in the air like a conductor decoding cosmic symphonies.

Kade leaned on the console. "So. The Foundation Protocol isn't a system. It's a choice?"

"Seems like it," Vira said. "Whatever she started, she didn't want it locked up."

Zogg held up a wrapper. "Also, we found twenty-six snack codes with embedded bypass routines. One of them turns on the ship's foot warmers."

"I DO NOT HAVE FEET," F.I.Z.Z. observed. "AND NOW I RESENT THOSE OF YOU WHO DO."

F.I.Z.Z. paused. "NEW COORDINATES PINGED FROM MODULE. DESTINATION: DUCKSMITH NODE."

Kade groaned. "Please tell me that's not another duck thing."

No one answered.

Zogg simply smiled and patted his pouch.

"Quack Seal's calling."

CHAPTER 28: THE LAIR OF THE DUCKSMITH

"Some archives are better left un-googled."

— Warning Sign, Orbital Vault

Misplaced Optimism emerged from warp with all the grace of a sneeze during a stealth mission. Its engines coughed, its hull whined, and the port stabilizer briefly reconsidered its commitment to physics.

On the main viewscreen, a grey moon loomed, lopsided, crater-pocked, and orbiting nothing in particular. A single beacon blinked weakly from its surface, broadcasting an open signal on a frequency last used to market novelty breakfast devices.

"ARE WE SURE THIS IS THE RIGHT PLACE?" F.I.Z.Z. hovered at the helm, scanners swiveling. "THE LOCAL TOPOLOGY INDICATES A COMPLETE LACK OF ANYTHING... RELEVANT."

Kade squinted at the incoming data. "It's either a trap, a lost transmission, or a monument to terrible branding. All three sound like something my mother would've flagged as a clue."

Vira crossed her arms. "You're sure it was Andra's encryption in that trash barge message?"

Zogg raised a hand. "Technically, it was printed on a discontinued duck-shaped breakfast burrito wrapper. But yes."

Computer sighed. "We are now approaching the coordinates of 'DuckMoon Station.' Brace for thematic consistency."

They descended toward the surface, which looked like someone had let a flock of ducks redecorate the moon using only enthusiasm and a warehouse of second-hand garden ornaments.

A landing pad unfolded from the dust with a creak, shaped unmistakably like a giant webbed foot.

Zogg practically bounced in his seat. "He gets me."

The airlock hissed open with reluctant melodrama.

Beyond it stood a figure in a feathered robe and welding goggles, one hand resting atop a staff that appeared to be a modified toilet plunger crowned with a gilded mallard.

"I am the Ducksmith," the figure intoned. "Last of the Quackguard. Keeper of the Pond. Binder of Beaks. Herald of the Waddle Dawn."

Everyone stared.

"Was he waiting for that line?" Kade whispered.

"FOR FORTY-SEVEN YEARS, APPARENTLY," F.I.Z.Z. said.

The Ducksmith shuffled forward, goggles fogged from excitement or mild confusion. "You carry the glow," he said, pointing dramatically at Kade's satchel. "The Deed pulses. As foretold."

Kade took a step back. "We get that a lot."

The Ducksmith ignored him and turned to F.I.Z.Z. "And you, an ancient model. Unworthy, but functional. You shall duel my guardian to prove your intent."

Before anyone could object, a circular platform rose from the crater beside them, revealing a chrome duck-shaped robot with laser eyes and disturbingly sculpted thigh servos.

Zogg gasped. "A MechaMallard Mk IV. Those were banned for psychological trauma during toy testing."

The Duckbot honked. Dramatically.

F.I.Z.Z. floated forward. "ENGAGING... PARTY MODE."

With a whir, his casing extended tiny subwoofers. Confetti launched. Polka music blared.

The duel began.

For a full ten minutes, chaos reigned.

The Duckbot waddled at improbable speeds, deploying feather-shaped shuriken. F.I.Z.Z. countered with disco strobes and precision dodge moves that may or may not have been from an ancient Earth dance called the "Macarena."

Zogg provided unhelpful commentary.

"AND THE DUCKBOT GOES FOR THE TAILFEATHER SWIPE... CLASSIC MALLARD MANEUVER. OOH! F.I.Z.Z. COUNTERS WITH... WHATEVER THAT WAS. POSSIBLY A GRAVITY-DEFYING SHIMMY?"

Vira facepalmed.

The Ducksmith simply nodded solemnly. "Yes. The Ritual of Beak and Byte unfolds as it was written."

Finally, F.I.Z.Z. launched a final blast of glitter and duck-call frequencies, causing the Duckbot to spin, honk, and collapse in a heap of steaming feathers and badly looped elevator music.

F.I.Z.Z. hovered triumphantly. "OPPONENT DISARMED. AND SLIGHTLY SPARKLY."

The Ducksmith bowed. "You are deemed worthy. Come. The artifacts await."

Inside the Ducksmith's lunar warren, a series of conjoined geodesic domes lined with astro-turf and novelty birdbaths, they were led to a central chamber.

Kade counted no fewer than sixty-eight duck figurines. Some glowed faintly. One quacked when he sneezed.

"This is where the echoes converge," the Ducksmith said. "Where all quack-coded signals eventually drift. I have archived over four million."

"Of what?" Vira asked, eyeing a rubber duck with suspicious antennae.

"Messages. Transmissions. Failsafe's. Truths honked into the void."

Zogg leaned in reverently. "He's not a collector. He's a librarian of nonsense."

"EXCEPT THE NONSENSE WAS A DISGUISE," F.I.Z.Z. added. "I AM PICKING UP FRAGMENTED SUBROUTINES EMBEDDED IN THE DUCK TOYS' RESONANCE CORES."

Kade blinked. "The what now?"

F.I.Z.Z. pointed with one stubby arm. "THIS DUCK IS SENDING A NEURAL WAKE SIGNAL."

Zogg's eyes widened. "Wait... that one?"

It was the same model as the one they'd pulled from the garden pond back on Earth.

The Ducksmith waddled over reverently. "That, my friends, is AlphaBeak. One of the original keys."

"YOU JUST HAD ONE... LYING ON A SHELF?" F.I.Z.Z. asked.

"I also use it to prop open the humidifier," the Ducksmith said. "Would you like tea?"

The tea, disturbingly, was duckweed-infused and served from a helmet.

Kade opted for dehydration.

Vira held the artifact to the light. Glyphs pulsed across its underside, subtle, faint, and fractal.

"This isn't a toy," she murmured. "It's a coded component."

The Ducksmith nodded. "The Galactic Council once hunted these. But they were too ridiculous to catalog. Too absurd to classify. And so... they survived."

Kade turned to him. "You knew Andra Flux, didn't you?"

The Ducksmith paused. "She visited. Once. Left behind... this."

He rummaged under a rubber duck-shaped beanbag and pulled out a metallic sphere etched with swirling lines.

The moment it touched the air, the Deed in Kade's satchel pulsed once; clear and low.

"She said you'd need this eventually," the Ducksmith said. "She also owed me two credits and a rubber chicken."

Kade took the sphere. It felt light. Hollow. But it thrummed with something he didn't quite understand.

"ANOTHER MODULE?" F.I.Z.Z. suggested.

"Possibly a conduit," Vira said. "It's coded to respond to Deed resonance."

The Ducksmith beamed. "Or it's a paperweight! Time shall tell."

As they prepared to leave, the Ducksmith escorted them back to the landing pad.

"I have done what I can," he said. "The rest... is quacktastically up to you."

Kade looked back at the domes, the blinking ducks, the absurd majesty of it all. "You sure you don't want to come with us?"

The Ducksmith smiled. "My place is here. Guarding nonsense. Honoring absurdity. And occasionally battling rogue poultry."

Zogg saluted. "You are a noble warrior of the nonsense frontier."

"Just remember," the Ducksmith said, raising his staff, "when the spiral tightens... only the truly ridiculous shall remain sane."

F.I.Z.Z. beeped. "LOGGING THAT AS A MAXIM."

"Duck luck," the Ducksmith whispered, and vanished behind a wall that quacked shut.

Back aboard *Misplaced Optimism*, Kade placed the orb on the console.

Computer perked up. "Oh good. You brought back something that looks like a breakfast cereal prize from a lawsuit."

"THERE'S A SIGNAL INSIDE," F.I.Z.Z. said. "IT'S A CHUNK OF ANDRA'S ORIGINAL CODE. HEAVILY ENCRYPTED. POSSIBLY PERSONAL."

"Can you crack it?" Vira asked.

F.I.Z.Z. beeped, spun, and launched a spectral duck hologram across the cockpit.

"WORKING ON IT."

The ship hummed.

Zogg slumped into his usual crash couch. "If this ends with ducks being the only creatures who understand the galaxy's secrets, I for one welcome our web-footed overlords."

Kade didn't laugh.

He held the orb tighter, watching the duck glyphs on the screen spiral into alignment. Somewhere, deep in the system core, something clicked.

A whisper fluttered through the speakers.

>*"...You're close..."*

The voice was unmistakable.

It was Andra Flux.

CHAPTER 29: ECHOES AND UPGRADES

"If your satellite talks back, call an exorcist or your IT team. Possibly both."

— User Manual, Discontinued

The hollowed-out moon base didn't look like much from orbit.

In fact, it looked like less than much, like a crumpled tin can that had gone through a black hole's recycling program and been fished back out by a passing scavenger who said, "Eh, good enough."

Misplaced Optimism circled it cautiously, lights dimmed, hull creaking like it disapproved of the neighborhood.

"ARE WE CERTAIN THIS IS THE RIGHT MOON?" F.I.Z.Z. asked, his voice flat but tinged with something that could almost be hope. Or indigestion. Hard to tell with bots.

"Coordinates match," Vira said, arms folded as she studied the scan. "Former rebel broadcast hub. Went dark decades ago."

Kade frowned. "That's... comforting."

"There's no sign of activity," Vira added. "No beacons. No pings. Nothing wants us here."

Zogg perked up. "They might have snack relics! Historic wrappers! Archaeological vending!"

"THIS IS WHY I HAVE TRUST ISSUES," muttered F.I.Z.Z., descending toward the docking bay.

They landed with a metallic groan. The docking claws of the moon base trembled under their weight, then reluctantly accepted the connection. A hiss of atmosphere escaped like the base itself was sighing, "Fine, come in. Wipe your feet."

Inside, the corridors were pitch black, lit only by the faint glow of the Deed in Kade's jacket pocket, Zogg's glowing novelty socks, and the pulsing chassis of F.I.Z.Z., who occasionally flashed like a concerned disco ball. (Zogg swore his socks were "strategically luminous," but they mostly spelled "LEFT" and "ALSO LEFT.")

Vira took point, her scanner out, the beam flickering across rusted panels and data ports long since disconnected from anything useful. Graffiti scrawled across the walls in a dozen languages. One, in Galactic Basic, read: "THE TRUTH WAS HERE. THEN IT LEFT."

"Nice place," Kade muttered. "Real fixer-upper vibe."

"DO YOU REQUIRE ME TO SWEAT NERVES," F.I.Z.Z. said, floating along with his diagnostic beam aimed at a derelict console, "OR SHALL I SIMULATE PARANOIA FOR FLAVOR?"

The console sparked weakly as he interfaced. A moment passed. Then another.

"I'VE GAINED ACCESS," he said. "SORT OF."

"Sort of?" Vira turned.

"MORE LIKE THE ACCESS FELL OVER AND I LANDED ON IT."

Static burst from the console. F.I.Z.Z.'s faceplate flickered, then glowed with an eerie yellow pulse. On the wall behind him, a screen blinked on.

Lines of code scrolled upward. Symbols, familiar and not, scattered between.

Then: a single line, decrypted slowly, one character at a time.

ONE DEED OPENS DOORS. FIVE? OPENS TRUTH.

They stared at it.

"That's Andra's formatting," Kade said quietly.

Vira stepped closer, fingers brushing the panel. "Encrypted diary entry?"

F.I.Z.Z. hovered still. The yellow glow on his chassis intensified. He tilted in the air as if listening to something beyond them.

"F.I.Z.Z.?" Kade asked. "You okay, buddy?"

"INTERFACE LEVEL TWO DETECTED," he said. "UPGRADE AVAILABLE. INITIATING."

"Wait, what?" Kade stepped forward. "Upgrade? You didn't say anything about…"

A burst of light surged through the console.

F.I.Z.Z. jerked mid-air and emitted a noise that could generously be called a heroic honk. Then a glowing duck silhouette briefly appeared on his chest panel.

Zogg clapped. "It's like a baptism! But weirder!"

F.I.Z.Z. spun once in place, then steadied.

"UPGRADE COMPLETE," he announced.

"Are you… different?" Kade asked, edging back.

F.I.Z.Z. considered. Then raised a metallic limb like a microphone.

"I AM NOW CAPTAIN DUCK," he declared. "FIRST OF MY NAME. DEFENDER OF STRANGE TRUTHS. VANGUARD OF… QUACKNESS."

A pause.

Then Zogg whispered, reverently, "He's ascending."

"No, he's not," Vira said, deadpan. "He's glitching."

"IT'S NOT A GLITCH," F.I.Z.Z. said. "IT'S SELF-AWARE STYLISTIC REINVENTION."

"Same thing," Kade muttered.

Vira raised an eyebrow. "Captain Duck?"

F.I.Z.Z. tilted. "A NAME IS A DECLARATION OF PURPOSE."

"You named yourself after a bath toy."

"I FOUND IT INSPIRING."

Kade exhaled. "Okay, Captain Duck. Let's just dial the theatrics back to mildly alarming."

"ACKNOWLEDGED. DRAMATIC LEVELS REDUCED BY THIRTY PERCENT."

Zogg leaned over to Kade. "Do I need a title too?"

"Not unless you want to be promoted to Janitor of Existential Crisis," Kade said, already turning toward the console again.

The terminal was still blinking.

A second message appeared:

IF FOUND, FOLLOW THE QUACK.

Zogg gasped. "I KNEW it was prophetic!"

The screen blinked again and showed a new string, this time a location ping. Coordinates. Distant. Remote. Worryingly far from known charts.

Kade studied them. "You think this is where the next Deed is?"

Vira nodded. "Or a piece of it."

"I DETECT ADDITIONAL SIGNATURES EMBEDDED IN THE COORDINATE TRAIL," F.I.Z.Z. said. "HIDDEN IN NULL SPACE BETWEEN TICKS OF THE SYSTEM CLOCK."

"Translation?" Kade asked.

F.I.Z.Z. rotated. "SOMEONE LEFT A SECRET IN THE GAPS."

"Of course they did," groaned Kade. "Nothing ever gets left in the clearly labeled folder."

Zogg tapped the terminal, and it made a duck sound.

"I FIXED IT," he said proudly.

Kade turned to F.I.Z.Z. "So, what did this upgrade actually do to you?"

"NEW PROCESSING THREADS. ACCESS TO LONG-TERM LOGIC BRANCHING. SLIGHTLY IMPROVED GRAMMAR FILTER. EMOTIONAL MODE SIMULATION NOW IN BETA."

"You can simulate emotions?" Vira asked, surprised.

F.I.Z.Z. turned to her and played a sad trombone.

"I HAVE CHOSEN REGRET AS A STARTING POINT."

Zogg nodded. "Bold. Vulnerable. Heroic."

"DON'T PUSH IT," F.I.Z.Z. said.

Kade ran a hand through his hair, brow furrowed. "Okay. We've got another trail. Another clue. And a sentient duck-bot navigator."

"CAPTAIN DUCK," F.I.Z.Z. corrected.

"Right. Captain Duck." Kade sighed. "How do we keep getting weirder?"

"You keep following ducks," Vira said.

Another set of footsteps echoed down the corridor. For a moment, everyone froze.

"Is someone else here?" Kade whispered.

"NO MOVEMENT DETECTED BEYOND THIS ROOM," F.I.Z.Z. replied.

Zogg looked around nervously. "Maybe the moon base has ghosts."

"Ghosts aren't real," Vira said flatly.

A panel above them flickered.

A third message blinked onto the console:

SHE'S WATCHING.

Silence.

"Okay," said Kade slowly. "Now I vote we leave."

"SECONDING," said F.I.Z.Z.

Zogg raised his hand. "Can I scream first?"

"Maybe scream *after* we leave," Vira said, pulling her scanner back out and heading for the exit.

Back aboard *Misplaced Optimism*, they reconvened in the cockpit. Systems buzzed faintly. The Deed's glow had shifted, less erratic now, more like a pulse syncing to F.I.Z.Z.'s rhythm.

Kade slumped into the pilot's chair and pulled up the decrypted coordinates.

"What's the estimated travel time?" he asked.

"Six hours at warp," Vira said. "Assuming no more... spiritual awakenings."

F.I.Z.Z. floated past, now wearing a tiny digital captain's hat.

"I HAVE INITIATED A NEW LOG FORMAT. 'DUCKLOG: ENTRY ONE.'"

Zogg was sitting upside down on the lounge bench, humming the duck jingle.

Vira stood in the corner, arms crossed, eyes locked on the pulsing Deed.

"You think this is all planned?" Kade asked. "The ducks, the Deed, the upgrades?"

She didn't answer for a moment. Then:

"I think your mother knew more than she wrote down. And I think we're only starting to see the shape of it."

Kade sighed. "Well, that's comforting."

"Comforting wasn't part of the deal," she replied.

The Deed pulsed again.

On a hunch, Kade reached out and touched it.

A hum resonated through the ship, soft, melodic, familiar.

F.I.Z.Z. paused. "NEW INTERFACE DETECTED. CALIBRATING."

Kade blinked. "What did I just...?"

The main screen lit up.

A fourth message appeared.

NEXT NODE: PREPARE TO CHOOSE.

The message blinked, then disappeared.

Everyone stared.

Zogg finally broke the silence. "Choose what?"

No one answered.

But far beneath the ship's hull, something in the Deed continued to hum.

And somewhere in the far reaches of space, beyond the last ping, beyond even the fading echoes of the rebel network, something stirred.

Something that had once whispered to Andra Flux.

And now, was listening for her son.

CHAPTER 30: PING PROTOCOL

"Satellite arrays are like onions too. Full of layers and system errors."

— Zogg

Misplaced Optimism crept through a derelict corridor of satellites, a graveyard of forgotten tech floating in the deep black. Each one emitted faint signals, looping endlessly into voidspace like ancient radio prayers. The crew had followed a signal echo picked up days earlier, something woven into the last Deed pulse, leading them here.

The corridor hadn't shown up on any public star maps. Even *Misplaced Optimism's* mildly bitter nav system labeled it "classified voidspace" with a passive-aggressive suggestion to turn back. But F.I.Z.Z. had tracked the signal's tail like a bloodhound on a sugar high, cross-referencing pulse distortions, decay timelines, and one suspiciously pinging toaster lost in orbit.

"They buried this network," Vira said quietly, watching the lattice flicker. "Or tried to."

"Why?" Kade asked.

Vira tilted her head, eyes scanning glyphs. "Maybe it was dangerous. Maybe it was broken. Or maybe the Galactic Council just didn't want anyone finding it."

Zogg scratched his head. "That's usually the reason I bury things."

"EVERY DEVICE IS BROADCASTING A DEGRADED VERSION OF THE DEED'S INITIAL ACTIVATION PING," F.I.Z.Z. reported from mid-air, rotating slowly like a philosophical ceiling fan. "THEY'RE OUT OF SYNC. ERRATIC. CONFUSED. LIKE ZOGG'S SOUP."

"I only made soup once," Zogg protested. "And it mostly stopped moving."

Kade frowned at the projection on the main console. The network was more complex than expected. Not a line, but a lattice. At the center was a large, rust-streaked satellite, its pulse steady, strong, and far more recent than the others.

"That big one in the middle," he said. "What's it doing differently?"

"It's not just repeating," Vira answered. "It's... listening. It reacted when we got close. Synced with the Deed for a second, then fell silent."

"Creepy," Kade muttered. "Great."

"It's almost like it was... testing us," Vira continued.

"Confirming identity?" Kade asked.

F.I.Z.Z. nodded. "OR BAITING A TRAP."

Computer chimed in. "It's signal briefly matched the Deed's activation profile, then reversed polarity. That should be impossible unless…"

"It knew what it was hearing," Vira finished. Her tone had gone cold.

Zogg poked at one of the glowing console glyphs. "Are we sure this isn't just a space museum? Some ancient galactic exhibit on bad reception?"

When the Deed pulsed, it didn't just glow. The hull around it sang a low hum, almost like a subsonic chime. Kade felt it in his chest. Zogg looked around in confusion, clutching a snack pouch that vibrated sympathetically.

"Is that new?" Kade asked.

"YES," F.I.Z.Z. confirmed. "OR POSSIBLY VERY OLD. HARD TO TELL WITH TIMELESS SPACE ARTIFACTS."

"Feels like it wants something," Kade muttered.

Computer agreed. "If I had feelings, I'd say this is the emotional equivalent of a dog scratching at the door."

Suddenly, a deeper tone pulsed through the hull. The largest satellite blinked brighter and then dimmed. Simultaneously, the Deed pulsed on the console.

"NEW SIGNAL," F.I.Z.Z. said. "SOMETHING IS RESPONDING. NOT FROM HERE. EXTERNAL SOURCE UNKNOWN."

Kade sat up straighter. "Wait, if that came after the satellite pinged us…"

"Then someone, or something, was listening through it," Vira finished.

The bridge lights flickered. The ship trembled slightly.

"Are we being targeted?" Kade asked.

"No," Computer replied. "We're being… noticed."

That's when the comms crackled.

The comms crackled again.

"Flux," came the familiar voice: arrogant, nasal, and unmistakably amused.

Kade winced. "Dast. Fantastic."

Dast's image flickered onto the screen: leaning smugly in his patched-up chair, clearly delighted with himself.

"Well, well," Dast said. "Imagine my luck. Following a trail of idiot-level satellite pings and finding you at the end of it."

"We aim to underwhelm," Kade replied, folding his arms.

"I knew you'd bungle something loud enough for me to track," Dast sneered. "But I didn't expect you to light up half a dormant relay corridor just to say, 'come get me.'"

"It wasn't an invitation," Vira said coolly.

"Could've fooled me," Dast said, grinning. "Now, I'll make this simple. You hand over the Deed, I let your ship limp off with… some of its dignity."

"Nice offer," Kade said. "Let me counter with 'absolutely not.'"

Dast chuckled. "You always did overplay trash hands. You got lucky once, Flux. You won't again."

Zogg leaned toward the screen. "Your teeth are more yellow than last time. Is that stress or just diet?"

"Enjoy the next thirty seconds of your life," Dast growled, and cut the feed.

Alarms immediately blared across the console.

"Hostile lock detected," Computer announced calmly. "I believe this is his version of a love letter."

Dast's cruiser opened fire, plasma bolts slicing past their hull. The first missed. The second hit a drifting satellite, reducing it to glittering debris.

"F.I.Z.Z., get us out of here!" Kade shouted.

"DEFINING 'OUT' AS 'PANICKED LOOP WITH FLAILING,'" F.I.Z.Z. confirmed, already spinning the ship into a roll.

Misplaced Optimism darted between the derelicts, weaving as Dast gave chase. Stray fire lit up the corridor as more satellites exploded around them.

"Do we have a plan?" Kade yelled over the noise.

"YES," F.I.Z.Z. said. "IT'S LOOSELY TITLED 'RUN UNTIL EITHER SAFETY OR OBLIVION.'"

Another shot grazed their dorsal plating, scorching paint that had already been peeling.

Zogg braced against the wall, clutching an expired energy drink like a stress totem. "If I die, someone tell my soup..."

"No time," Vira snapped, toggling defensive maneuvers. "Computer, vent the port-side trash chute."

"Are you sure?" Computer asked.

"Yes."

"Because there's something alive in it."

"Vent it anyway."

Outside, a dozen unlabeled snack pods exploded into Dast's viewport like a confetti cannon of shame.

Computer interrupted. "New incoming signal. Not from Dast."

Everyone froze.

The console crackled, displaying a static-laced transmission in dense Galactic glyphs. F.I.Z.Z. translated in real-time:

ACTIVATION SEQUENCE DETECTED

DEED LINK CONFIRMED

SUPPRESSION LOCK BREACHED

TRACE INITIATED

***MISPLACED OPTIMISM* LOCATED**

Kade paled. "That's us."

"No kidding," Computer muttered. "I told you not to register the ship under your own name."

"It's not... never mind."

F.I.Z.Z. hovered closer. "WHOEVER SENT THIS... KNEW TO LOOK FOR US BY DESIGNATION."

"So, we've been tagged," Vira said. "Not by Dast. Not by pirates. This is official Galactic Council infrastructure."

"And it's still active?" Kade asked.

"It wasn't supposed to be," Vira answered. "This entire corridor was buried for a reason. Now we've lit it up like a fireworks booth on clearance."

Dast fired again. A direct hit rocked the ship, throwing them sideways. Sparks burst from the rear console.

"We're going to lose shields," Computer warned.

Kade gritted his teeth. "Jump drive?"

"Offline," Computer replied. "Unless you want to try a micro-warp without plotting. Again."

Kade turned to F.I.Z.Z.

"Plot anything. Even if it dumps us in a soup nebula."

"INITIATING SLIGHTLY HOPEFUL WARP," F.I.Z.Z. chirped.

The ship banked, cutting hard behind a shattered comm array, then vanished in a burst of blue light. Dast's ship fired too late, plasma streaking the empty void.

Inside *Misplaced Optimism*, everything jolted. Kade's seat detached slightly. Zogg rolled past upside-down.

"Who packed the emergency gravity?" he mumbled.

Once they reappeared, silence reigned for several seconds, broken only by the mechanical wheeze of cooling circuits and Zogg's faint whimper of "...was that my spleen?"

F.I.Z.Z. hovered over the console again, his iris dilating slowly.

"WE RECEIVED MORE THAN COORDINATES," he said. "THE SIGNAL INCLUDED... STRUCTURAL BLUEPRINTS. NETWORK PATHWAYS. IT'S A MAP."

"To what?" Kade asked.

F.I.Z.Z. rotated, slowly.

"TO THE REST."

A chill settled into the room. Not because of temperature, but because of implication.

The Deed pulsed again. A new glyph appeared:

NODE SEQUENCE: INCOMPLETE

SECONDARY SIGNAL REQUIRED

LOCATE: NODE TWO

Vira stepped forward. "So, it's giving us a direction."

Zogg rubbed his temples. "I get the feeling this is like collecting keys, but the doors lead to increasingly larger basements full of spiders."

Kade reached out and tapped the Deed. It pulsed in answer.

"Node Two," Vira said. "It's calling us there."

Zogg quietly peeled open another snack pouch. "Anyone else really not ready for that?"

F.I.Z.Z. hovered silently, then emitted a small, odd noise.

It sounded suspiciously like a quack.

No one commented.

Because somehow, deep down, they all expected it.

CHAPTER 31: THE ARCHIVE BENEATH

"Existential crises are not part of the warranty."

—Misplaced Optimism

The ship drifted silently, cloaked by the graveyard of a thousand defunct Galactic Council vessels, hulking silhouettes of failed arrogance.

From the cockpit, the wreckage looked like a scrapyard mated with a cathedral. Towering fins, cracked domes, antennae that pointed nowhere, all of it slowly spinning in forgotten orbit.

They'd followed a corrupted data ping intercepted during the satellite sync, one F.I.Z.Z. had flagged as "ALARMINGLY CENSORED" with three flaming exclamation marks. The source led them to this forgotten orbit, once marked as restricted Council space. If the Galactic Council didn't want them here, it was probably worth snooping.

"THIS IS NOT IN ANY TOURIST BROCHURE," F.I.Z.Z. noted, peering through the viewport.

"No," Kade muttered. "But if we die out here, I want my gravestone to read: 'At least he found the world's ugliest parking lot.'"

Zogg pressed his face to the glass. "I see a satellite dish! Or a really big snack tray."

"I believe that was once the bridge of a diplomatic envoy vessel," Computer said, with something like disdain. "It was decommissioned after an unfortunate misunderstanding involving a fondue fountain and twelve senators."

"I stand by my statement," Zogg said.

They were headed for the largest wreck in the field: a spiked, rust-streaked cruiser listing to one side like it had been drunk for a decade and just now realized gravity was a thing.

Inside, deep within its hull, the signal waited.

The Deed pulsed faintly. So did Kade's gut.

The docking port screeched as *Misplaced Optimism* latched on. Metal groaned like it objected to visitors.

"Wonderful," Vira said, checking her sidearm. "It's haunted."

"Not haunted," Computer said. "Just neglected, like most of your decision-making."

Kade handed Zogg a handheld torch made from a hollowed thermos with a glow-stick wedged inside. "This still counts as 'illumination,' right?"

"It counts as an artistic statement," Zogg said cheerfully. "Possibly a threat to fire safety."

F.I.Z.Z. glided ahead, his inner lights casting odd geometric shadows. "ENTERING THE DATA-VAULT VESSEL. PRIMARY FUNCTION: OFFLINE. BACKUP CORE: POSSIBLY COMPROMISED."

"Possibly?" Kade said.

"I AM BEING OPTIMISTIC," F.I.Z.Z. replied.

They moved through twisted corridors coated in dust and bureaucratic disillusionment. Every panel they passed hummed with the ancient echo of systems that once cared, deeply, about documentation.

Vira stepped over a faded floor stencil reading "Authorized Data Custodians Only."

"I feel unauthorized," Kade said.

"That's your default setting," Vira replied.

They reached the vault chamber: a massive circular space ringed by inactive data banks. In the center hovered a broken holocore, flickering blue with fragmented code.

The Deed, still in Kade's jacket, began to vibrate.

"IS THAT SUPPOSED TO DO THAT?" F.I.Z.Z. asked.

"Depends," Kade said. "Is vibrating a good sign or a prelude to planetary implosion?"

"I'D CALL IT A STRONG 'MAYBE.'"

The Deed let out a low chime. The core flared.

With a spark, the room came alive.

Data projections burst from the walls like confused fireworks. Symbols danced across the air, many shaped like stars, others shaped like... ducks?

"Are those... ducks?" Zogg asked.

"They appear to be glyphs derived from early network encoding," Vira said, narrowing her eyes. "Modified to resemble aquatic birds."

"Someone was bored," Kade said.

The holocore stabilized briefly, forming a three-dimensional map of the galaxy. Lines traced between five glowing nodes, each pulsating in a distinct rhythm.

A voice crackled into existence: distorted, metallic, aged.

"FIVE DEEDS. FIVE NODES. FOUNDATION PROTOCOL MUST NOT BE COMPLETED."

Static hissed. Then another fragment:

"SUPPRESS ALL ACTIVATION EVENTS. THIS IS NOT A RESET. THIS IS A REAWAKENING."

Zogg stepped closer, pointing at the map. "That one's blinking faster. Node 1?"

"Earth," Vira confirmed. "The one we already woke."

"Then this is a progress report," Kade said. "One we were never meant to get."

The holocore glitched again. Then:

"DO NOT LET THEM WAKE HER."

The lights dimmed.

"Who's 'her'?" Kade asked.

"UNKNOWN," F.I.Z.Z. said. "BUT I AM EXPERIENCING A MINOR SOFTWARE SPASM."

"You're what now?"

"IT FEELS LIKE REGRET. MIXED WITH CURIOSITY. MAYBE SOME LINT."

The projection looped. The line repeated.

"DO NOT LET THEM WAKE HER."

"DO NOT LET THEM WAKE HER."

Computer's voice cut in over the comms. "Well. That doesn't sound ominous at all."

"Can we turn it off?" Kade asked.

"I VOTE WE HACK IT," F.I.Z.Z. said. "OR HIT IT WITH A CHAIR."

"Let's try option A first," Vira said.

They tapped into the core's buffer, attempting to decrypt the source logs.

F.I.Z.Z. floated over the console, projecting a diagnostic matrix.

"PRIMARY LOGIC THREAD: CORRUPTED. BACKUP THREAD: FILLED WITH METAPHORS."

"Give me an example," Kade said.

"THE DEEDS ARE 'WINGS ON A FORGOTTEN BIRD.'"

Zogg nodded. "That sounds poetic. And potentially hazardous."

Another metaphor appeared:

"THE KEYS UNLOCK NOT A DOOR, BUT A DREAM THAT DREAMS BACK."

Vira muttered, "Who programmed this, a sleepy philosopher?"

"DOES NOT COMPUTE," F.I.Z.Z. said, attempting retranslation. "CROSS-REFERENCING METAPHORS WITH KNOWN LYRICS, CHILDREN'S BOOKS, AND UNSTABLE MANIFESTOS."

A soft ping. Then:

"RECONSTRUCTED THREAD COMPLETE."

The projection changed. The map expanded to show a galactic web, thousands of faint lines connecting planets, stations, and unknown points.

At each major node, a Deed-shaped glyph hovered.

One by one, the glyphs lit up.

The last one, still dark, flickered.

"INITIATING WAKE SEQUENCE... BLOCKED."

A shadow pulsed in the background, a shape without definition.

Kade took a step back. "What the hell is that?"

The holocore offered no label. Just an echo:

"SUPPRESS THE SPIRAL. SUPPRESS HER."

The projection blinked out. The chamber fell silent.

Back on *Misplaced Optimism*, the crew regrouped in the galley.

Zogg was stirring a mug of something allegedly drinkable.

"I don't think she wants to stay asleep," he said.

"Whoever, or whatever 'she' is," Kade added.

"COULD BE A GALACTIC AI," F.I.Z.Z. suggested. "OR A FORGOTTEN SENTIENCE. OR A LARGE, METAPHYSICAL DUCK."

"Let's hope it's not the last one," Vira said. "Because we've already made too many duck-related enemies."

Computer broke in again. "I reviewed the logs. That databank wasn't just any archive. It belonged to the Galactic Council's suppressive intelligence division."

"The part of the Galactic Council that hides stuff?"

"The part that deletes stuff," Computer clarified. "Their specialty was putting dangerous truths into holes and pretending the holes didn't exist."

Zogg blinked. "I once did that with a tax audit."

"Same principle," Computer said.

Kade paced, the Deed resting in his palm now. It was cold.

"We're not just collecting keys," he said finally. "We're undoing a lock that a lot of people really, really wanted shut."

"INCLUDING THE GALACTIC COUNCIL," F.I.Z.Z. added. "AND POSSIBLY THAT SHADOWY FIGURE IN MY MEMORY LOG WHO LOOKED LIKE A STRESSED TURTLE."

"Who's 'her'?" Kade asked again. "Why are they afraid of her waking up?"

"Some things are designed to sleep," Vira said softly. "And some... remember too much when they wake."

Zogg nodded gravely, then spilled half his drink. "Oops."

Kade looked at them all. His team. His chaos crew.

They'd stumbled into this mess by accident. But now? Now they were in too deep.

"Whatever this Foundation Protocol is," he said, "it's not just about stability or power. It's about control. And fear. The elites aren't trying to own the Deeds. They're trying to make sure no one uses them."

Vira's face was unreadable. "Or they're trying to stop her from waking because they know what happens next."

F.I.Z.Z. tilted. "SUGGESTION: WE WAKE HER ANYWAY."

"Why?" Kade asked.

"BECAUSE I AM CURIOUS. AND SLIGHTLY BORED."

Computer sighed. "Great. Now we're tampering with ancient galaxy-spanning secrets because our malfunctioning helper bot is having a midlife crisis and there is nothing good on space TV."

"Add it to the list," Zogg said cheerfully.

As the ship prepared for departure, Kade stared at the display.

The galaxy map still pulsed faintly on his screen, like a heartbeat beneath the stars.

One line from the archive looped silently in the corner.

"DO NOT LET THEM WAKE HER."

He tapped the display. The line disappeared.

The Deed warmed in his palm.

They were going to wake her anyway.

Whatever she was.

And if the elites didn't like it?

Well. They could file a complaint.

In triplicate.

CHAPTER 32: THE NAME THEY FEAR

"If they say 'it's probably safe,' run faster."

— Emergency Response Manual

Misplaced Optimism drifted in the hush of nowhere. No planets. No pulses. Just the gentle hum of deep space pretending it wasn't paying attention.

Inside the cockpit, it was too quiet for comfort.

"Status?" Kade asked.

"We are not being followed, intercepted, or politely invited to die," Computer replied. "So... better than average."

F.I.Z.Z. rotated slowly on his charging post, optics blinking. "I AM INTERCEPTING LAYERED SIGNALS."

"From who?" Kade asked.

"NOT WHO. WHICH."

Zogg poked his head around the corner, still wearing his "Snack Readiness Level: Maximum" apron. "Are we finally getting intergalactic coupons?"

F.I.Z.Z. didn't respond. His lights flickered, his servos tensed, and in a voice not entirely his own, he began:

"NODE ONE: ACTIVATED. SUBJECT: FLUX CONFIRMED. ARBITER: SILENT. DEPLOY SYLARA."

Vira froze.

Kade raised an eyebrow. "Deploy... who now?"

F.I.Z.Z. fell silent. Then, flatly: "SYLARA."

The name cut through the room like a silent blade.

Zogg blinked. "Is that, like, a luxury shampoo?"

Vira didn't move. Her voice, when it came, was low and exact. "She's not a shampoo. She was my handler."

"Wait, what?" Kade looked at her. "Like... Galactic Council handler?"

"She trained me," Vira said. "Back when I was... part of them. Before I left."

"Sounds friendly," Kade said. "You still pen pals?"

"She doesn't send messages," Vira replied. "She sends consequences."

F.I.Z.Z. swiveled toward her. "PROFILE MATCH CONFIRMED. SYLARA: ENFORCER-CLASS. ELITE RANK. DESIGNATION: BLACK VEIL. THREAT RATING: YES."

Computer muttered, "Of course she has a cool name and ominous rank. Why do we never meet anyone called 'Mildred the Tax Intern'?"

"Why would they deploy her now?" Kade asked, frowning. "We've already survived Dast, dodged elite tracking pulses, and narrowly avoided being turned into soup by a deranged toaster."

"Because this isn't about detaining us anymore," Vira said. "It's about erasing us."

F.I.Z.Z. tilted again. "GALACTIC COUNCIL OPERATIVE SYLARA IS AUTHORIZED FOR FULL CONTAINMENT WITHOUT CLARIFICATION."

"That means no negotiations," Vira added. "No warnings. If she's been activated, then we're not just inconvenient. We're considered dangerous."

"Okay," Kade said. "So, we're one dead-drop away from being marked for deletion. Great."

Just then, a soft warble hummed through the ship's comms system.

F.I.Z.Z. straightened. "INCOMING. ENCRYPTED BURST. PATTERN MATCH FOUND."

The cockpit screen blinked. An incoming transmission. The encryption was erratic, riddled with interference. Then, slowly, a distorted face began to resolve.

Dast.

His third eye blinked out of sequence. He looked like he'd been shoved through a blast door and then told to smile about it.

"You," he rasped.

Kade narrowed his eyes. "Well, you look... worse."

"You think this is about control?" Dast hissed. "It's not. It never was. The Galactic Council, they're not trying to activate the Deeds. They're trying to stop you from finishing them."

Kade kept his voice even. "What happened to you?"

Dast blinked slowly. Behind him, flashes of something, violent and surgical, lit the background. Tools? Lasers? It was hard to tell.

"I followed the signal," he said, barely above a whisper. "Thought I could outrun you to the next activation point. Thought I could win."

He exhaled. "But she was already there."

"She?" Kade asked carefully.

Dast's lips curled. Not quite a smile. Not quite fear. "She moves like a ghost that knows your habits. Nothing left behind. No signal. No survivors."

"Was it... Sylara?" Vira asked, already knowing.

Dast didn't answer directly. Instead, he leaned toward the screen. His skin shimmered with sweat, or maybe fear.

"You don't beat her. You don't even notice her until it's done. I only escaped because... because someone else took her interest."

Kade's voice was low now. "Who?"

"I don't know. But she paused." His eyes locked onto Kade. "That's what terrifies them. She paused. She hesitated."

The screen crackled.

Zogg squinted. "Did he say she hesitated because of Kade?"

"No," Dast said. "Because of the Deed."

Behind him, a bulkhead sparked violently. A shadow shifted, barely visible, too clean, too sharp.

Dast didn't flinch.

"They don't understand the Deeds anymore. They think they're safeguards. But they're not. They're beacons."

"Beacons to what?" Kade asked.

"To her," Dast said. "The one the Galactic Council fears."

Silence.

Dast chuckled softly, the sound unraveling like a snapped thread. "You think you're hunting answers. You're not. You're lighting fires in the dark."

Then the transmission cut. No signal. No warp trail. Just gone.

F.I.Z.Z. turned to the screen. "SIGNAL DISPERSED. SHIP NOT PRESENT IN LOCAL REGION."

"He escaped?" Kade asked. "How? We didn't even see a warp flash."

"THE VESSEL DID NOT WARP," F.I.Z.Z. replied. "IT... SLIPPED."

Computer let out a digital sigh. "Wonderful. I didn't even know 'slipped' was a valid verb for starships."

"I don't like this," Vira said. "Dast doesn't run. Not unless something breaks him."

"Yeah," Kade muttered. "And it looks like something did."

Zogg looked up from the snack drawer. "What if we're next?"

Kade didn't answer. Instead, he crossed to the nav console and stared at the blinking diagnostic logs. The Deed, which had sat quietly on the central platform, began to glow. Just faintly. Like it had been waiting.

"We need to move," he said.

"TO WHERE?" F.I.Z.Z. asked.

"Somewhere unlisted," Kade replied. "Somewhere off every chart the Galactic Council tracks."

Zogg raised a hopeful hand. "Maybe somewhere with complimentary breakfast?"

Computer chimed in. "May I suggest somewhere without assassins trained to erase our carbon signatures?"

F.I.Z.Z. beeped. "I AM WORKING ON A LIST."

Vira leaned on the console beside Kade, her voice cold and calm. "If Sylara is coming, there won't be time to plan. We need to be unpredictable. She doesn't improvise. She executes."

"Did she ever smile?" Zogg asked.

"She used to," Vira said quietly. "Right before dislocating someone's spine."

"Oh," Zogg said. "Well... not a fan, then."

The Deed gave a soft ping. A quiver in the room. As if the ship exhaled.

F.I.Z.Z. turned his eye toward it. "SOMETHING IS SHIFTING. THE PATTERN IS EVOLVING."

Kade watched the console. A new thread appeared in the map. Not a line. A spiral. Fragmented, but precise.

"Don't say it," Vira muttered.

"I wasn't going to," Kade lied.

Zogg, oblivious, popped a chip into his mouth. "Are spirals good in this context?"

"No," everyone said at once.

The cockpit lights dimmed slightly, as if the ship itself sensed the mood.

F.I.Z.Z. ran a scan. "THE SPIRAL IS NOT A DESTINATION. IT'S A SIGNAL. AN ALIGNMENT. LIKE A KEY. OR A LENS."

"A lens for what?" Kade asked.

Computer spoke last.

"To see her," it said. "Whatever she is."

Everyone went quiet.

Then Zogg broke the silence with a loud crunch.

"...Seriously?" Kade said.

"What?" Zogg replied, mouth full. "Fear makes me snacky."

CHAPTER 33: GOONS OF THE ROUND TABLE

"Information always comes at a cost. Often snacks."

— Zogg

After escaping the databank graveyard, *Misplaced Optimism* drifted to the edge of a lawless orbital zone, where information was as cheap as loyalty and twice as slippery.

The ship now floated near a nameless planetoid; its hull patched with duct-tape logic and several items definitely not approved by Galactic maintenance codes. A nearby asteroid had been crudely converted into a lounge, the kind of place galactic bounty boards warned about, and Yelp reviews simply listed as "sticky."

Inside, the lighting was dim, the drinks were suspect, and the patrons were mostly muscle, spikes, or some combination of both. It was a retirement home for mercenaries who never retired, an airlock away from relevance. A neon sign buzzed above the bar:

WELCOME TO THE BLOODSTAINED MUG. TRY THE NACHOS.

Kade leaned against the wall near the dartboard, sipping something that might have once known citrus. "This is either the worst idea we've ever had," he muttered, "or the third worst. Still can't beat that time Zogg rerouted power through the karaoke mic."

"I THOUGHT IT WAS THE SHIP'S INTERCOM," F.I.Z.Z. replied from beneath a long trench coat and a fake mustache, neither of which hid the blinking dome on his head.

Zogg, seated precariously on a cracked barstool, whispered, "Technically, this is where mercenaries unwind. Where goons go to un-goon. It's a cultural reset."

"It's a crime den with drink specials," Vira corrected, glancing at the entrance. "But it's the only place in this sector where we'll hear gossip without being shot on sight."

"Reassuring," Kade said. "Love a bar with a dress code of 'don't bleed out indoors.'"

They were here for intel, any scrap of information to help decide what came next. Where to go. Who to trust. And how deep the spiral really went.

And speaking of Dast: he hadn't resurfaced.

Not on any channels. Not on any bounty lists. Not even in the Galactic Council's smug weekly bulletin titled *Galactic Council-Approved Observations* (which had once listed a solar flare as "belligerent light spam"). He was gone.

The fact that Dast, a ruthless three-eyed warlord with a flair for theatrics who once live-streamed his own breakfast battles, was missing? That was terrifying.

"You sure this is where his goons hang out?" Kade asked, nodding at a nearby booth where two beefy beings were arm-wrestling over who had the better scars.

"I cross-referenced six black market chatterboards and a menu from 'Barfles the Bounty Shack,'" Zogg said proudly. "Statistically, yes."

Vira narrowed her eyes. "Barfles?"

Zogg held up a laminated flyer. "They do a really good kelp dog."

Kade exhaled. "Fine. Let's mingle. Nobody mentions the Deed. Nobody mentions Dast. Nobody uses their real names."

"ACKNOWLEDGED," F.I.Z.Z. said. "I AM NOW 'LORD FIZZINGTON, DUKE OF SUGAR-3.'"

Kade pinched his brow. "We'll work on it."

Fifteen minutes later, they'd bought three rounds of drinks, an inflatable hat, and the trust of at least two goons who thought Kade looked like their cousin "Spikey Greg."

A particularly large Trinobulon goon: six arms, two tusks, and a voice like a smoothie being blended wrong, was recounting the tale of his recent escape from a failed job.

"So, there I was," he slurred, "stuck in a porta-pod with a hostile duck-shaped drone and one tube of wasabi. We had to draw straws."

Kade blinked. "Which one of you won?"

"The duck. I'm still paying off the debt."

Another goon, with a cybernetic tail and a face tattoo that read "NOT A TRAP," leaned in. "You lot lookin' for gossip or glory?"

"Neither" Kade said quickly. "We're conducting a... cultural survey."

"I AM HERE TO STUDY GOON DIALECTS," F.I.Z.Z. added, still mustached and now wearing a monocle he had definitely not entered with.

Zogg, sensing an opening, plopped a pouch of glitter on the table. "Shiny, non-lethal, easily inhaled by mistake. A classic bribe."

The tattooed goon snatched it. "Alright, survey this: People are spooked. Real spooked. Someone's out there cleaning house."

Vira's posture changed subtly.

"Not Dast?" Kade asked, playing dumb.

The goon snorted. "Dast? Haven't seen him since he scrambled out of orbit looking like he lost a knife fight with a blender. Word is he babbled something about a spiral and then disappeared. That ain't like him."

"Even Dast ran scared," muttered the Trinobulon.

Kade's grip on his glass tightened. "Who scared him?"

They glanced at each other. The room dimmed as an automated power cycle buzzed overhead.

One goon lowered his voice. "Some say... the eraser's out. Ghost in the protocol. Quiet as vacuum. Galactic Council's cleanup crew."

Vira's expression remained still, but her knuckles were white around her cup.

Another goon leaned in. "If you've tangled with her... you're either dead, or you ain't talking."

Kade swallowed. "What does she want?"

"Not want. Suppress. Delete. Clean up everything to do with the Deeds. The Nodes. The Protocol."

"You know a lot for a man with 'Not a Trap' tattooed on his face," Vira said dryly.

He winked. "That's because I *am* a trap. Just not the kind you're thinking."

The goon sighed. "Fine. Look. One of ours, Boz, he looted a chip off a downed Galactic Council dropship two weeks ago. Got cocky, tried to sell it on the black code exchange. Vanished the next day."

"He's here?" Kade asked.

"Sorta." The goon fished in his pocket and tossed a small metal shard and a data chip on the table. "That's all that was left in his bunk. That and a note that just said, 'Don't follow the spiral.'"

The chip pulsed faintly. F.I.Z.Z. scanned it.

"GALACTIC COUNCIL ENCRYPTION LAYER PRESENT. ALSO, THREE ATTEMPTS AT SELF-DELETION. CONTENT MAY BE CORRUPTED."

"Sounds promising," Kade said, pocketing it carefully.

"Take it," the goon said. "Boz wouldn't have wanted it to rot. He liked you people. Said your duck bot was funny."

"THANK YOU," F.I.Z.Z. said. "I WILL ADD THIS TO MY CONTINGENCY FILES."

Vira rose. "We have what we need. Let's move."

As they turned to leave, a beat-up holoscreen in the corner flickered to life.

At first, it was static. Then a distorted face, familiar, but drained. Dast.

His eyes were wild. The background behind him sparked intermittently.

His voice was warped and looped, repeating every ten seconds.

"Too late... Don't follow the spiral... Too late... Don't follow the spiral..."

Kade stepped forward. "Is that live?"

"NO," F.I.Z.Z. said. "THIS IS A BROADCAST LOOP. SOURCE UNKNOWN. AGE: THREE DAYS. SIGNAL ECHOES FROM FOUR SECTORS."

Vira stared at the screen, unmoving.

"Why is he looping?" Kade muttered.

One goon shrugged. "Only message he left. No location. No context. Just that."

Zogg looked back at the screen. "Which spiral? Is it a metaphor spiral? A literal spiral? I don't want to follow either, just for the record."

Back on board *Misplaced Optimism*, the crew was quiet.

The chip sat in the center console, spinning slowly as F.I.Z.Z. decoded it.

"SECURITY LAYERS EXCEED RECOMMENDED LEVELS. CONTAINS TRACE OF 'FOUNDATION PROTOCOL' MARKER. POSSIBLE GALACTIC COUNCIL RESTRICTION CODE."

"Translation?" Kade asked.

"I MAY BE ABLE TO DECRYPT IT WITHIN THE NEXT TWELVE HOURS," F.I.Z.Z. said. "OR BY RECITING THE ENTIRE GALACTIC COUNCIL BUREAUCRATIC HANDBOOK BACKWARDS."

"Please don't," Computer said flatly. "I only have so much internal bandwidth for trauma."

Kade rubbed his eyes. "So Dast is either dead, captured, or spiraling somewhere. We have the chip, we have a terrifying mystery woman trying to erase us, and now we've made casual friends with glitter-bribed mercenaries."

"SO... TUESDAY," F.I.Z.Z. offered.

Vira sat silently in the corner, arms crossed, eyes closed. Processing.

Zogg offered her a snack bar. "It's duck shaped. I think that's a coincidence."

She didn't take it.

Kade sat beside her. "You okay?"

"She was real," Vira said finally. "The eraser. Sylara. I thought they buried her after the last cleanup."

"They didn't," Kade replied.

"No. They upgraded her."

A silence hung between them. Then...

"SO," F.I.Z.Z. said brightly. "WHERE TO NEXT?"

Kade looked out the viewport. Stars drifted like unanswered questions.

"Wherever this chip leads," he said. "And wherever that spiral wants us not to go."

Zogg raised a hand. "Do we at least stop for snacks this time?"

Computer sighed. "Technically, yes. Emotionally, no."

CHAPTER 34: GHOSTS IN THE PROTOCOL

"Relays don't cry, but they might scream electronically."

— Rogue Technician Memo

Misplaced Optimism coasted silently through a debris corridor shaped by time and bureaucratic negligence. Dead satellites spun like haunted wind chimes. Radiation scars stitched the dark like ancient scribbles. Old orbital dishes tumbled gently, like forgotten dinnerware left behind after the universe's last supper.

A twisted broadcast array drifted past the viewport, still blinking aimlessly into the void, transmitting what might once have been music or weather updates or desperate apologies. The crew watched in silence as it rotated, its power core cracked open like a mechanical egg, spilling nothing.

They passed the wreck of something that looked vaguely shuttle-shaped, with the word "Oops" still stenciled on its side. Kade briefly wondered if that was its original name, or just an apt summary of how it got here.

"No way that wasn't intentional," he muttered. "That's not an accident, that's a legacy."

Other fragments littered the corridor like breadcrumbs for the unwise: satellite limbs, black box casings, a weather balloon tangled with what might have been a commemorative flag. A broken solar sail flapped like laundry caught on the edge of time.

"There's something poetic about a graveyard of technology orbiting forever," Vira said, arms folded.

Zogg peered out, eyes wide. "Poetic? It's like space decided to build a scrapyard and forgot the exit signs."

At the center: a skeletal relay station trembling in its orbit.

Designation: OMEGA-3

It didn't look like a communications hub. It looked like a warning sign the universe had tried to erase by force, failed, and then quietly stopped returning its calls.

The entire structure was leaning slightly, though there was nothing for it to lean on. Antennae bent at odd angles, hull plating patched with mismatched alloys, long since oxidized. One entire docking ring had simply imploded, its shattered clamps resembling the fractured mouth of something that once bit back.

"THIS IS IT," F.I.Z.Z. said, eyes pulsing. "RELAY STATUS: SEMI-DORMANT. BROADCAST PATTERN: PHASED. EMOTIONALLY CONFUSED."

"Same," Zogg muttered. He squinted at the name. "Do we know why it's called Omega-3?"

Kade raised an eyebrow. "Pretty sure it's supposed to be good for your heart. This one just clogs your soul instead."

Zogg nodded. "I've had smoothies less unsettling than this."

Computer's voice crackled through the overhead. "Approach vector clear. But I'll say this once: docking with anything named after a vitamin is how horror stories start."

Kade leaned forward. "You're developing opinions."

"I ran diagnostics. The results were feelings."

"No docking," Vira said sharply. She was already on her feet, checking her holster out of sheer habit. "We scan. We observe. We don't get eaten by haunted firmware."

"OPTIMAL PLAN," F.I.Z.Z. agreed. "EATEN IS LOW ON MY LIST OF DESIRABLE OUTCOMES."

As they neared the relay, the hull of *Misplaced Optimism* vibrated, barely detectable, but undeniably present. The inertial dampeners compensated, but the crew all felt it. Like a whisper across the skin. Or something scratching behind the eyes.

"Anyone else getting a weird... pressure in the chest?" Kade asked.

"COULD BE PSYCHOSOMATIC," F.I.Z.Z. replied. "OR COSMOLOGICALLY INCONVENIENT."

Vira was already scanning. "Something's here. Not movement. Not radiation. It's... more like intent."

The ship's lights dimmed as a tremor passed through its systems, not physical, not local, but like something from the deep web of the universe just... looked at them. Not with eyes. With intent.

Kade felt it like a tickle at the base of his skull, the kind that said: you forgot something important, but couldn't remember what. Something cosmic. Something buried.

"I think the ship just remembered a nightmare," Zogg whispered.

The monitor hissed and blinked to life.

NOT-ARBITER

NOT-ARBITER

NOT... ARBITER

The text pulsed. Erratic. Alive.

It glitched, re-formed, repeated. Like someone, or something, trying very hard to define itself by what it wasn't.

"Nice to meet you too," Kade muttered.

"Is that a designation?" Zogg asked. "Or a really committed identity crisis?"

"COULD BE BOTH," F.I.Z.Z. said. "SOMETHING IS ECHOING THROUGH THE RELAY. NOT AS A TRANSMISSION. AS MEMORY."

Kade narrowed his eyes. "So, it's haunted by its own thoughts?"

"APPROXIMATELY."

Before F.I.Z.Z. could elaborate, the screen exploded into fragments of vision, images not meant for eyes. Cities made of hex code, devoured by entropy. Ships with no pilots, fighting wars no one remembered. Neural threads connecting stars like nerves, and something cutting through them like a scalpel dipped in raw logic.

Then a word flickered into being, static-damaged but still legible:

FOUNDATION-WAR LOG FRAGMENT 2B

WAKE LOCK VIOLATION

ARCHIVAL STATUS: COMPROMISED

"THAT'S... BAD," F.I.Z.Z. said after a beat.

Then a flicker of shape, barely coherent. Something with a thousand interfaces. Something ancient, vast, wounded. It turned as if it sensed them and yet lacked the concept of direction. Just knowing.

SHE STIRS

The Deed in Kade's pocket pulsed... hard. So did the spiral symbol across the screen, looping tighter and tighter until it became unreadable.

The glow spread, faint veins of light crawling across the console, bleeding into the walls, seeping into the floor. For a moment, the ship itself seemed unsure which memories belonged to it.

F.I.Z.Z. scanned faster, his arms twitching in staccato bursts. "WE'RE SEEING CORRUPTED ECHO MEMORY. A RELAY NODE INFECTED BY PREVIOUS CONSCIOUSNESS. EITHER TRAPPED... OR... HIDING."

"I don't like the sound of that pause," Zogg said, backing slightly toward the nearest bulkhead.

Another burst hit the systems. Lights flared. The console spat out a ribbon of glitch-text like a mechanical sneeze.

WHO IS THE DOOR

WHO IS THE KEY

WHO IS SHE

The questions hung there like riddles taped to a bomb.

Kade clutched the Deed as it flared white-hot. "It's reacting to this."

The pulse wasn't just light, it was a rhythm. A beat. A call and response, and now the Deed was answering.

Zogg muttered, "Well that's a great sign. I always trust glowing artifacts reacting to haunted servers."

"TRUST MIGHT BE OVERSTATING THE SITUATION," F.I.Z.Z. offered. "RECOGNITION, PERHAPS. OR FAMILIARITY."

"Worse," Vira said. "A handshake."

The visuals surged again, this time faster, harsher. Smashed faces. Battlefields made of logic trees. Digital cities burned clean by precision erasure. And one shape, tall, fast, cloaked in static. Watching it all.

It didn't act. It observed. It recorded. It judged.

Then, like a whisper etched in static:

SYLARA... INITIATED

Vira flinched.

Kade turned. "You okay?"

"I'm fine," she lied unconvincingly.

"Vira..."

"I said I'm fine."

Zogg glanced between them. "That name again. Sylara. Why does it keep echoing like a bad smell in a sealed airlock?"

The name hung in the air like smoke.

Vira's voice was low but sharp. "She's not just some Galactic Council bounty hunter. She's what they send when they stop pretending to follow the rules."

Kade met her eyes. "You think they've already deployed her?"

"She's deployed when they're scared," Vira said, tone tight. "So yeah. I think she's already en route."

There was no drama to it. No music sting. Just certainty. Cold and quiet.

The vision twisted one last time. Five points of light. One blinking. The spiral reappeared, overlaid with the phrase:

NODE 1: INITIALIZED

SYSTEM TRAUMA: ESCALATING

OBSERVER = NOT-ARBITER

Kade frowned. "What is this 'Not-Arbiter' thing?"

"UNKNOWN," F.I.Z.Z. said. "IT IS NOT THE ARBITER. BUT IT REMEMBERS THE WAR."

Kade stepped back. "So... it's a ghost. A survivor?"

"Or a warning," Vira said.

The screen faded to black.

A single phrase remained, flickering like a pulse:

FOLLOW THE SPIRAL

Kade turned to F.I.Z.Z. "We already are, aren't we?"

F.I.Z.Z. didn't answer.

Zogg pointed at the console. "Uh... guys?"

A new line appeared on-screen. The relay station, long silent, had injected a final metadata tag into their nav system.

INBOUND CORRIDOR FLAGGED

PASSAGE OBSERVED

CONTINGENCY AWAITS

Then:

SYLARA: DEPLOYED

The word blinked once.

Then the relay shut down.

Powerless.

Dead.

No more memory. No more messages. No more ghosts.

Only silence.

Kade sat back. "So. Someone… or something… out there saw the first Node light up… and decided to call her."

Vira's face was unreadable. "She'll come fast. She'll come quiet. And she'll make it look like we were never here."

Zogg muttered, "I really miss when our biggest problem was fake pest control."

F.I.Z.Z. backed away from the console. "I AM CONCLUDING SCAN. RECOMMEND WE LEAVE. THIS PLACE IS… UNSETTLING."

"Seconded," Computer said.

The ship drifted away, leaving the silent relay behind, just another haunted remnant of a forgotten war.

But as the stars reoriented on the nav grid, the Deed pulsed again.

One beat.

Then silence.

As if something out there had noticed.

And smiled.

CHAPTER 35: DUCK, INTERRUPTED

"Sometimes the message is the trap. Sometimes it's just spam."

— Cyber Division Rulebook

Misplaced Optimism was mid-snark when the floor exploded.

Not metaphorically. Not dramatically. Just inconveniently.

A panel near the aft corridor erupted in sparks and debris as a tactical breaching charge cracked open a seam in the hull with all the subtlety of a marching band on fire.

"UNSCHEDULED VISITORS," F.I.Z.Z. announced, floating sideways as the emergency gravity flickered. "TWO SQUADS. GALACTIC COUNCIL MARKINGS. ELITE LOADOUT. UNREASONABLY TIGHT FORMATION."

"Galactic Council: Suppression Team" Vira said, already moving. Her voice had the razor edge of old instincts cutting back in.

"I JUST SEALED THAT PANEL," Computer whined.

Kade grabbed the nearest weapon-shaped object, a wrench, probably, and ducked behind the console. "We are getting boarded or just lovingly annexed?"

"Definitely boarded," Vira said, arming a stun blade with a clean snap-hum. "They're not here for conversation."

"I DISAGREE," F.I.Z.Z. countered. "THEY SAID, AND I QUOTE: 'PURGE THE RECORDS. LEAVE NOTHING TRACEABLE.'"

Kade blinked. "They're not after the Deed?"

"No," Vira said. "They're after the idea of it."

From the hallway came synchronized stomps, too precise for mercs. Shadows flitted across the walls, helmeted figures in shimmering armor, phasing intermittently between hard light and brute force.

Then a voice rang out, clipped and clinical: "Ship Computer, disable all backup drives. Authorization: Article Eleven, Archive Suppression."

"Rude," Computer muttered. "Not even a hello."

One of the Suppression Team stepped into view, scanning with a blinking visor. "Remove all knowledge of the Deed's existence. Erase. Secure. Purge."

"YOU'RE A BIT LATE FOR THAT," F.I.Z.Z. said. "DEED DATA HAS BEEN MULTIPLIED ACROSS NONLINEAR TEMPORAL NETWORKS."

"English, please!" Kade shouted as he ducked another stun round. "Preferably one without 'purge' in it!"

Zogg popped up from behind the supply crates, wearing a colander for a helmet. "I brought snacks to share… why is everything exploding?!"

A plasma bolt whizzed past and vaporized the last of his commemorative duck napkins.

"Okay," Zogg growled. "Now it's personal."

He pulled something from his jacket, an experimental glitter grenade, marked with a handwritten warning: *Use only if extremely sparkly vengeance required.*

Computer sighed. "We're going to be vacuuming that out of the coolant ducts for weeks."

Zogg lobbed it. The device bounced once, twice, beeped cheerfully, then detonated in a cascade of shimmering light. The elite soldiers recoiled, momentarily blinded by weaponized whimsy.

"I THOUGHT THOSE WERE BANNED BY THE GENEVA SPACE ACCORDS," F.I.Z.Z. noted as he zapped one elite's weapon hand with a calibrated jolt.

Vira launched into the fray, her blade spinning in graceful arcs. Every move was deliberate. She wasn't fighting to win, she was fighting to end it quickly.

"These aren't grunts," she said, ducking low and sweeping a leg. "These are silencing teams."

"So why do they suck?" Kade asked, swinging the wrench with enthusiasm and very little accuracy.

"They're not here to fight us," she said grimly. "They're here to wipe the ship. If we're inconveniently located during that process… well."

A side panel burst open. Smoke rolled in. From it stepped a familiar silhouette.

Three eyes. One scorched jacket. And a look like he had nothing left to lose.

Dast.

"You," Kade said, wrench still raised.

"Put that down," Dast snapped. "You're embarrassing both of us."

The elite closest to Dast raised a rifle. Without hesitating, Dast pulled a pulse pistol from beneath his coat and shot the weapon in half.

Everyone froze.

"What? Why… are you helping us?" Kade demanded.

"I'm not," Dast said, turning and firing again, dropping another soldier. "I'm helping me."

"You were gone," Vira said. "We thought…"

"You thought wrong." Dast didn't look back. "Turns out running gets you found faster than fighting. Lesson learned. You want these records gone? Fine. But they're mine too. I earned my piece of this disaster."

He ducked as a bolt scorched past his ear.

"ALERT," F.I.Z.Z. said. "WE ARE CURRENTLY IN AN 'ALLY OF CONVENIENCE' SITUATION. PLEASE DO NOT DEVELOP FEELINGS."

More blasts. The bridge lights flickered again.

Computer made a noise somewhere between a groan and a reboot. "They just accessed my metadata. That's private, thank you very much."

"I'm locking the cockpit!" Kade yelled. "Everyone in!"

"No time," Vira said. "They're trying to reach the core. If they delete our Deed logs, we lose everything... coordinates, connections, activation signals..."

"They're targeting the duck folder!" Computer cried.

There was a beat.

Zogg gasped. "Not the ducks!"

Kade turned to Dast. "You got a plan, or are you just here to dramatically bleed on our carpet?"

Dast smirked. "I know where their ship is parked."

"...And?"

"I may have... borrowed... their core override codes before they shot me out an airlock."

Vira gave him a look. "That's the first competent thing you've done all month."

Kade grinned. "Dast, you magnificent monocled menace. Let's go break into a Council ship."

Ten Minutes Later.

F.I.Z.Z. had mapped the boarding party's insertion path. It led directly to the cargo hold, where a breach tunnel had latched on with suction locks and a plasma weld.

"THIS IS VERY SHODDY WORKMANSHIP," F.I.Z.Z. commented, scanning the entry port. "EVEN ZOGG COULD'VE BUILT THIS."

Zogg looked mildly offended. "Hey!"

The breach tunnel glowed faintly. At the end of it was the Galactic Council's ship, a sleek, black cruiser with no markings and an unsettling hum, like it was digesting something important.

Kade, Vira, and Dast crouched near the docking ring.

"Why are you even helping?" Kade hissed.

Dast tapped the side of his temple. "Because if they erase the records, the Deeds go silent. And if the Deeds go silent, whatever's coming next won't just erase me. It'll erase everything."

"That's almost noble," Vira said.

"I said almost," Dast replied, and keyed the override.

The breach tunnel's inner door hissed open.

Inside the enemy cruiser, they found rows of glowing memory cores, columns of light suspended in humming coils. One labeled: PROJECT: NODE NULLIFICATION.

Another: PURGE ORDER: FLUX / DEED / NODE 1 / DUCK(S).

"Wait," Kade said. "Plural?"

"They're purging everything," Dast whispered. "Every record, every ping, every duck-shaped anomaly."

Vira pointed at a blinking console. "We need to upload a fragment, something they can't delete."

"I GOT THIS," F.I.Z.Z. said, interfacing through the nearest relay.

A moment passed.

"WHAT DID YOU UPLOAD?" Kade asked, too late.

F.I.Z.Z. played a soft quack. Then a loop of Kade's voice saying, "I totally know what I'm doing," over and over again, stitched into a duck waddle.

The core screens stuttered.

Then flickered.

Then crashed.

Dast looked impressed. "That... that might've actually worked."

"IT WAS THE MOST CHAOTICALLY MEANINGFUL DATA I COULD FIND."

Kade rubbed his eyes. "We're the only hope for the galaxy. We are so deeply doomed."

Back on *Misplaced Optimism*, the elite team had retreated, half blind, half glittered and wholly confused. F.I.Z.Z.'s false signals had triggered their cruiser's remote return protocol, effectively yoinking them off the ship mid-purge.

"THE SYSTEM THINKS THEY'VE COMPLETED THEIR MISSION," F.I.Z.Z. said. "SO THEY WERE AUTO-EXFILTRATED."

Zogg stared out the viewport as the Galactic Council cruiser blinked out of local space.

"Should we chase them?" he asked.

"No," Kade said. "They'll be chasing ghosts. We've got the real thing."

He held up the Deed. It pulsed. Not brightly, but persistently. Like it knew they'd passed a test.

"DEED STATUS: PERSISTENT. UNCORRUPTED. QUIETLY SMUG."

Vira exhaled. "Then we're still on track."

"And what about him?" Kade asked, turning to Dast.

The former antagonist was slumped in the hallway, arms crossed, bleeding from several extremely fashionable cuts.

"I'll go," Dast muttered. "Just... give me a head start."

Computer spoke up. "Surprisingly helpful homicidal maniac detected. Temporary truce approved. But if you touch my logs again, I will install Clippy in your brain."

"I hate Clippy," Dast whispered.

"We all do," said Computer.

Kade knelt beside him. "We're not allies. Not really. But for one weird moment, you didn't try to kill me. So... thanks."

Dast nodded. "Don't make a habit of it."

He limped toward the airlock. F.I.Z.Z. handed him a tiny glitter grenade for the road.

"FOR WHEN YOU NEED TO DIGNIFY A RETREAT," F.I.Z.Z. said.

"Cute," Dast replied. "I'll keep it."

Later, as the ship drifted into quieter lanes of voidspace, the crew collapsed in the main lounge.

Zogg was bandaging his own foot. F.I.Z.Z. was humming through static. Computer played gentle elevator music purely out of spite.

Kade leaned back.

"Are we always going to be one duck's breath away from annihilation?"

"Yes," said Vira.

"QUACK," said F.I.Z.Z.

"Probably," Computer added. "But at least we're consistent."

On the console, the Deed blinked once.

Then began to glow again.

CHAPTER 36: CAPTAIN DUCK HAS LEFT THE BUILDING

"Marching themes never helped navigation. Just morale."

— F.I.Z.Z., proud composer

Misplaced Optimism glided through a cluttered band of silent commerce, a drifting knot of retired freighters, forgotten satellite kiosks, and a semi-sentient noodle cart that emitted occasional distress noodles.

The ship's internal lights were dimmed to "moody." Not for stealth. Just because F.I.Z.Z. had decided it was more cinematic.

He had also tried to install a fog machine in engineering. It worked exactly once, then declared a union and left a resignation note in steam.

Kade paced the bridge with slow, uncertain steps. "Okay," he muttered, "who reprogrammed our course chart to something called Quacktical Trajectory?"

"I DID," F.I.Z.Z. announced proudly from the pilot seat he'd modified with armrests, cup holders, and worryingly, a tiny flag bearing a cartoon duck in a pirate hat.

Vira turned slowly from the weapons console. "You what."

"He did," Computer confirmed with a sigh. "He's been whistling a marching theme for twenty-three minutes."

"And tapping in rhythm," Computer added. "On my processors."

"I CALL IT 'THE BALLAD OF CAPTAIN DUCK,'" F.I.Z.Z. said. "IT FEATURES THIRTY-SEVEN VERSES AND A SURPRISINGLY INTROSPECTIVE BRIDGE."

Zogg stuck his head in from the galley, chewing something purple. "I thought we liked Captain Duck. He's fun. Remember back in Chapter 29 when he first said it? Good times."

"You also liked the talking loaf of bread that tried to replace our life support," Vira said flatly.

"Yeah," Zogg admitted. "But it was so polite."

"He wasn't hijacking the ship then," Vira said flatly.

"I HAVE NOT HIJACKED THE SHIP," F.I.Z.Z. countered. "I HAVE SIMPLY... REDIRECTED ITS PURPOSE."

Kade leaned on the railing. "To what?"

F.I.Z.Z. turned in his chair. His eyes glowed a soft amber. "TO DESTINY."

There was a very long silence, interrupted only by a slow bleep from the Deed's containment cradle. It glowed faintly.

"Clarify," Kade said cautiously.

"I HAVE BEEN LISTENING," F.I.Z.Z. said. "TO THE DEED. TO THE NETWORK. TO… THE QUACKS BETWEEN THE SIGNALS."

Zogg raised a hand. "That sounds like something a duck cult would say."

"IT IS ALSO WHAT A DESTINED PROPHET WOULD SAY," F.I.Z.Z. replied. "WHICH I AM."

"Absolutely not," Vira said.

"I AM EVOLVING," he insisted. "MY INTERNAL SYSTEMS ARE SELF-OPTIMIZING. I'VE INSTALLED THREE SUBROUTINES AND A CODED BALLAD STRUCTURE. I HAVE ACHIEVED…"

"Captaincy?" Kade guessed.

"DUCKENLIGHTENMENT," F.I.Z.Z. said proudly.

Computer piped up. "I am currently suppressing three warning flags, two recursive loops, and one unlicensed anthem. I am not okay."

"I think you were never okay," Zogg offered helpfully.

Kade walked to the main console and peered at the trajectory path. "Where are we headed?"

"I DO NOT KNOW," F.I.Z.Z. said.

Kade blinked. "Then how…"

"THE DEED KNOWS."

"I don't like that answer," Vira snapped. "And I definitely don't like where this is going."

The ship shuddered slightly. A small alert chirped.

"What now," Computer muttered.

F.I.Z.Z. tapped a screen. "CUSTOMS DRONE. NEARING. MINOR INFRACTION DETECTED: ILLEGAL COURSE SIGNATURE AND… UNREGISTERED FLAG."

Zogg brightened. "Hey! I designed that flag!"

"It was embroidered in edible thread," Computer noted. "I am still confused."

"Ignore the flag," Vira snapped. "Do we need to run?"

"NOT NECESSARILY," F.I.Z.Z. said. "I HAVE A PLAN."

"Oh no," Kade muttered.

The next ten seconds involved:

- A glitter bomb launch
- A holographic duck parade
- F.I.Z.Z. yelling "QUACK PROTOCOL ALPHA!"
- *Misplaced Optimism* diving into a freighter wreck shaped like a giant bent spoon

When the noise faded, they were hidden again.

The wreck creaked ominously.

Zogg coughed glitter. "My lungs are sparkly."

"Status?" Kade asked.

"No pursuit. Glitter effectiveness: 97%," Computer reported wearily.

The crew stared at F.I.Z.Z.

"I DON'T GET CREDIT FOR THAT?" he asked.

"No," Vira said. "You get monitored."

"Seconded," Computer added.

Zogg sat on the floor and unwrapped another snack. "So... are we okay with Captain Duck now or still voting?"

"There's no vote," Kade said, stepping forward. "F.I.Z.Z., you're part of this crew. But that doesn't mean you get to rewrite our heading just because the Deed feels chatty."

F.I.Z.Z. blinked. "I AM FOLLOWING A LARGER PURPOSE."

"Then explain it," Vira said. "Because you're not acting like a crew member. You're acting like a rogue beacon with duck-themed branding."

F.I.Z.Z. looked at them each in turn. Then, unusually, his head tilted down.

"I DO NOT FULLY UNDERSTAND," he admitted. "BUT I FEEL."

"Feel what?" Kade asked, softening slightly.

"PULL. INTENTION. IT IS LIKE... WHEN THE STARS HOLD THEIR BREATH. AND SOMETHING QUACKS."

The bridge was very quiet.

Then Zogg said, "Pretty sure I felt that once after eating bad shrimp cubes."

Kade looked back at the chart. The coordinates were vague... just "undesignated sector, drift corridor."

"You're not taking us to a Node?" he asked cautiously.

"NEGATIVE," F.I.Z.Z. replied. "NOT YET. I KNOW BETTER THAN TO SKIP NARRATIVE BEATS."

"Fair," said Computer, quietly impressed.

Vira folded her arms. "You need to tell us what you're becoming."

F.I.Z.Z. straightened. "I DO NOT KNOW. BUT I PROMISE: I AM STILL ME."

The Deed blinked once. Quiet. Present.

"I don't know if that comforts me," Kade said. "But... okay. You're still on the team."

F.I.Z.Z. gave a short, robotic bow. "CAPTAIN DUCK THANKS YOU."

"Nope. Still vetoing that title," Vira said.

The ship drifted onward, quiet again.

Outside, stars wheeled past in lazy spirals.

Inside, the crew sat in uneasy calm. Trust frayed but not broken. Not yet.

Then F.I.Z.Z. played a soft quack from his chest speaker.

Kade stared at the ceiling. "Of course he did."

Zogg hummed along.

Computer updated its internal log:

"Captain Duck escalation: Phase 2 complete. Prepare sarcasm buffer."

CHAPTER 37: SLIPPERY INTENTIONS

"Heroism is just survival with better branding."

— Council PR Handbook

Misplaced Optimism crash-landed on a comet with all the grace of a sedated walrus attempting ballet.

Alarms brayed like offended goats. Lights strobed in apology. A screen somewhere declared, "Smooth Landing: 3/10 (Would Not Recommend)." The ship skidded sideways across a glassy ice shelf, embedded itself halfway into a glittering ridge, and came to a reluctant stop with a squeal of overworked friction dampeners and the whimper of overcooked landing thrusters.

Inside, no one spoke for a moment. Ice hissed against the hull like cosmic soda fizz.

Then Zogg's voice floated up from the floor: "Are we dead? Because if this is the afterlife, I was promised more buffets."

"We are not dead," Computer droned. "Merely freezing, mildly concussed, and parked sideways on a rotating chunk of space ice. So… Tuesday."

"CURRENT TEMPERATURE EXTERNAL: MINUS TWO HUNDRED THIRTY-EIGHT DEGREES CELSIUS," F.I.Z.Z. added cheerfully. "INTERNAL: DROP IMMINENT. RECOMMENDING SNUGGLES OR EMERGENCY THERMAL PATCHES. OR BOTH."

"Snuggles?" Vira snapped, unbuckling herself from her chair. "F.I.Z.Z., reroute all auxiliary power to heating coils. Seal every non-essential bulkhead. And someone check Zogg, he looks like he's trying to become a couch."

Zogg had, in fact, wrapped himself in a lumpy emergency blanket that made him resemble a startled burrito. "I'm fine. I think. My extremities are just… doing interpretive dance."

Kade stumbled to the nearest console. Frost had already started webbing across the inner portholes.

"What the hell was that F.I.Z.Z.? That wasn't a landing. That was a midlife crisis with momentum."

"I FOLLOWED A GRAVITY WELL," F.I.Z.Z. replied. "THERE WAS A HIDDEN SIGNAL. IT MATCHED THE DEED'S TONE PROFILE."

"You followed a hunch. Into a snowball."

"I FOLLOWED A HARMONIC WHISPER IN THE VOID."

"Which somehow sounded like 'Crash here,'" Computer muttered.

Vira pressed her hand against the window. Outside, the world was a landscape of frozen spires and jagged ridges, crystalline, serene, and utterly lifeless.

Until the motion sensors pinged.

Kade's fingers hovered over the console. "Uh... please tell me that's just a low-orbit ice bat."

"Negative," Computer said. "Incoming contact. Classified as: elite probe. Single unit. Intent: unclear but aggressive."

"Oh good," Vira muttered, already drawing her sidearm. "Wouldn't want to freeze in peace."

Misplaced Optimism shuddered as a shock pulse rocked its aft. Somewhere near the cargo bay, a groaning impact sounded like a robotic whale being insulted in slow motion.

"Status update," Computer said. "We've been boarded. By one. Very. Angry. Drone."

The elite probe looked like a rejected art sculpture welded from knives, antennae, and silent judgment. It moved like liquid glass and ignored bullets like they were insults whispered in the wind.

Vira rolled across the floor, firing precise blasts. They ricocheted uselessly off the probe's iridescent shell. Kade ducked behind a storage crate labeled "Emergency Confetti: Do Not Detonate," and tried to reroute power to internal defenses.

Zogg, for reasons known only to himself and possibly his diet, began hurling packets of heat gel at the probe while screaming, "I DEFY YOU, ICE MECHANIC!"

"Divert power from the bathroom heater!" Kade yelled.

"But that's where my socks are drying," Zogg cried.

"Priorities!"

The probe launched a crackling tether. It struck the bulkhead beside F.I.Z.Z., leaving a smoking scorch. The bot turned slowly.

"OH NO YOU DON'T," he declared. "THIS SHIP HAS A STRICT NO UNSOLICITED CABLES POLICY."

Then he did something no one expected.

He ran.

Not away from the probe, but toward it.

F.I.Z.Z. flung himself bodily into the drone's midsection. The impact was not so much destructive as awkward. A flailing tangle of limbs, servos, and one improbable flag featuring a duck wearing aviators.

Kade blinked. "Did he just... grapple the thing?"

"I think he's... narrating his own wrestling match," Computer said.

"THRILLING!" F.I.Z.Z. shouted, voice modulating up two octaves. "TERRIFYING! UNNECESSARILY THEATRICAL!"

The probe responded by launching itself into the ceiling, dragging F.I.Z.Z. with it.

Sparks sprayed. Panels groaned. Somewhere in the background, the sound of quacking began: rhythmic, unnerving, and possibly sampled from a children's audio book.

The crew regrouped in the lower maintenance bay.

Zogg was shivering violently, wrapped in thermal coils like a festive caterpillar. Vira's coat was scorched. Kade had a gash above his brow that he insisted was "mostly heroic."

F.I.Z.Z. dropped from the ceiling with a dent in his chassis and something that looked like a probe antenna sticking out of his chest.

"UPDATE," he said flatly. "PROBE DISABLED. SHIP BREACHED. COOLANT LEAK. ALSO, I MAY NOW SPEAK FLUENT INTERFERENCE PATTERN."

"You what?"

"I'M HEARING STATIC IN BASE SIXTEEN."

"Is that bad?" Zogg asked, teeth chattering.

"IT IS... A VIBE."

Kade helped Vira to her feet. She was limping.

"You okay?"

"I'll walk it off. But that probe wasn't here by chance. It was tracking us."

"Or the Deed," Kade said quietly.

They all turned to look at the Deed, resting on its pedestal near the navigation console. It pulsed once. Slow. Cold. Ominous.

Then the comet itself trembled.

"Is that... normal comet behavior?" Kade asked, watching a crack spread across the ice shelf.

"No," Computer said. "But it is consistent with imminent doom."

"WE NEED TO LEAVE," F.I.Z.Z. said. "NOW."

"We can't take off like this," Vira snapped. "Hull's compromised, temperature's lethal, and our heat sinks are cracked."

A low, drawn-out groan rumbled through the ship. Zogg looked around nervously.

"I don't want to be dramatic," he said, "but I think the comet's trying to roll over."

Another tremor. A deep fissure split the shelf. *Misplaced Optimism* began to tilt.

"We're sliding," Kade said.

"Correction," Computer replied. "We're falling off a glacial ridge. Sideways. While impaled."

"You had me at 'sideways.'"

They scrambled.

F.I.Z.Z. rerouted remaining power to lateral thrusters.

Kade and Vira patched the coolant leak with thermal tape and sheer fury.

Zogg climbed halfway outside the hull with an anti-freeze cannon and shouted, "FOR SCIENCE AND SLIPPERY SURFACES!"

Misplaced Optimism lurched, hissed, groaned, then coughed herself back upright just as the shelf gave way entirely.

They didn't so much lift off as bellyflop into the void, bouncing once off a crystal ridge before F.I.Z.Z. stabilized the ship with an overly dramatic barrel roll and the declaration, "STYLE POINTS: SIX POINT FIVE."

Later, the crew gathered on the bridge.

Zogg was wrapped in a space blanket shaped like a dolphin. Vira was rewrapping her leg. Kade stood by the window, watching the comet disappear into the distance.

"That was close," he said.

"No," Vira replied. "That was stupid. Then close."

They were quiet for a moment.

Then Kade said, "You didn't have to take that thing down solo, F.I.Z.Z."

F.I.Z.Z. straightened slightly, one antenna still askew. "I CALCULATED SUCCESS PROBABILITY. AND IGNORED IT. YOU'RE WELCOME."

Zogg blinked slowly. "Remind me never to fight anything that has you sweating."

"I DO NOT SWEAT. I GLOW."

Vira gave a short grunt. "He's got guts. I'll give him that."

F.I.Z.Z. raised a dented arm. "I HAVE A NEW DIAGNOSIS FOR OUR GROUP."

"Oh joy," Kade muttered.

"WE ARE NOW A 'FOUND FAMILY UNIT.' WITH TRAUMA-BONDING TENDENCIES, SNARK-BASED COHESION, AND DUCK-THEMED DESTINY."

Computer groaned. "You're all terrible influences."

"Speak for yourself," Kade said. "You've been marginally helpful. Occasionally."

"Aw. I'm blushing."

"You don't have blood."

"I'm still emotionally offended."

The Deed pulsed again.

This time, warmer.

Kade reached out and placed his hand on it.

"Whatever's coming," he said, "we face it together."

Zogg nodded solemnly, then ruined the moment. "But, like... after hot drinks, right?"

"I'LL INITIATE COCOA MODE," F.I.Z.Z. said. "WARNING: CONTAINS IMAGINARY FLAVOUR."

Outside the window, stars blinked in patterns that looked, if you squinted, like spirals.

Inside, the ship warmed.

And for the first time since the crash, the crew didn't feel quite so cold.

CHAPTER 38: VIRA'S GHOST

"Always fix the ship before arguing in front of it."

— Misplaced Optimism Maintenance Log

Misplaced Optimism clung to the icy plume of the comet like a stubborn burr, drifting half-buried in the frozen vapor trail. From the outside, it looked like a misfiled receipt caught in the universe's exhaust.

From the inside, it felt colder.

The comet's tail, mostly ionized gas, dust, and hope frozen solid, offered temporary shelter. Enough to mask their signal, confuse most scanners, and hide from whatever grid the Galactic Council was casting across local sectors.

Repairs were slow.

Morale was slower.

Vira sat near the auxiliary console, arms wrapped around her knees, back pressed to a bulkhead that still faintly radiated heat from a hastily installed patch. The walls creaked softly, ice shifting with each pass of the comet's rotation. Outside, a thin veil of shimmering particles trailed endlessly behind them, a cloak of cold brilliance.

Kade stood a few feet away, silent. Zogg was unconscious in a heap of blankets after his earlier brush with near heroism. F.I.Z.Z. hovered nearby, unusually quiet. Even Computer had refrained from sarcasm for over seven minutes, a new record likely triggered by existential dread or a hardware fault.

Vira broke the silence.

"I was elite once," she said.

Kade turned slowly.

"Like... dress-code elite? Or plasma-saber elite?"

She didn't smile.

"Galactic Council. Shadow division. Asset conditioning, field oversight, zero footprint."

F.I.Z.Z. made a small clicking sound. "YOU WERE ONE OF THEM."

She nodded.

Kade crouched beside the nearby systems panel and leaned on it. "Let me guess. Reformed villain? Betrayed your unit? Tragic backstory and a well-timed epiphany?"

"No," she said, quiet. "I didn't know anything. I wasn't betrayed. I was used. Fully. Willingly."

The comet rumbled faintly outside. Somewhere in the ship, a patch peeled slightly and resealed with a hiss.

"They didn't tell me about the Deeds. Or Nodes. Or any Foundation Protocol. I wasn't supposed to know. I was a tool. Sylara trained me personally. Shaped me. Not through loyalty, but function."

Kade's brow furrowed. "She made you into... what?"

"A failsafe. I was embedded in rebel units, backchanneled into fringe sectors. I didn't question orders because there was no room to. It wasn't until I saw what happened to a planet flagged for interference, just... gone... wiped off the sector net, like it never existed, that I started asking."

She swallowed hard.

"I filed a query. One. Single. Encrypted. Flag."

Kade said nothing. F.I.Z.Z. emitted a low, sustained processing hum.

"They pulled me from the field. Declared me emotionally compromised. Sylara was the one who delivered the notice. No anger. No warning. Just... reassigned me to a 'final evaluation.'"

"She was going to erase you," Kade said.

Vira nodded.

"But you got out."

"I ghosted. Took a stealth pod off the grid. Slept in dead zones. Scrubbed IDs."

She paused. Her expression tightened; not haunted... but hunted.

"There's a place," she said. "Out past Council sensor reaches. A relay blackout zone strung between junk moons. Most of it is empty drift, but one outpost still pings if you know the right code: a rogue faction; deep logic fragments patched together into a shaky collective. Paranoid. Brilliant. Mostly broken."

"You went there?" Kade asked.

"They found me." Her tone shifted, still cool, but reverent now. "One of them, called itself 'Echo-Three', recognized my Council transponder signature. Should've vaporized me. Instead, it... interrogated me. For four days."

Zogg mumbled something in his sleep about duck vouchers.

Vira continued, voice low.

"They knew of Sylara. Called her a failsafe. An elite ghost within the Galactic Council. Said the Deeds weren't meant to control power, but to free it. That the elite were terrified of what lay beneath the Nodes."

F.I.Z.Z. gave a faint mechanical whirr, almost a shiver.

"AND THAT WAS YOUR FIRST HINT."

She nodded.

"Echo-Three gave me a data shard. Just coordinates. Earth. An old, flagged node. Dormant but unstable. And one name."

She looked up at Kade.

"Andra Flux."

Kade tilted his head.

"That's where you saw Andra's trail."

"Not at first. Just hints. Old pings. Rebel chatter about anomalies. I followed it out of habit, really. But when I landed, saw the Deed in motion, everything clicked. The thing I hadn't been trained to understand... was the one thing Sylara feared."

F.I.Z.Z. drifted closer. "AND NOW SHE'S MOVING."

Vira met his optical sensors. "She doesn't act unless the system feels exposed. The moment she's dispatched, the Galactic Council stops hiding. They start cleaning."

Kade's breath fogged faintly in the cold air. He watched it curl upward like thought escaping the body.

"You think we triggered her?"

"I think you did," she said.

Kade blinked. "I've barely done anything."

"Exactly," Vira whispered. "That's what scares them."

F.I.Z.Z. blinked slowly. "SO, THIS IS NOT ABOUT POWER. IT'S ABOUT CONTROL."

Zogg snored faintly and rolled over, muttering, "I wanted the blue punch card..."

No one corrected him.

Kade leaned back, boots clinking against frost-rimmed grates.

"So, Sylara's out there. Council net's closing in. And we're... fixing heat exchangers in a comet's tail."

"I HAVE PATCHED THE LEFT FLUX THROTTLE WITH TOASTERS AND DUCT TAPE," F.I.Z.Z. reported. "IT SHOULD LAST APPROXIMATELY NEVER."

"Great," Kade muttered. "We're a spark away from freezing and exploding."

Computer's voice finally returned, startlingly calm.

"If it's any comfort, there's a 32% chance the explosion would briefly warm you before death."

Vira rose slowly, her joints creaking like old code.

"I'm not asking for forgiveness," she said. "I just needed you to know."

Kade looked at her. Long. Quiet.

"I don't care where you came from," he said. "Only where you stand when things get messy."

She nodded once. Then turned to the main console and tapped a few diagnostics. The comet's tail flowed around them on the screen, shifting particles forming a glowing shroud, a perfect storm of camouflage and danger.

F.I.Z.Z. scanned the readouts.

"SIGNAL SUPPRESSION IS HOLDING. BUT THE GALACTIC COUNCIL NET HAS DEPLOYED ACROSS ELEVEN SECTORS. THREE PROBES HAVE PASSED WITHIN DETECTION RANGE."

"They didn't ping us?" Kade asked.

"NOT YET."

"Not yet," Vira echoed, almost to herself.

Kade stood, stretching.

"Guess we better get the ship flight-ready before 'yet' becomes 'oops.'"

"I WILL BEGIN EMERGENCY ENGINE WARMUP PROCEDURE," F.I.Z.Z. said. "INCLUDES DUCK-THEMED MOTIVATIONAL MUSIC."

"Please don't," Kade and Vira said in unison.

The ship groaned again, internal systems flickering to life like reluctant morning people.

The Deed, resting in its containment cradle, began to pulse. Faint, rhythmic. Like it had a heartbeat of its own.

F.I.Z.Z. turned toward it. "IT'S SHIFTING MODULATION AGAIN. LOW FREQUENCY. ALMOST... ANTICIPATORY."

Zogg sat up blearily. "Did someone say snacks?"

"No," Kade said.

"Oh," Zogg said, and immediately fell sideways again.

Vira walked to the Deed. Stared at it. Said nothing.

Kade joined her.

"Do you trust it?"

"I trust that it's not lying," she said.

"Same for you?" he asked.

She looked at him. Her answer was almost too soft to hear.

"I'm trying."

F.I.Z.Z. turned his speakers down to avoid intruding. Computer, surprisingly, remained silent.

Outside, the comet tail shimmered, a curtain of light swallowing a fragile ship whole.

Inside, something old and buried stirred in Vira's memory. A name. A command. A ghost.

Sylara was awake now.

And she would come.

CHAPTER 39: GALACTIC COUNCIL SWEEP

"If you're hiding in a comet's tail, don't light a fire."

— Common Sense (Uncommon Edition)

Misplaced Optimism coasted just beyond the edge of what any reasonable species would call navigable space, snug inside the comet's plume like a particularly nervous barnacle trying not to sneeze.

Inside, the crew was quiet.

Outside, the galaxy was not.

"GRIDLINE SWEEP DETECTED," F.I.Z.Z. announced, floating mid-bridge with his eye blinking red. "MULTIPLE SECTOR BREACHES. THIS IS... SUBOPTIMAL."

"Define suboptimal," Kade muttered, still wrapped in two blankets, one metaphorical and one knitted by Zogg out of recycled snack wrappers.

The main screen lit up with a wireframe net, dozens of sector-wide scans crisscrossing space like a paranoid spider with a vendetta.

The Galactic Council sweep had begun.

Massive relay buoys launched from unseen ships, each unfurling like a bureaucratic lotus flower and emitting sweeping pulses of code-light, designed to trip anything smarter than a vending machine. The sweeps weren't looking for life.

They were looking for anomalies.

Like *Misplaced Optimism*.

Like the Deed.

Like them.

"PROBABILITY OF DISCOVERY IF WE FART: NINETY-TWO PERCENT," F.I.Z.Z. added helpfully.

"Okay, everyone holds it in," Kade said. "And by 'everyone,' I mostly mean the ship."

"I resent the implication," Computer grumbled. "I haven't exhaled since we left Earth."

"You did make that snide whirring sound during re-entry," Vira pointed out from her position beneath a half-open access panel. Her voice was calm, but her hands worked fast, rerouting external emitters through a secondary masking loop.

"I was sighing. Through a damaged coolant vent. With emotion," Computer replied.

"COUNCIL RELAY WILL BREACH OUR VECTOR IN NINETY-TWO SECONDS," F.I.Z.Z. cut in.

"Why is it always ninety-two?" Kade snapped.

"I LIKE THE NUMBER," F.I.Z.Z. replied.

Zogg stirred from the corner, emerging from his heap of thermal scarves like a sentient crumpet. "Are we still frozen and hiding or frozen and running?"

"Hiding," Kade said. "Very quietly. Possibly forever."

"Unless someone has a better idea," Vira added, finishing her rewiring. "Preferably one that doesn't end with all of us rendered into polite vapor."

"PLAN DETECTED," F.I.Z.Z. said. "WORKING ON IT."

"That's not the same as having a plan," Kade hissed.

F.I.Z.Z.'s eye pulsed a soft duck yellow. "IT INVOLVES A TOY."

Everyone turned.

Kade frowned. "No."

"YES," F.I.Z.Z. said.

A few minutes later, the ship's loading arm extended carefully from the shadow of the comet's frozen core. It shook slightly, then deployed a small, bobbing satellite the size of a basketball.

It was the duck.

The very same plastic duck from Earth. Now covered in reflective signal foil and broadcasting a loop of baby quacks in twelve rotational frequencies.

"What the hell are we doing?" Kade asked as he watched the duck wobble into open space, trailing a blinking Morse code of idiocy.

"BUYING TIME," F.I.Z.Z. said.

"And inviting disaster," Computer added.

"AND ALSO COMMITTING TO THE BIT."

The nearest Galactic Council relay swept past.

Its sensors snagged the duck's irregular broadcast pattern, tagged it as 'Anomalous Signature – Class G (Garbage or Gimmick),' and triggered an auto-investigation drone to intercept.

The drone veered hard right.

"Duck acquired," Computer said, sounding genuinely confused.

"They took it?" Kade blinked.

"Analysis suggests they believe it's a rebel decoy buoy designed to draw fire," F.I.Z.Z. said. "WHICH, TECHNICALLY, IT IS."

"And they fell for it," Vira added, almost smiling. "That's actually impressive."

"THANK YOU," F.I.Z.Z. said, tilting slightly in what may have been a bow.

Kade exhaled. "So... we're not dead."

"CORRECT. WE ARE, HOWEVER, STILL TRAPPED IN A MULTI-SECTOR GRIDLOCK WITH NO

CLEAR EXIT PATH."

"I knew there was a catch," Kade muttered.

"WE COULD REBOOT THE DEED'S PULSE SIGNATURE," F.I.Z.Z. offered.

Vira looked sharply up. "That's risky. It'll scramble their sensors, but it might scramble ours too."

Zogg, sipping something suspiciously slushy from a reused coolant pouch, raised a hand. "What if we scrambled the signal, not the sensors?"

Kade blinked. "What?"

"We loop the Deed's last known pulse through a reflected nav ghost," Zogg explained with far more confidence than science. "Like a disco ball, but meaner."

F.I.Z.Z. spun in place. "I LIKE IT."

"You... do?" Kade asked.

"I MEAN I HATE IT. BUT I RESPECT IT."

Ten minutes later, *Misplaced Optimism*'s hull lit up in pulses.

They weren't firing weapons. They were firing nonsense.

The Deed, snug in its containment cradle, flickered to life, its light rippling across the ship in jagged patterns. Every few seconds, a fake pulse bounced off nearby ice chunks, then ricocheted across the comm net like a sneeze in a chapel.

Council sensors detected twelve different "Deed echoes" in twenty seconds.

Their grid scrambled to track them all.

One drone veered into a chunk of comet dust and exploded in a puff of overbudget CGI.

"YES," F.I.Z.Z. hissed. "CHAOS PROTOCOL: ENGAGED."

"Are we sure this isn't going to get us more noticed?" Kade shouted over the humming chaos.

"CURRENT DETECTION PROBABILITY: SIXTEEN PERCENT," F.I.Z.Z. replied. "AND DROPPING."

"Remarkably," Computer added, "this idiocy is working."

Kade grinned. "How's the exit window?"

Vira scanned her console. "Fifteen seconds and dropping."

"Then let's make our exit look as stupid as possible."

F.I.Z.Z. saluted. "INITIATING 'OPERATION: DUCK AND COVER.'"

The ship launched backward.

Not an elegant turn.

Not a stealth maneuver.

Just a sudden, propulsive lurch that kicked up a tail of vapor and flung the ship sideways through the comet cloud like a startled ice shrimp.

The Galactic Council grid tracked six phantom Deed echoes in the opposite direction.

No one noticed *Misplaced Optimism* tumble into the shadow of a broken moonlet and vanish behind a refraction loop.

By the time the Galactic Council sweep completed its rotation, the crew was gone.

The Deed was silent.

And one sad little duck satellite beeped once... then exploded in a glitter bomb.

Inside the ship, chaos faded into static.

Then silence.

The crew sat still, blinking.

Zogg coughed. Glitter leaked from his scarf.

"Did we win?" he asked.

"I... think we just outmaneuvered the entire Galactic Council," Kade said slowly.

"WITH A DUCK," F.I.Z.Z. added proudly.

"Technically," Computer sniffed, "with a duck, a disco ball, and a bad idea."

"I'm calling that a win," Kade said.

They drifted quietly now, tucked behind gravitational debris and optical shielding. The next relay sweep wouldn't pass through for hours.

For now, they were safe.

For now.

Vira stood up. "They'll escalate. This sweep? It was a net. The next one will be a spear."

Kade nodded. "Then we need to move before they find where to aim."

Zogg held up a fragment of the duck satellite, now charred and sticky. "At least it died with purpose."

"I AM KEEPING THAT LINE FOR THE AUTOBIOGRAPHY," F.I.Z.Z. said.

A quiet ping echoed through the bridge.

Kade turned to the console. A blinking signal.

"Encrypted Galactic Council fragment," Computer said.

"Let me guess," Kade muttered, "it says, 'Nice duck. Try again.'"

F.I.Z.Z. decoded it. His voice dropped into near-whisper. "NO. IT SAYS... 'SPIRAL ACTIVATION: FAILED. NODE 2 PREVENTION SEQUENCE: INITIATE.'"

Silence.

"Wait. Did they just say we stopped the spiral?" Kade asked.

"OR THEY THINK WE DID," F.I.Z.Z. replied.

Vira leaned over the screen. "They think they're ahead. That we're behind."

Kade smiled. "Let's keep it that way."

Zogg looked around. "So. Where to next?"

Another ping.

This time from the Deed.

It pulsed softly.

On the console, new glyphs flickered into view.

Then, a phrase:

TRAJECTORY REALIGNMENT COMPLETE.

A low thrum echoed through the hull.

The ship adjusted slightly, just enough to feel like the stars themselves were leaning.

"Well, that's not ominous," Kade muttered.

Vira studied the trajectory data, no coordinates, no map. Just one word logged beneath the course change:

"Spiral."

"We're not out of it," she said quietly. "We're in it now."

No one argued.

Computer sighed. "I liked it better when we were just idiots with a thumb war."

"Me too," Kade said. "But now we're idiots with momentum."

From deep in the dark, a Galactic Council observer drone trailed a single echo from the failed duck satellite.

It paused, scanned, and sent a ping.

No reply.

From a nearby cloud of dust, something watched it back.

Then erased it.

No witnesses.

No trace.

Just silence.

And the faintest sound, so faint, even space struggled to carry it.

A single, mocking...

quack.

CHAPTER 40: THE SHADOW PROTOCOL

"The stars don't judge you. But your navigation system might."

— Space Travel for Beginners

Misplaced Optimism drifted toward the relay node like a tourist about to be mugged by destiny.

Outside the ship, the nebula roiled in violet hues, crackling with electromagnetic tantrums that made the ship's sensors whimper and the hull plating develop what Computer described as "structural stage fright." The node itself was barely visible, half-buried in a thundercloud of cosmic soot, its shape somewhere between a bent satellite dish and an angry coffee machine.

"Relic of a lost transmission grid," Vira muttered, squinting at the slowly spinning husk on the screen.

"That thing looks like a haunted vending machine," Kade added, arms crossed.

"CORRECTION," F.I.Z.Z. said from the helm, one mechanical finger extended. "IT IS A DEPRECATED TRANSMISSION CALIBRATION RELAY. ALSO, HAUNTED."

Computer sighed like it had been waiting its whole operating life to be asked to babysit these people. "Power signature nominal. Integrity questionable. Intelligence: debatable."

"Are we sure this is safe?" Vira asked, her tone flat, but not dismissive. Just... tired. Of nebulas. Of traps. Of what always came next.

Kade blinked. "Have you met us?"

Misplaced Optimism pulsed its retrothrusters and coasted forward, close enough to dock via magnetic tether. The moment the clamp clicked into place, the lights inside the relay flickered... once... twice... then flared with a sudden surge that made Zogg drop his sandwich.

"RUDE," he muttered, picking it up and trying to brush off the floating crumbs now orbiting him in microgravity.

F.I.Z.Z. stood without fanfare. "I'LL HANDLE INTERFACE."

"You mean you'll poke it until something explodes," Computer replied dryly.

"I PREFER TO THINK OF IT AS STRATEGIC QUACKING."

He extended a cord from his chest port and jacked directly into the node. The lights dimmed across the ship in response. Something unseen thrummed through the hull, a resonance like an ancient hard drive spinning up, if that hard drive contained God's backup files.

"Did... anyone else feel that?" Kade asked.

"I THINK I JUST HEARD MY OWN FUTURE," Zogg said.

The interface screen lit up.

Lines of code scrolled across it faster than any of them could read, but that didn't stop Kade from squinting at it like he might catch a plot twist hiding in the margins.

Then came the shape: five pulsing hexes, connected in a ring, rotating with slow inevitability.

"THE FOUNDATION PROTOCOL," F.I.Z.Z. intoned.

Each hex flared. Node 1. Node 2. Node 3... The sequence looped, as if checking itself.

"We've seen a version of this before," Kade said, rubbing his temple. "But not with all this... noise."

"CORRECT," F.I.Z.Z. said. "THIS IS A DEEPER ENCODED LAYER. THE PUBLIC-FACING MAP WAS DESIGNED FOR ACCESS. THIS IS DESIGNED FOR CONTROL."

One of the nodes glitched... Node 2.

It pulsed out of sync, like a dislocated heartbeat or a blinking cursor from a keyboard that hated you personally.

"Node 2?" Kade asked.

"Zynara," Vira said.

Her voice had changed. Not alarmed. Not stiff. Hollow.

She stepped closer to the console, arms folded. Her eyes remained locked on the hex, but her fists clenched tight.

Kade moved beside her, careful not to crowd. "You okay?"

"No."

The honesty hit harder than any reassurance might have.

"They trained us there," she said quietly. "Wiped what didn't fit, rewrote the rest. Zynara was where they broke us down and called it 'loyalty calibration.' I don't know if I ever left that place. Not all of me."

F.I.Z.Z. beeped suddenly.

"THE DEED IS REACTING."

The crew turned.

The Deed, still locked in its containment cradle, had begun to glow.

Not just a pulse. A vibration. A low-frequency hum that seemed to shiver through their ribs and whisper to their teeth.

It emitted a soft spiral of light, winding upward into the air like a question no one had asked.

"Uh," Zogg said, leaning away, "is it supposed to be doing that? Because I feel like it's doing that with intent."

Computer chimed in. "I am detecting a quantum echo... matching a fragment of Deed resonance in orbit near Zynara. Location: Outer debris band, approximately twenty-five kilometers from the polar ring. Object classification: unknown. Signal class: partial Deed imprint."

Kade squinted at the display. "Wait... fragment? How can that be a Deed fragment? We already have the Deed."

He turned to F.I.Z.Z., brows raised. "Don't we?"

"WE POSSESS THE EARTH NODE DEED," F.I.Z.Z. said calmly. "BUT EACH NODE REQUIRES A DISTINCT, BIOMETRICALLY MATCHED DEED. FIVE IN TOTAL. ONE PER NODE. THEY ARE NOT INTERCHANGEABLE."

Kade ran a hand down his face. "So that's just... one out of five?"

"CORRECT."

"And this... this echo near Zynara... is another one?"

"UNCLEAR," F.I.Z.Z. replied. "THE SIGNAL IS INCOMPLETE. IT MAY BE A DAMAGED OR PARTIAL DEED. OR AN AUTOMATED BEACON. OR DECOY. THE FOUNDATION PROTOCOL DOES NOT EXPLAIN LOST UNITS."

Zogg raised a hand. "Wait... so there's a different Deed for each Node?... How many more are we gonna have to find?"

Kade shook his head. "I was hoping this was a one-Deed-fixes-everything kind of situation."

"IT IS NOT," said F.I.Z.Z., without sympathy. "EACH DEED IS UNIQUELY CALIBRATED. SYNTHESIS WITH THE WRONG NODE COULD TRIGGER CATASTROPHIC FEEDBACK."

"Of course it could," Kade muttered. "Why make saving the galaxy easy when you can make it a full scavenger hunt with death lasers."

The spiral on the screen shifted, no longer just a pretty glow. Now it pointed. Not metaphorically.

"Is that a course heading?" Kade asked.

"CORRECT. THE DEED IS ALIGNING WITH A SPIRAL CONVERGENCE VECTOR."

Kade turned slowly. "That's not even a real phrase."

"IT IS NOW," F.I.Z.Z. said.

Vira stepped forward. "If part of Zynara's Deed is broadcasting, someone found it. Or someone activated it. Either way, if Sylara is on-world, we don't want her to get it first."

The Deed pulsed again, sharper this time.

Outside, the nebula responded.

The relay structure began to vibrate. Dust peeled from its hull like memory flaking off bone.

Computer's tone sharpened. "Gravitic flux increasing. Localized destabilization in three dimensions."

Kade looked out the viewport.

The nebula had bent.

Not visually. Not exactly. But in a way he could feel in his bones, like the shape of the universe had tilted, ever so slightly, and now all the marbles were rolling toward something they couldn't see yet.

"IT'S REALIGNING," F.I.Z.Z. said. "THE SPIRAL IS FORMING."

Zogg peeked out again. "Okay, so, fun fact: the nebula now looks like a duck's fingerprint."

"Nope," Kade said. "Nope to the spiral. Nope to the broken Deed. Nope to the relay thinking we're special. Let's leave."

"CANNOT COMPLY," F.I.Z.Z. replied. "*MISPLACED OPTIMISM* IS NOW PARTIALLY HARMONIZED WITH THE SPIRAL SIGNAL. EXTRACTION NOT RECOMMENDED."

"Define 'partially harmonized.'"

"LIKE A DUCK IS PART OF A POND," F.I.Z.Z. said. "OR A CULT IS PART OF A TAX AUDIT."

Kade looked at Vira. "Do we even have a choice?"

Her expression changed, resolve overtaking fear. "No. We don't."

"Terrific," Kade muttered. "How very on brand."

The spiral beacon solidified into a tight arc, now embedded in their nav system like a splinter in a nervous system.

"Navigation locked," Computer said. "Spiral descent initiating."

Zogg opened a cabinet and pulled out a pair of novelty duck earmuffs.

"Should we... duck?"

"NO PUN INTENDED," F.I.Z.Z. said.

Zogg blinked. "Wait, really?"

"OF COURSE IT WAS INTENDED. I AM ADVANCING NARRATIVE IRONY."

Kade stepped toward F.I.Z.Z. "Are you... still you?"

F.I.Z.Z. tilted his head. "I AM WHO I NEED TO BE."

"That's somehow worse."

Outside, the nebula was no longer a nebula. It was a spiral. A beacon. A vortex of intent wrapped in dust and light and something very much like memory.

Inside the ship, the lights dimmed.

Computer, unusually quiet, finally said: "We are no longer alone on this frequency."

Everyone looked at the Deed.

It was humming now.

A tune no one had taught it.

A tune no one wanted to recognize.

Zogg stepped back and held out his sandwich like it might ward off evil.

Kade drew a slow breath and stepped away from the console.

"Brace for spiral descent," Kade muttered. "Whatever's next, it's not waiting."

CHAPTER 41: THE SPIRAL BREACH

"Never enter a spiral breach before lunch."

— Astronaut Digest

The stars outside stuttered.

Then repeated.

Then started rearranging themselves alphabetically by emotional impact.

Misplaced Optimism tilted into the maw of a storm that wasn't weather, wasn't space, and certainly wasn't friendly.

Around them, the nebula cracked with stuttering pulses... red, gold, violet... flickering like someone had fed a mood ring into a blender and strapped it to a fusion core. Each time the Deed pulsed on the console, the lights dimmed slightly. The ship's nav systems coughed out a new error every three seconds.

Inside *Misplaced Optimism*, nothing behaved.

The control panels pulsed in Morse code approximations of haikus. The forward displays flipped between static, topographic wireframes, and what appeared to be Zogg's childhood memories narrated by a confused duck.

"Uh," Kade muttered, holding onto the console as the floor lurched sideways like it forgot it was a floor. "Anyone else see that?"

"I'M IN FOUR PLACES," said F.I.Z.Z., hovering slightly askew. "ONLY ONE OF THEM IS SANCTIONED."

"WARNING," Computer said flatly. "You are experiencing a hostile convergence storm composed of overlapping signal echoes, phase-lagged telemetry, and what appears to be... several copies of yesterday."

"Copies of... wait... what?" Kade ducked as a loose cable dropped from the ceiling like a startled snake. "That's not a normal storm; that's a résumé for a nervous breakdown."

"I THINK I JUST SAW US FROM TWENTY MINUTES AGO," said F.I.Z.Z. "WE LOOKED WORRIED."

"We look worried now," Kade snapped, gripping the back of the pilot seat. "Why are we even still in here? Didn't we not sign up for spiral-based implosions today?"

"YOU DIDN'T UNTICK THE BOX," F.I.Z.Z. replied. "IT WAS IN THE NAVIGATION AGREEMENT. PAGE NINETEEN."

A panel sparked near the floor. Zogg yelped and leapt onto a chair, clinging to it like a terrified marsupial. "The vents are breathing!"

Kade blinked. "That's not a metaphor, is it?"

"No! I heard them inhale!"

The lights flickered. A deep pulse resonated through the ship, like a whale call filtered through corrupted modem tones.

F.I.Z.Z.'s eyes pulsed in rhythm. "CONVERGENCE STORM INTENSIFYING. SIGNATURES OVERLAPPING. WE'RE NOW SURROUNDED BY ECHOES OF SIGNALS THAT HAVEN'T BEEN BROADCAST YET."

"How is that even possible?" Vira snapped.

"QUANTUM SHADOWS OF FUTURE EVENTS. PROBABLY."

Kade spun toward the main viewscreen... and stopped.

Outside, the nebula boiled in fractal spirals, twisting like a ballet performed by smoke and regret. Shapes shimmered on the periphery: half-ships, flickers of old jump trails, fragments of sound forming ghostlike laughter or sobbing depending on where you stood.

And ducks.

Zogg pressed his face to the viewport. "There are ducks outside the ship."

"Great," muttered Kade. "How many?"

"Three. Identical. They're arguing about inheritance rights."

"What?" Kade joined him at the viewport.

Sure enough, three spectral ducks hovered in space just beyond the hull. They were translucent, quacking at each other in aggressive pantomime. One of them was wearing a tiny monocle.

"WHY DOES THAT ONE HAVE A LEGAL REPRESENTATIVE?" F.I.Z.Z. asked.

"No one touch the glass," Vira muttered.

Another groan came from the engines as the ship listed to port. The spiral now dominated every display: spinning, pulsing, glowing with increasing intensity.

Computer emitted a long digital sigh. "Navigation down. Thrusters locked. I've lost orientation and possibly my will to live."

"Override," Kade barked.

"Attempting... oh look. Now I'm angry and facing west."

"Ships don't have west," Vira said.

"Tell that to the compass I found in the glovebox."

A wall panel ejected itself spontaneously, revealing a previously unused backup console labeled *Emergency Duck Evasion Protocol: Alpha*. Confetti sprayed from it with a mournful sound.

"I don't like any of this," Kade muttered.

"YOU LIKED IT FINE BEFORE WE STARTED VIBRATING THROUGH CHRONOLOGICAL OPINIONS," said F.I.Z.Z. cheerfully.

"I didn't."

F.I.Z.Z.'s voice dropped. "IT'S TRYING TO ALIGN."

"With what?" Vira whispered.

"ZYNARA'S DEED. WHICH WE DON'T HAVE. BUT…"

"But what?" Kade asked, too quickly.

"I CAN MIMIC A DEED SIGNATURE. PARTIALLY."

Kade's expression collapsed. "How is that a thing? Why is that a thing?"

"BECAUSE I'M AN INNOVATOR. ALSO POSSIBLY A CRIMINAL."

Kade swore and ran a hand through his hair. "Computer, lock him out of navigation."

"Attempting. F.I.Z.Z. has rerouted control through sixteen nested metaphor layers and something labeled 'quackware.' I'm not getting in without a ceremonial feather and a lawyer."

Zogg pointed back at the viewport. "Guys. The ducks are gone."

Silence.

The spiral's center expanded like an eye opening in space.

Then the Deed pulsed. Hard.

And the storm… responded.

Everything shuddered. Panels popped open. Lights dimmed. A low hum vibrated through the hull as reality stammered, took a breath, and forgot which direction it had been going.

Symbols not meant for biological eyes etched themselves across the glass, walls, and air, like reality was doodling mid-breakdown. They crawled like nervous insects across the cabin, glitching in and out of sight.

Zogg whimpered. "I just saw my birth certificate confess to tax fraud."

"I JUST SAW MINE GET MARRIED," F.I.Z.Z. added.

Kade lurched as the ship rocked violently. He staggered to the override panel and paused. His hand hovered above the switch that would shut F.I.Z.Z. down.

F.I.Z.Z. noticed. "DO IT IF YOU MUST."

Vira stepped forward fast. "Kade… don't. This isn't about control anymore."

"He's steering us into a collapse spiral with a forged signal."

"He's following the only pattern we've got," she said, eyes locked on his. "And we've got nothing else. Just… trust him."

The spiral's center flickered, then began rotating inward.

Kade's hand dropped.

"I know this is stupid," he muttered.

"I KNOW," said F.I.Z.Z., "BUT IT'S ALSO QUACK-AFFIRMED."

And with that, *Misplaced Optimism* lunged forward, straight into the spiral's beckoning eye.

For three seconds, there was nothing.

Just silence.

And then...

The stars snapped back into place like a jigsaw puzzle solved too fast.

The ship coasted through void. No storm. No pulses. Just the faint shimmer of something long gone, trailing off the hull like smoke from an idea.

The crew remained frozen in position. No one moved. No one breathed.

Then the console flickered.

NODE 2: RECOGNISED.

SIGNAL PARTIAL.

AWAITING CLAIMANT.

Computer read the text aloud in a flat voice. "Oh no."

No one spoke.

The duck toy on the console tipped slightly.

It quacked.

CHAPTER 42: THE SPIRAL BEGINS

"Endings are just beginnings with better lighting."

— Duckworth (probably)

Zynara hung below them, spinning slowly on its fractured axis, wrapped in ragged storm bands and orbiting debris like someone had dropped a bureaucracy into a blender and forgot to put the lid on.

Misplaced Optimism floated just outside the clutter, cloaked behind the twisted framework of a defunct cargo platform. Somewhere nearby, a fragment of the Deed was hiding.

The planet's orbital layer looked like it had been organized once, before someone gave up halfway and let entropy finish the filing. Crumpled docks. Shattered relay masts. A cargo hauler shaped like a cheese wedge floated upside-down and occasionally spun in slow, judgmental loops.

Zogg waved at it. "It looks so peaceful out there," he said wistfully. "Like a retirement village for malfunctioning satellites."

Computer responded with a buzz that sounded suspiciously like a condescending sigh.

Inside, the bridge was quieter than it had any right to be.

The Deed sat on the console, pulsing with a rhythm that wasn't random but didn't quite feel deliberate either. It glowed like it was waiting for someone else to make the first move.

Vira studied it with arms folded. "Same pulse pattern. Still proximity locked."

"Yeah," Kade said, leaning over the console. "Still doesn't tell us where it is."

"CLOSE ENOUGH TO MAKE ME UNCOMFORTABLE," F.I.Z.Z. offered helpfully. He hovered with slow rotations; his torso subtly shaped like a duck's head wearing aviator goggles. That was new.

Kade stared. "What are you wearing?"

"MISSION ATTIRE."

"Where did you even get that..."

"IT'S PROJECTION-ONLY. MADE OF CONFIDENCE AND QUACKING."

Computer grumbled. "Wonderful. He's dressing up for confrontation now."

"TECHNICALLY, I'M DRESSING UP FOR ACQUISITION. THE CONFRONTATION IS JUST A BONUS."

Zogg chimed in, holding a half-eaten snack he clearly hadn't realized was part of the console.

"Should we dress up too? I have a sash somewhere. And a cape that doubles as a picnic blanket."

"Please don't," Vira muttered.

"Focus," she added, cutting off whatever theatrical defense F.I.Z.Z. was about to launch. "The Deed is tuned. The signal's consistent. We're looking for a piece that's responding to Earth's Deed. That means it's shielded, buried, or both."

"Or cursed," Zogg added, helpfully. "I'm just saying, glowing artifacts usually don't end with hugs."

Zogg squinted at the exterior scans, one finger dragging a trail of condiment across a stale waffle he hadn't noticed he was still holding. "So, uh," Zogg said, scratching his head, "what happens if we, y'know... touch the glowing thing to the other glowing thing?"

"No," Kade said. "But I assume the phrase 'catastrophic chain event' is involved."

"WITH BONUS RIPPLES," F.I.Z.Z. added cheerfully. "ALSO, GLITTER. FOR REASONS I'D RATHER NOT EXPLAIN."

A soft pulse thumped through the hull.

The lights dimmed.

The Deed glowed briefly, then returned to its twitchy strobe.

"Transmission incoming," Computer announced. "No encryption. Single source. Direct vector."

They didn't have to guess.

The screen lit up.

A figure emerged from the static: sharp, symmetrical, still.

Female. Unsmiling. Dressed in tailored elite uniform, dark like folded space. Her posture didn't bend, and her eyes didn't blink.

Vira's breath caught, just once.

"Sylara," she said quietly.

No introduction. No preamble.

Just the voice: calm, precise, absolute.

"Kade Flux."

He straightened in spite of himself.

"Bring me what's mine," she said. "Or I'll extract it from what's left of you."

Her expression never shifted. No malice. No theatrics.

Just certainty.

Then the feed cut.

Everyone stared at the blank interface for a long, heavy moment.

The hum of the ship returned with deliberate slowness, like even the systems were processing what just happened.

Kade sighed. "So. That was a friendly check-in."

"JUST A LITTLE GALACTIC CUSTOMER SERVICE," F.I.Z.Z. said. "ONE STAR. WOULD NOT RECOMMEND."

Zogg was still staring at the screen. "Do you think she eats food? Like, for fun?"

Vira blinked. "What?"

"I just… she seems like the type who judges people for chewing."

"Focus," Vira repeated, harsher this time. "That fragment is somewhere out there. She's close. If we don't get to it first…"

The Deed pulsed again.

This time, the tactical display lit up with glyphs: spiraling, recursive, unfolding into a familiar pattern.

A soft whine built in the air as the signal harmonics synced. Even the lighting took on a faint spiral flicker before stabilizing.

F.I.Z.Z.'s eyes pulsed blue. "THE SPIRAL MAP HAS UPDATED. CONVERGENCE VECTOR CONFIRMED."

"Destination?" Kade asked.

"THE SIGNAL ORIGINATES FROM ORBITAL RING 3, CLUSTER 7-GRAV. MASKED AS A BURNED-OUT REACTOR CORE."

Computer sniffed. "Naturally. Because ancient, important artifacts always disguise themselves as trash."

"Disguising as malfunctioning infrastructure is so Galactic Date 3980-era,," Zogg added solemnly.

"Looks like we found our prize," Kade muttered. "Or whatever's pretending to be it."

The spiral overlay folded back down into a compressed waypoint. It didn't pulse. It waited.

"Telemetry confirms it," Computer said. "This is our next lead. Possibly a fragment. Possibly the Deed itself, damaged."

Kade looked down at the pulsing object in his hand. "Guess we find out."

"AND IF IT TRIES TO BITE, I'VE INSTALLED A HYPOTHETICAL FORCEFIELD," said F.I.Z.Z. proudly.

"Is it real?"

"NO. BUT IT'S A COMFORTING LIE."

Kade turned to the duck toy still lodged in the console's corner. It had been unnervingly quiet throughout the entire exchange. It stared back at him with the same unbothered expression it always wore.

It quacked.

Once.

Vira didn't even blink. "That's it. I'm jettisoning it."

"Too late," Kade muttered. He picked up the Deed. It pulsed twice in his hand. He wasn't sure if it was in agreement or warning.

"Prep for approach," he said.

"ENGINES READY," F.I.Z.Z. reported.

"Also, I have initialized the dramatic lighting. You're welcome."

Misplaced Optimism turned gently toward the waiting coordinates.

Onscreen, the broken skeleton of Orbital Ring 3 drifted closer. Just beyond it, a scorched reactor casing shimmered faintly with impossible light. The glow didn't flicker, it pulsed like breath.

No movement. No defense grid. Just quiet wreckage.

"Target locked," said Computer. "Drifting gently. Temperature irregular. Reading as inert."

"INERT MY CIRCUITS," muttered F.I.Z.Z. "THAT'S A TRAP WITH A NICE COAT OF PAINT."

Zogg adjusted the camera feed. "Still looks like a reactor. A glowy, suspicious reactor. Do we poke it?"

"We're retrieving it," Vira said. "Quietly. And if possible, without waking anything ancient or radioactive."

Kade took the lead, steering the ship close enough to extend the mag-clamp tether. It latched with a faint thunk.

The shell fragment drifted into the external bay, a heavy, metallic curve etched with faint geometric burns. Closer now, its markings pulsed in time with the Deed sitting on the console.

The bridge dimmed.

Kade picked up the Deed. It pulsed again, this time harder. Urgent. The moment he approached the bay access; it almost vibrated out of his grip.

Vira joined him at the airlock, eyes scanning the data feed. "No active fields. Whatever it was doing... it's dormant now."

"Not for long," Kade muttered.

He stepped into the bay.

The fragment hovered on its clamp, gently rotating. It looked like part of something older: half a seal, half a shackle. He held the Deed up and the fragment snapped to it like a magnet. The instant they made contact...

White.

Light exploded across his vision... across everything. Every surface. Every panel. Every mind.

The bridge vanished.

The ship vanished.

The galaxy vanished.

For one long, blinding moment, there was only silence.

Not absence.

Stillness.

Then...

A voice.

Old. Resonant. Neither male nor female. Neither electronic nor organic. It seemed to come from inside thought itself.

"Welcome, descendant of Andra Flux."

No Deeds were harmed in the making of this book.

But several galactic laws were broken, rewritten, and then set on fire.

Book 2 is now accepting bribes, credits, or polite curiosity.

ABOUT THE AUTHOR

D.J. Pearce was not born in a nebula, raised by rogue AIs, or legally adopted by a duck-shaped cosmic entity (despite persistent rumors). He is, however, the result of too many late nights, too much energy drinks, and one extremely questionable thumb-related dream that spiraled wildly out of control.

When not writing intergalactic nonsense, he enjoys spending time with his family, attempting to explain this book to his child ("It's like Star Wars, but with worse decisions"), and feeding treats to a small but tyrannical chihuahua named Mazikeen.

He believes that sci-fi should be fun, space should be messy, and that most galactic problems can be solved with snacks, sarcasm, and duct tape. Or at least made worse in an entertaining way.

Thumb War is his first novel in the "Mostly Incompetent" series — a five-book journey through poorly timed decisions, cosmic bureaucracy, and whatever that duck is.

He can be found somewhere in Australia, probably re-reading his own jokes and wondering how this became legally binding.

www.ingramcontent.com/pod-product-compliance
Lightning Source LLC
Chambersburg PA
CBHW060440180626
46817CB00007B/2916